The Book of Commentary /
Unquiet Garden of the Soul

THE GERMAN LIST

The Book of Commentary /
Unquiet Garden of the Soul

ALEXANDER KLUGE

TRANSLATED BY
ALEXANDER BOOTH

LONDON NEW YORK CALCUTTA

This publication was supported by a grant from the Goethe-Institut, India.

The translator's work on this text was supported by the Deutscher
Übersetzerfonds within the framework of the NEUSTART KULTUR programme
of the Federal Government Commissioner for Culture and Media (BKM).

Seagull Books, 2023

Originally published as Alexander Kluge,
Das Buch der Kommentare / Unruhige Garten der Seele

© Suhrkamp Verlag, Berlin, 2021

All rights reserved by and controlled through Suhrkamp Verlag Berlin

English translation © Alexander Booth

ISBN 978 1 8030 9 260 7

British Library Cataloguing-in-Publication Data

A catalogue record for this book is available from the British Library.

Typeset by Seagull Books, Calcutta, India
Printed and bound by Hyam Enterprises, Calcutta, India

CONTENTS

• STATION 12

THE MURMURING OF THE PILOT FISH

THREE STORIES AS A PREFACE

PERHAPS A PART OF PERCEPTION IS LOCATED NOT IN THE YOUNG WOMAN'S HEAD BUT BETWEEN HER AND HER CHILDREN WHO HAVE LONG BEEN SITTING AND STUDYING SOMEWHERE ELSE

The bathroom floor was wet. The impression of wet feet, the sign of those children who, just a little while ago, had been splashing about nearby. Footprints already indistinct. Touched by these traces of her loved ones' presence (who in the meantime should already have reached the classroom), the mother wiped these 'documents of vitality' away with cloth and brush (though dedicated to order, regretfully) until the floor was dry again. For a while, she preserved in her mind the impressions of the padding feet on the wet tiles. Until that impression too began to fade. She would not have been able to explain it to anyone else. How do you describe the sound of splashing feet? You'd have to bring the 'joy of wetness beneath children's feet' into the words of the report. Words are often poor when meant to directly describe sensory impressions. It's hard for them to manage the combination of exact impression on the nerves (the moment) and empathy, which isn't located in the nerves but in the past and within inner connection (duration). Only the two together contain 'modern sensuousness'.

AT 90, THE SOUND OF SIRENS STILL UNNERVES ME

Because the municipal authorities' fire department service regulations still stem from before 1945, once a week test sirens sound across all the schoolyards of the city, calling schoolkids and teachers outside. There they stay put for a bit before going back to their rooms. Obedience, the smooth exit from the building in case of danger, is only of secondary importance. Of primary importance is testing whether these public warning systems, the sirens, still function.

This custom was only abandoned 11 years ago. Since then, the sirens have only been examined internally. They are no longer activated. No one can be sure that in the case of an emergency, an air raid on the city, say, they will be able to raise their Cassandra-like voices. What would those gathered together in alarm do if they really were in danger? It depends on the type. A catastrophic fire or gas leak nearby? The outbreak of war? For today's students and teachers an unimaginable exercise. In the case of a pandemic, the sirens' sounds would be useless. And if the earth opened up in an earthquake? That is unlikely in Opladen, a district of Leverkusen.

COMMENTARIES ARE SPRINGS

Commentaries are not linear narratives. They work vertically. They are mines, catacombs. In Volume 1 of Jürgen Habermas' *This Too a History of Philosophy*, I read with astonishment about the tradition of the glossators of Bologna, who would enter explanations, glosses and notes into the ancient collections of law, the most important surviving example of which comes from the time of the emperor Justinian. Later, during the period of High Scholasticism when the first universities were founded, these glosses were expanded by commentaries. The working form of commentary is closer to the idea of collecting than to that of shaping. Closer to the poetics of the Brothers Grimm than the dramatic or novelistic form.

Putting this particular form of narration to the test excites me. Peter Schäfer has shown us how, in the interpretation of the Talmud, such commentary serves to PERPETUALLY UPDATE SELF-PERPETUATING TEXTS. It has to do with the modes of expression of the cooperative public sphere, even that public sphere which bridges heterogeneous times. Not least respect for the principle of FRAGMENTATION, respect for the particular and for the individual (and its defence against the merely generally available), speaks for attempting something like this over and over. The call to such an effort belongs to the lines of Frankfurt School–style critical theory. Observing our 'torn reality' grants permission to the incomplete message. The word *attempt* obtains fresh élan. To keep up with the algorithmic behemoths of the Big Five in Silicon Valley, any modest means will do. Commentary's formal principle has always been the working method of poetic critique.

THE CHALLENGE
WHICH BEGAN THAT GLOOMY
ADVENT OF 2020

FIGURE 1 (ABOVE). 'Christmas Eve 2020'
FIGURE 2 (BELOW). 'A pale blue planet'. False colour.

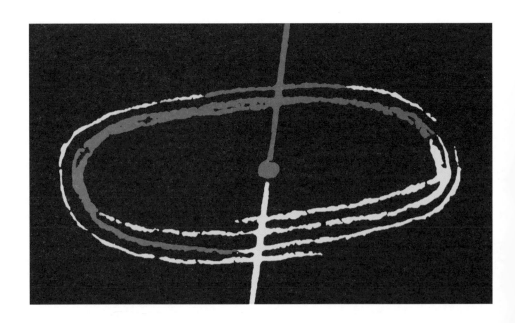

LOOKING AT A PECULIAR DEMON
UNLISTED IN ANY ANCIENT BOOK OF LEGENDS

Under the electron microscope, the virus that had just broken out of the lung cell had a desolate appearance. The virologist stared dumbfoundedly at the turbulent image. Throughout its adventurous trip, not to mention its many divisions, the being had committed numerous errors in transmitting its genetic code. Hence this—one cannot say animal—piece of RNA's, this thing's, this 'architecture's', 'alien's' or 'mutation's' rather strange look. Shreds of the host cell's cellular material wrapped around the once geometrically elegant body, the impression of a tiger's mouth moving about the remains of a felled sheep—that's what it looked like to the virologist, the moment's lone witness. In place of the missing molecules that the virus had tossed off or simply lost, a group of foreign molecules had gathered, in hump-like fashion, into the protein sheath which now curved outwards. Hardly any resemblance to the being that had originally wandered into the human bloodstream, and that more or less corresponded to the textbook images.

From now on, further mutations were to be expected at a rate of less than a billionth of a second, and lead to unexpected fractions of several million individuals within a short span of human time. The virologist saw it all—it was the night before Christmas Eve—in her microscope, not as individual detail but as that swarm of billions which, through partition, has since emerged from the original. Each with both original and foreign tissue around it; in-between, the virus' protective, protein-rich skin, which nothing but strong soap can defeat.

PECULIAR LOCATION OF A—TO US—
FOREIGN INTELLIGENCE

Viruses, the virologist said—and at the same time pointed out that the term *virus* always refers, even in the sharpest electron microscope, to a clump, to a quantity of a few million, billion or even trillion specimens—are condemned to association. A single individuum of its kind does not live long. As a crowd, they have been 'intelligent' for millions of years now. Although we could by no means say that virus-masses have anything like 'reason', 'will' or 'motive'. Viruses mutate at random when they divide. They agglutinate their work-spaces behind them. Indeed, the virologist added, one cannot even pinpoint exactly *where* these tiny 'bodies' contain *life*. Pipsqueaks. Ultimately, it is the reaction of the outside environment they've blundered into in order to perform their mutations—unintention-ally, accidentally, out of the boundless preparedness to make mis-takes—that determines the failure or success of their reproduction, that determines their destruction or survival on a gigantic scale. One generation is not identical to another, though it stands in rela-tion to its own continuation, so that one could indeed speak, as the virologist put it, of a continuous thread running through almost 3.5 billion years. You could say that these are simply random sequences. But they are sequences all the same . . .

CHALLENGE TO OUR NATIONAL DEFENCE

The virus' (temporary) indomitability casts us human beings back upon ourselves. We count our weapons. We change our habits. 'Isolating out of insight'. We are capable of learning.

Our Bundeswehr has sent soldiers to protect senior-citizen homes. But even with their training and their weapons, there is little they can do against the enemy. They are skilful, if occasionally clumsy. Like 'unskilled help'. Despite their marksmanship, they are inferior to the adversary.

A central problem, according to virologist Karin Mölling, is our urban way of life. One of the prerequisites of the crisis is the constant flow of people across the planet, a luxury that doesn't fit with the term 'state-of-war'. Pandemics demand a decentralized way of life.

There are no plans for the evacuation of metropolises in the event of a military conflict, one possibly involving the use of nuclear weapons or hitherto unknown military equipment.

INDECISVE WEATHER BEFORE
AND AROUND CHRISTMAS IN CENTRAL EUROPE

In mid-December the weather's emerging westerly flow gradually causes a warm spell. Both the horizon and the skies above Germany become damp. We who in November pulled out our winter things and dressed accordingly now sweat all over and our armpits stink.

Winter's hesitancy here during the season of Advent, as if something unexpected were on its way, has led to anxiety. To the expectation of a definitive cold spell. That kind of cold (which, however, usually first appears in January) can be calculated in days or weeks, which is another way of saying that just such an articulated period of weather ends with absolute certainty. But the lackadaisical, indecisive weather of mid-December (from the 24th through the 31st) seems as if it will never end. It weighs on one's soul like a 'mud season of the spirit'. Mud is not an element. It isn't solid, finite or hard, it is neither indecisive nor decisive.

OUR DOG'S DISORIENTATION ON CHRISTMAS EVE

My dog is waiting. Waiting for a bite, something from 'the master's table'. He has already eaten: a dish of canned chicken and calf meat in safflower oil (mixed feed for dogs up to a size of four decimetres). This, in any event, is different from what 'falls from the master's table'. The latter has the added excitement of surprise, the unexpected, the sovereign. I often notice that our dog sees our behaviour as some kind of slip. The slip consisting of the fact that we don't perceive him to be a human being, a member of the society of human beings, which indeed he is. He only experiences sympathy as a family member when he is unwell or has injured his paw.

Normally, he is deprived of such participation. He is not sitting in a chair at the table. All this touches upon misunderstanding.

As a result, on Christmas Eve, he only gets a tiny piece off the plates from which the adults are eating. He sits nervously under the table, visibly disappointed, even humiliated. For him, this Christmas, damaged and limited by the virus, holds only confusion. The presence of people he doesn't know. One simple chunk of beef and he'd be reconciled with Jesus. He doesn't know any dogs by the surname of Christ. As a dog, you sniff other creatures out, from behind. A spiritual being from more than 2,000 years ago has no smell of any kind.

THE REMOVAL OF UNNECESSARY HOLIDAYS AT A MOMENT THE THIRD REICH REQUIRES MAXIMUM EFFORT / CONFIDENTIAL INFORMATION RIGHT FROM THE FÜHRER'S MOUTH AT TEATIME

Yesterday, at the Horcher restaurant, Undersecretary Berndt of the Reich Ministry of Public Enlightenment and Propaganda—a member of Goebbels' most trusted staff—laid out the Führer's thoughts regarding the 1942 Christmas Eve celebrations. As soon as there was time, the Führer said during a round of tea, they would turn to the question of the Church. The nonsense of the ecclesiastical holidays (above all, their frequency during the turn of the year) had to be done away with. Bismarck had only got half the job done with his turn against the Vatican's machinations throughout the Reich. The eastern front is turning to ice. The enemy is threatening our position in North Africa. And across the Reich, the most pressing emergency measures, the most decisive tasks, are being held up by a chain of Saturdays, Sundays and statutory holidays. And every single time, that fighting spirit which connects front and Heimat withdraws into downright medieval-style caves. The Führer had just been informed—sipping his tea and nibbling biscuits, Hitler completely flew off the handle while listening to the report—that, during

Christmas, large-scale operations would be completely suspended.
Only one emergency service was planned. Instead of self-defence in
an all-out war, days of sentimental intimacy. The Führer categorically rejected the veneration of a weak and penitent preacher, a
victim of Roman justice.

–Does the fact that Jesus was Jewish play any role?

–As far as the Führer is concerned, Jesus wasn't a Jew.

According to Berndt, it's quite possible that a higher Roman officer, possibly of Gallic or Germanic origin and transferred to the
Orient, impregnated the Aramaic or Kurdish Mary. The point, however, was: no wailing over 2,000 years later for a single sacrificial
death! The Church leadership had been informed of the Führer's
opinion: no result or response. Getting rid of medieval Church
power, the Führer believed, would also have effects on the 'the future
world of opera'. There, too, it would not do for all those sopranos to
continue dying in the final acts, their sacrificial deaths blocking the
audience from paying attention and responding to current events.
The Führer repeats: 'Since the Day of Prayer and Repentance and
All Souls' in November (which, during the war, he had already moved
to a Sunday), there has been an unbroken chain of unnecessary days
off for Church reasons.' Berndt counted: four Sundays in Advent,
three holidays. Does the Führer count Sundays as well? 'Of course,'
Undersecretary Berndt replies. The Führer was appalled by the sheer
number of Saturdays and Sundays in a year. Question: Could one
not call off Christmas celebrations in such a crisis-ridden year? Or
postpone it to after the peace agreement? Pass a law in the Reichstag
or have the Führer give a special command? Or a ministerial ordi-
nance perhaps?

Berndt didn't want to talk about the question of the form with
which the ecclesiastical blocking of 'wartime' was to be removed in
the future. The waiters brought the second course, refilled glasses.
How easy it would be for a foreign agent or a simple windbag to be
among them, ready to pass on the information.

'It has to do with confronting the Church itself,' Berndt said, changing the subject. Christianity has to be replaced by National Socialist conviction wherever we find it. This internal struggle of youth competing against an outdated generation of old believers is the fundamental content of a new 'Night of the Long Knives', a second National Socialist revolution which the German Reich has been awaiting since 1934. In any event, a thorough 'revolution of the calendar' is part of the programme, and one of its components is the 'freeing up of the turn of the year for use in the combat mission'. Of course, consideration had to be given to certain regions in Southern Germany, as had been the practice with the white-flour allocation for Vienna, which is to say, local habits and preferences had to be taken into account. Having said that, it is imperative that we stop glorifying this weak-kneed Jesus, and child to boot. 'With that miserable flesh wound of his in the lower abdomen' which would not be recognized as 'invaliding' by any present-day military doctor. Strange, how the holidays are so frequent in the winter, always at the point when the initial cold snap in November is replaced by slack, damp weather that is good for nothing but the spread of various influenzas.

THE TAXI DRIVER LOOKING
FOR THE REPUBLIC OF PHILOSOPHY

My wife didn't want anything to do with the bearded man at the door. She didn't trust him. She sent me one floor further down, where the man was waiting. Due to Corona, he offered to put on a mask. I stood there, leaning against the railing in the stairwell.

He turned out to be a taxi driver who'd once given me a ride. He had remembered the address. He held a black-bound book by Sloterdijk which dealt with heaven. He had written down in pen on certain pages his impressions and comments. Lived experiences, he said. He showed me the pages. A late descendant of the twelfth-century GLOSSATORS.

Where, he asked, would he be able to find a group of similarly minded individuals with whom he could discuss his observations, his 'glosses', of the philosopher's book? In the city of Munich, off the top of my head, I have no idea where to send him. In ancient Athens, coming out of the suburbs, the Axial Age at his back, my visitor would certainly have found companions, maybe even a PUBLIC QUESTIONER like Socrates. And maybe today too, within the institutions of adult education, there is a philosophy-discussing circle of long standing that would welcome the bearded man with his observations. He could read his glosses out loud, and a debate could follow.

Conversely, a search for ADEQUATE CONTACTS ACROSS THE CITY'S CENTRAL SQUARES, in Stachus, in Lenbachplatz or any of the other centrally located traffic circles would no doubt be in vain, for not a single one of them hosts any kind of AGORA or has place for a philosophical discussion.

For me too, intellectual contact is coming undone. Habermas on the telephone earlier today: agitated, distracted, interrupted by a call on his second phone. We'd agreed to a chat today, Thursday. Our talk, he said in a nervous tone, will have to be postponed until Saturday morning. His publisher was calling at that same moment. Since yesterday, the philosopher said, 'unexpected complications have arisen.' It turns out he has to have three or four pages of his book *This Too a History of Philosophy* ready for a French publication tomorrow. The excerpt still has to be translated. He is completely taken.

RECALLING A MOMENT FROM 53 YEARS AGO
WHEN ANYTHING SEEMED POSSIBLE

In December 1968—after the topsy-turvy, revolutionary late autumn at Frankfurt's Karl Marx University (in the meantime, again rechristened Johann Wolfgang Goethe University), including the occupation of the Sociological Institute in Myliusstrasse—a small circle of comrades from the SDS (Socialist German Students' League) with-drew to the countryside. Into a farmstead in North Hessen and, together as a commune, studied Immanuel Kant's three powerful critiques under the guidance of Hans-Jürgen Krahl. Looking for spirited debate, direct activity, even fistfights with the police (who defended themselves with shields), in other words, floods of adrenaline, solid ground beneath their 'intellectual feet'. Time rushed on.

WILL THE ANGELS' ADMINISTRATIVE OFFICES DISAPPEAR WHEN THE LAST JUDGEMENT IS OVER OR JUST THOSE OF CERTAIN HIGHER ANGELS?

In the relationship of angels among themselves, there is the differ-ence between their nature and the grace in which they stand in rela-tion to God. Supposing that, at the moment of the Last Judgement, all the previous work of the 'messengers', that is, the official angels, becomes superfluous, would the angels themselves be destroyed? Would they disappear? the twelfth-century scholar who calls himself Anonymous and presumably travelled to Paris from Oxford asks. Or would they be active underground? Would they be transferred to a particular state of beatitude? To a rest home? Or something else entirely? Thomas Aquinas' answer to the question is as follows: None of this will happen, and, in the event of the Last Judgement, neither will the angels be destroyed. The exercise of their administrative offices, on the contrary, will indeed come to an end.

In commentaries accompanying this debate, there is reference to the fact that, at the moment of the Last Judgement, the angels will be responsible for gathering all the living and the dead to be judged. Some of the most decrepit creatures have to carry them on their backs. Loaded down under the weight, their wings are useless. And so, on they plod like pack mules. But reliably, 'as if by magic', they ensure the COMPLETENESS OF THE ASSEMBLY OF ALL THE LIVING AND THE DEAD.

Giorgio Agamben recently posed these questions anew. He tends towards a Latinate sceptical tone. One might almost be tempted to think that he believes instead in the resurrection of the maritime sea gods, magical Mediterranean beings. Be that as it may, whatever we know about angels comes from the Orient and the Nile.

WHAT CAN ANGELS DO?

PURGARE ('purify')

ILLUMINARE ('illuminate', in the celestial sense 'speak')

PERFICERE ('perfect', help, save)

THE LONG PRE-HISTORY OF CREATION
AS A SCHOLASTIC TEMPORAL FORM OF AETERNITAS
(ETERNITY)

Midrash says, '2,000 years before the creation of heaven and earth' (which is always calculated in God-time, that is, over a period of more than 14.7 billion years of cosmic time), God created seven things:

–The Torah

–The throne

–Heaven

–Hell

–The heavenly temple

–The name of the Messiah

–And the voice: 'Return, ye children of men.'

Over the following 2,000 years (once again, the conversion of God-time into cosmic time or that of evolution is necessary), God consulted the Torah and made OTHER WORLDS (which is why the existence of string theory's parallel worlds is not only mathematically but also theologically justified). In addition, He got into it with the letters of the alphabet. Which letters will cause creation? Only thereafter the creation and beginning of the world.

KEYWORD: EDUCATION (ERUDITIO)

In my first book, *Lebensläufe* (*Case Histories*), there is the story of a cathedral-school principal, Eberhard Schincke. During the time of the Third Reich, he was evacuated with his students to the country-side. An urbanite himself. Shy with strangers. 'He felt there was dear evidence that the quadruple constellation of Charlemagne, Alcuin, Theodulf and Am had produced a cultural nucleus of which, within 30 short years, nothing but fossils remained. It was the brief life of this precious plant to which he wanted to give literary form and whose laws of existence he wanted to describe.' Following the DARK AGES, Charlemagne re-established contact with the writings of antiquity. Education meant naturalizing the barbarians of Central Europe into a continuum of 'conscious exchange'. Discourse instead of swordfights. The story ends in the following way: 'During the day, Schincke was at work again on his paper on the cultural reforms of the Carolingian empire, which he had started planning in 1932 and writing in 1934.'

Children who drink in education through their eyes and ears move me. What does education mean? The letters children first start to paint and then use to write? The agreement to climb common stairs into a main building called school?

Education = eruditio. To carve something out of the wild wood.

Educatio = to lead out of the wild woods. Orientation. Knowing the routes, for children, for adults too. Becoming familiar with paths through the woods, animal trails and, last but not least, streets which make their way through the woods as well. The danger of EDUCATION is that the woods will be ravaged by hacked-out lanes. And yet, untrodden woods are no kind of property for people. There has to be some kind of balance between the destruction of the forests and the impenetrability of wild growth. We have attracted the raw minds of the barbarous Saxons with cathedral schools. We have preserved education despite all the challenges from local leaders. We have concentrated it in the books, priming and customs of the teaching profession. We have often concealed them, promoted them in private, reworked them horticulturally. We, the philologists, educational artists, lovers of grammar and the word, their curators, the administrators of LANGUAGE, of the only humane mechanism of power of our CONSTITUTION which lives and works before and within all given *constitutions*.

EXAMPLE OF AN *INCISIVE SCHOLASTIC EXPERIENCE* AS EDUCATION IN A FORMAL SENSE, THAT IS, OF EDUCATIONAL IMPACT FOR A WHOLE LIFETIME

On 6 February 1945, about 600 metres from the stone stairs I had climbed seven years earlier on my first visit to school, the grounds of Gotha's main train station were heavily bombed. The Allied bombing squadrons' plans saw them moving systematically towards Central Germany; on the one hand, systematically in the geographical sense and, on the other, as far as destruction specifically was concerned, with regard to traffic routes, transportation hubs and key industries.

After a pre-alarm for the whole of Gotha that day, one school class was led into the air-raid shelter of an insurance building on Bahnhofstrasse. Under their teachers' supervision, they settled into the cellars. One hour later, the students were dead. The blast waves from the bombs had shredded their lungs. All 11-year-olds.

Already during the move towards the insurance-building air-raid shelters, that is, during the pre-alarm, which consisted of three sustained siren hisses, two of the students—one of them spoke about his experience in his memoirs which Sigrid Damm recorded in her book *Im Kreis treibt die Zeit* (Time drifts in a circle)—distanced themselves from the group without permission. Probably out of the desire to look for things in the basement rooms of strangers. That's how they ended up making their way through the cellars of the neighbouring buildings. They might also have been planning some 'naughty games' (touching each other's naked bodies). So much was easily doable in those buildings' subterranean side rooms and storage areas. A tunnel and wall opening led from one tall building close to the station to another. The building above the two 11-year-olds who had broken away collapsed on them during the bombing. They escaped through the basement and got out into the open. The region around the main station lay in ruins, under a cloud of dust. Signs of fires.

The paramedics and firefighters who lined up the bodies of the dead schoolchildren on the pavement didn't know their names. The two 11-year-olds, who had left without permission and had thus been saved, had been looking for their classmates. They were now tasked by the other teachers, who had rushed out of the school as well, with identifying the dead. Handouts with the names of the deceased were made and attached with pieces of wire and threads at the level of their ankles. This was easier with the boys' short socks than with the girls' wool stockings which covered the skin up to the thighs.

In my friend, educational researcher Wolfgang Edelstein's published studies, teaching is differentiated into EDUCATION IN THE FORMAL SENSE and EDUCATION IN THE MATERIAL SENSE. Education in the material sense refers to material skills and knowledge of practical use in life. Education in the formal sense, on the other hand, develops skills of the mind, the ability to recognize horizons and form centres and make distinctions, quite independently of the educational process experienced in the 'formal sense'.

One of the two 11-year-olds rescued from the inferno, Hans von Frankenberg, later called the morning of 6 February 1945, and in particular the hours during which he, instructed by his teachers, had to attach the name tags (on cardboard and paper) to the limbs of his schoolmates, the 'most intensive lesson of his life'. Edelstein describes the literary account of this former pupil which he, like me, knows only from Damm's narrative, as a 'prime example of education in the formal sense'. The educational experience, he says, is a learning experience for life. It is learning about material that is intrinsically remote from this life, that perhaps happens only once in a lifetime or that never becomes reality at all. This is how, during Latin lessons, an all-round ability to distinguish accurately develops in the student, even if no one ever speaks Latin with them later in life. Von Frankenberg described the 'horror, still in my bones, of what I experienced'—the seconds of the bombing, the collapsing buildings, the derealization from all he was familiar with—as incisive and as a 'learning process' (though he is unable to give any indication of how he applied the experience). This kind of perception had not been extinguished, but had gradually reawakened in his nerves, body and mind while he made the little name cards as instructed and—also as an activity he had never performed before—attached them to the bodies of his comrades who only a short time before had formed a school class with him, and who had been closely and quasi-physically connected with him during the current school year. At times, they could hardly distinguish between themselves as the rescued and the dead they were properly lining up, uninjured on the outside but killed by ruptured lungs. None of his experiences, whether at school or in life, were as 'dense' and 'obscure', von Frankenberg wrote, as that lesson on that day 'when we didn't actually have school'.

'BASIC FORM OF TELLING A STORY'

For me, the basic form of telling a story is the piece of paper from the prescription pad that my father, a doctor, would use to write down, in five or six hard-to-decipher words, the stories he would then present to the guests of his 'cosy evening of wine punch', as though improvised on-the-spot. The fact that my father made such an effort to prepare the telling of a story still moves me. All he needed was a keyword, an 'intonation' of sorts. He was sure that a tone of voice would set in once he began to tell the story, without any long groping about.

FIGURE 3. A photograph of me by French photographer Gilles Pandel. 'This is what I will look like when I am dead.' The facial features of my father are now emerging in my old age. I had always thought I looked like my mother. Gilles Pandel took the photo in bright sunlight. My heartbeat was normal.

'A BACK-AND-FORTH, HALBERSTADT-STYLE'

Two waiting people are standing at the counter of a bar, talking. This is a story in the form of INTERJECTIONS. The interjections are preliminary answers that respond to the interlocutor's interjections in the form of quick sentences. They are feeling out the scale of reciprocal interest. It's a case of 'preparations for a conversation'. Sometimes the conversation doesn't come about. It is unnecessary, as everything has already been said. There is AGREEMENT. I have also been able to observe that the basic current of a collective 'conversation, Halberstadt-style' or even a soliloquy—namely, the major direction of interest being talked about on a given day in the city—leads into such a 'pre-talk in the form of interjections'.

–Böttcher's got it in her lungs.

–Hopeless?

–The doc says, Potentially. It could also help something.

–She'll manage.

–She'll manage or her husband will.

–Or the engine driver she had something with half a year ago. Her husband was friends with him.

–A threesome?

What remains unstated is how complex cooperation becomes in the workplace once rivalry enters the intimate sphere. A third party sparks into one's intimate web of relations. In the nineteenth century, dramas were made of such conflicts. Like the scene at the tobacconist's in the first act of *Carmen*. Or a murder like the one caused by the relationship of the solider Woyzeck in Leipzig. Now, under the pressure of the planning specifications, and considering the political struggle of the district administration against confusion in the work process and in daily life as a result of 'reckless relationships', in other words, private conflicts, the facts and the way they are talked about have changed. Cooperation has increased in both areas, in the work process as well as in terms of intimacy. The observation of the 'conversation, Halberstadt-style' dates to the time of the GDR. That was more than 40 years ago. This type of conversation, however, hasn't changed, nor has MODIFICATION REGAR-DING THE DE-DRAMATIZATION OF CONFLICTS.

'Epic, Dramatic, Lyric, Critical'
'Commentary, Epic, Dramatic, Lyric'

SUGGESTIONS FOR EXPANDING THE CLASSICAL
DIVISION OF THE ART OF POETRY
INTO FOUR CATEGORIES

A postdoctoral student from the circle surrounding Prof. Joseph Vogl at Humboldt University, Berlin, subjected the classical division of poetry (epic, dramatic, lyrical, critical) to a reconsideration. Instead of the word *epic*, whose orientation to GREAT FORM irritated her, she suggested the designation 'poetical gardens'. In gardens, it is necessary to plant. The term 'cooperative gardens' is familiar enough. The Iliad consists of a collection of narratives of various origins and times and temperaments; indeed, a portion of the text comes from anonymous reports and 'sub-collections' not originating with an author, a self-confident narrator, but with what 'one tells oneself'. In the replanting of narrative in the modern era, it would be a relief if the constraint imposed by classical prescriptions on an individual author to produce large narrative complexes on their own were to be overtaken by the possibility of linking different authors as well as already-existing textual concentrates. Wool, the academic continued, originates on the body of different animals before coming together in carpets and cloths through the art of weaving. She cites the mythical figure of the weaver ARACHNE from antiquity as the heraldic animal of this type of text.

'Cooperative gardens' primarily have to do with the replanting of the plebeian public sphere. The 'miscellaneous news' section of the paper would disappear. It is known that fairy tales have not been told anew in more than 200 years, nor the elderly listened to nor their stories collected. Stories, however, could arise out of the vocabulary of Schlager songs. But this doesn't happen all that often. The author lists 87 projects: all of them plantations, factory-like workshops, generators for practical storytelling. 'The poetic means collecting,' the young academic writes.

One has to be able to 'tell stories from out of Eve's rib'. At another point, the academic remarks: Telling stories through the means and spirit of music. It is indeed clear that there are such things as snapshots of speech which recall the buzzing of the spirit, the rhythms of the body, the nuances of language, so that they have a contagious effect on the course of speech. All of a sudden, speech becomes fluid. But this is precisely the beginning of epic storytelling.

From a narrative point of view, building rafts is better than building steamers. Building a steamer functionally degrades the material. The same holds true for personal experience in literary narratives. In the postdoc debate, the young academic was accused of verbosity and digressiveness in her choice of examples. She, however, doubled down on the 'unfolding of infinite melody as the motor of the epic method'.

THE CONCEPT OF RAW MATERIAL HAS RUTHLESSLY CHANGED IN THE SECOND AND THIRD NATURE IN WHICH WE LIVE. 'Second nature' is to be understood as social nature, in other words, the industrial age. 'Third nature' is that of the digital age, of algorithms. Poetical horticulture thus responds to innovative centres. And to changing horizons. At that point, it was clear to the participants of the seminar that the academic (who, like Vogl, spent half the year at Princeton and half at Humboldt) had come out of critical theory à la Frankfurt. That clarified the fronts. The majority of participants belonged to other factions of literary studies than Frankfurt's classical one or today's 'practical philosophy'.

The rebellious postdoc student (who in the meantime had just about finished writing her habilitation thesis) suggested—expressly as *complementary*, not as a replacement of the classic four types—the following division of the art of poetry as a so-to-speak productive orientation for the making of modern stories:

POETICAL HORTICULTURE / COMMENTARY
METAMORPHOSES / CONSTELLATIONS

'PLUMB LINE ORIENTED TOWARDS THE CENTRE OF THE EARTH'

At one of the subsequent meetings of the postdoc seminar, the academic had armed herself with a drawing by Paul Klee. The sketch showed (suggested) elemental relations like 'mountains', 'water', 'air'. From their horizontal depiction, energetic VERTICAL arrows. The drawing was used in lessons at the Bauhaus. Next to the vertically placed arrows Klee had noted: 'Plumb line oriented towards the centre of the earth.'

The young scholar (who despite the pandemic was packing her things for Princeton) maintained that neither the lyric nor the dramatic form allowed excavations into the vertical, through towards the thorough, to a sufficient extent. 'Networked times' in particular are tough to represent. And what are networked times? The mood in the seminar again turned against the speaker who was using terms without explaining them. She didn't answer, but pointed out that the narrative of drama, which aims at *suspense*, lays itself like a layer of lava across the 'multiplicity of times'. 'It makes invisible the ways in which times come to us.' Without any transition, as if controlled by an inner force, she briefly spoke about drones. Automatic weapons of Turkish production, paid for with Azerbaijan's oil wealth, which flared and incinerated the steel constructions of artillery and tanks (produced by the Russian arms industry) with which the Armenians were defending themselves in Nagorno-Karabakh.

The academic continued to speak in a raised voice, seeking to drown out her opponents. Commentaries are like voles.

How is a narrator like a vole? The image of the mole, the attacked academic replied, does not refer to a vole but rather to a burrowing animal active inside the earth. She referred to Marx, who compared the revolution in its downtimes to just such a mole. How would the master—referring to evolution's box of examples—have illustrated the expression: 'permanent revolution'?

One fault within the method of commentary, a speaker in the seminar interjected, has to with the volatility of words. Language itself does not permit commentary in this far-fetched form of association. Then it would have to be supplemented by mathematics, music or other distinctive narrative structures, the young woman replied stroppily. And was off again, linking remote things together. In a few sentences, she had spoken of the non-identity of oil, dependant on who was extracting it from the ground. In other words, the origin of oil judged not geologically but in terms of ownership and power relations. Then she went on to talk about the fifth act of Halévy's opera *La Juive* (The Jewess), in particular, the scene in which a girl who believes she is Jewish (but is in fact a Christian saved by a Jew 30 years previously) is being burnt alive in a kettle of boiling oil. The drama takes place during the Council of Constance in 1414. The way the opera progresses steadily increases the audience's tension before culminating in a musical imitation of the girl's scream. Such agitative influence on the emotions of the audience reminds her, the academic said, of the upward curve of stock-market prices. In fact, this opera had been the favourite of the Parisian public for almost a hundred years. The cardinal who signs the death sentence at the end and orders the execution, and who presides over the Council of Constance, is the biological father of the executed soprano. Thus, the possibility of finding a way out of the disaster narrows 'dramatically'. According to the committed doctoral candidate, the advice of dramatist Heiner Müller was to be taken into account here. It's a matter of 'digging tunnels'. It is necessary, in the midst of the dramatic constellation, to create an understanding of what the 'kettle filled with boiling oil' means. It is obvious that this kettle, this oil, is not the same as the oil produced today in the Baku foothills, which varies slightly in price from North Sea or Venezuelan oil. Both kinds of oil, the one of 1414 and the one of 2020, however, are similarly combustible and deadly on the skin of humans, and this skin has remained equally sensitive throughout the evolution of the human race: as equally sensitive today in the warlike conflict in Nagorno-Karabakh (the Turkish-Azerbaijani fuel is sprayed by drones) as it was in 1414 in Constance. In the seminar, the habilitand was told that to understand such leaps one would have to add a commentary immediately. They're not jumps, but excavations or tunnels, the attacked one replied. Besides, she was pleading for commentary!

But how does the format of commentary differ from that of metamorphoses? They are synonymous terms, the dedicated one answered. Something that changes, even mutates, during the telling of the story under the influence of the others' reactions is both a metamorphosis and the consequence of commentary.

It is not the rhymes, the rhythm, the language that are able to 'screw together' the contents of experience, the wise woman continued, but rather the knowledge of the ways out, the ability to connect something both tightly and loosely at the same time. And that is supposed to be an art of narration in its own right? Certainly, the questioned one replied, or more than poetry, at any rate.

But now we need to consider the fourth grouping of art: criticism. For this, the rebellious speaker claimed, one must supplement the category of criticism with the category of 'constellation'. In the short time available during Advent, however, as the end of the semester had been set prematurely due to the Corona crisis, this was no longer possible, either in the current seminar or in its continuation.

FIGURE 4. Supporters of the Enlightenment leading evil to prison.

THE NECESSITY OF REINTRODUCING
GHOSTS INTO EUROPE

In the eighteenth century, those hunting officials who'd been employed by princes or the State shot too many foxes and wolves. But what was even more grave was the decimation of ghosts and spectres by means of a populist, lay-driven 'Enlightenment' which involved the quoting of misunderstood philosophers.

The different parts of the soul (which change constantly throughout a human being's lifetime) need nourishment. Every child experiences the animistic phase. This phase, with its own eeriness and secrecy, is followed by the phase of trying to master that ghostly world in which all bushes, all things, have their own life. This is the phase of magic. Both phases give rise to spiritual forces, an undercurrent, a deep body of water in which ghosts and spirits live on, long after the animistic and magical parts of the soul have ceased to exist. No ratio, no EMOTIONAL INTELLIGENCE, without such elementary supply. The 'unproven', even the 'uncanny' is of vital importance to our souls and sense of self-assurance. And this supply system is precisely what a rapidly expanding company, a start-up from the Bavarian Forest on the border to Bohemia, is working on: FREISCHÜTZLAND. Paid by this company and on its behalf, ghosts are captured in Japan (where they sit behind every hill, even in earthquake-endangered high-rises in cracks in the floors). They can also be found in the lift shafts of skyscrapers, in places where the lifts aren't running. These ghosts must be brought to Europe, the start-up claims, and released if there is ever to be a generous, self-aware EUROPEAN COMMUNITY.

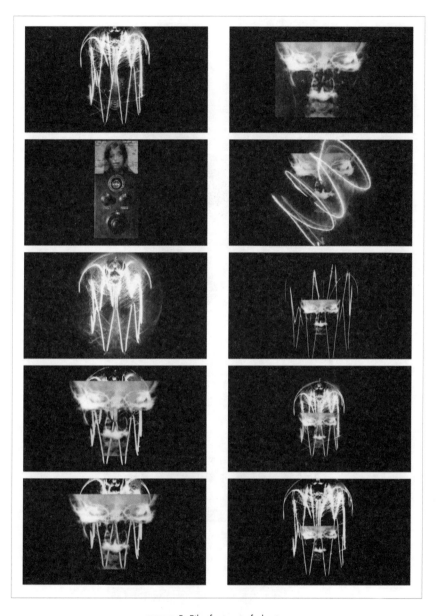

FIGURE 5. Film footage of ghosts.

FIGURE 6. One of Master Hokusai's last artworks:
An apparition of a dragon beyond a snow-covered Mt Fuji.

A DESCRIPTION OF WHERE I AM WRITING

I am a son. From the rib of my mother, Alice. All my body's cells tuned to her cells, and in agreement. Perhaps the vibrations, the priming of nerves and cells are identical. Perhaps it is also only a case of a majority of them agreeing that the vibrations, the strings, fit one into the other. My text flows from the tip of my pencil, the brown-coloured progeny of the Faber-Castell company (due to the high amount of lead, it writes both quickly and softly). My mother Alice's breath, her rapid pulse, her skin (her greatest organ), her nervousness—all that is within me as I sit here, and my writing quickens.

Moreover, I am my sister's brother. She determines me authoritatively. She's an Aries. She is responsible for a good half of my soul's salvation and my joy in writing. I do not belong to myself. Something within me listens to foreign voices. It would be arrogant to speak of 'I' or 'me'. It's not really a case of hearing foreign voices, but that a number of foreign voices within me are struggling for dominance in my texts. A lot of negotiation is required. At constant risk of an internal civil war, I can only create the 'I of the narrator' through great effort.

My father: a doctor. I can hear his footsteps throughout the first floor of our earlier home on Kaiserstrasse—although they date from 1941 or 1943—as if he were just above me or in the room next door. My father has short legs. He is lively. He has a quick pace too. That rhythm goes into my text. But under this influence the words drip from the pencil tip a little more slowly, calmly, hesitantly. I suspect that the spiritual influence of my father, in whose presence I would never write a word—as he was the storyteller—doesn't make me more critical, but, rather, enriches my ideas, the inflow. More comes to me. In the rhythm of my sister or mother, on the other hand, the walls retreat. The view more general. My father's footsteps move between his doctor's office, i.e. the rooms facing the street which are open to the public, the bathroom and my parents' bed-and-dressing-room facing the Harz mountains. Intimate places. I can feel how my father is my metronome, his medical practice the centre. Whenever I write, this centre, unchanged, lies, geographically speaking, 500 kilometres away from me and, chronologically, 76 years in the past. This is the now.

MY GOOD WILL IN WRITING IS NOTHING BUT THE GOOD WILL I HAD AS MY PARENTS' RUNNER

I am going to have to get going soon. In the meantime, it's 1946. With a tote bag off to Gebhardt, a food retailer, in the lower part of town, on the corner of Hoher Weg. A shop. There I have to say: 'I am coming from Dr Kluge and am supposed to pick something up.' The package is ready under the counter. Black-market goods. My father does not charge his patient Gebhardt. I bring the package home.

The period in which I was a runner for my mother, who was involved in a black-market chain, lies in a different period than that of my willing activity for my father. The texts which have been collecting on the paper of my DIN A4-sized ring binder are by no means as willing as I once was as a runner. Again and again, they get tied up. I start over. What I have described as the rhythm between my mother and I is a humming of nerves and cells. What I have referred to as the metronome of my father is no such tone at all, but a kind of interval, a regular, recurring stutter, a pause or sudden torrent of words forcing their way into the text. I would describe the gravity-like influence my sister exerts upon me when I write as a whispering against them, and a voice, an alternating voice, a contradictory spirit too.

STATION 2

WHENEVER I THINK OF MY HOMETOWN, IT HAPPENS THROUGH THE EAR

SNOW SHOVELS IN HALBERSTADT

On those January days of my childhood when massive amounts of snow had fallen overnight, I'd be awoken by the sound of the iron shovels the adults would use to move the snow onto the sides of the street, away from our houses and off the pavements. As the weather moves in circles, the snow-heavy clouds would usually come from the west, the south, from the east and then the north. Iron on stone, a hard sound, in-between the scraping of shovels or spades striking the snow- or ice-covered ground. The lumps of snow themselves toppled off the shovels onto the mountains of snow with a muffled sound. A week later, there are two peak-like walls of snow on either side of the street. They tower over the bicycle path, blocking direct access to the other side of the road. You can only cross at the intersections. We children scale these mountain ridges which in the meantime have become hard and crusty. You can get wounded in the process.

I EXPERIENCE THE PHYSICAL CONDITIONS OF MY CITY THROUGH MY EAR WITHOUT LOOKING OUT THE WINDOW

Every Tuesday morning, the thud of the heavy draught horses' hooves on asphalt wakes me up early. It's the beer truck coming to deliver the weekly beer supply and a case of non-alcoholic malt for me. The sound of the wheels—made of rubber—on the asphalt is soft and a little like the 'smacking' of lips. Over the course of the morning, the traffic out on the street grows heavier. The trucks and other vehicles create a continuous drone. When an artillery division moves through town, the cannons' metal wheels clatter and scrape the asphalt 'unnaturally'. Like a warning signal. One gets the impression that the street will be damaged. The impression is deceptive. The column passes through town without leaving a trace. It takes six hours, with long interruptions whenever they stall and become disorganized.

LOUDSPEAKERS ABOVE THE CITY

On Holzmarkt and 32 other public places throughout the city of Halberstadt, one of the Führer's speeches is being broadcast over loudspeakers. A five-year-old, I hear the sound filling the town. My steps slow and swing from Lindenweg into Heinrich-Julius-Strasse. With that backdrop of sound, you cannot simply keep walking. It breaks apart against the buildings and in the alleyways. A wax-and-wane of speech. It is difficult, if not to say impossible, to differentiate between the words. Of course, what's important is not the words but the dominance that tone exerts over everything in town. The people move slowly. In that sense you could say: the city has fallen into a deep silence.

It lies in a kind of 'open prayer'. As an adult, I can interpret the five-year-old's assured sense of hearing. There is an intimation of 'impending danger', of an 'urgent call to dress reality in black and get serious'.

THE SOUND OF WORK REPLACES
THE SOUND OF BELLS

It's a Protestant part of the country. Every Sunday morning, full of the rising and falling sound of church bells from a profusion of churches. The town is flooded by the summons to unhesitatingly populate their bare interiors. The number of my friends who go to church is small. And though the sound really impressed me, I didn't follow it anywhere either. All the same, it sets the rhythm of my week. Nothing of this massive acoustic experience survived 1945. The sound of a Sunday morning in 1946 is no longer defined by any church bell. The city is still. The quiet, however, is pervaded by natural sounds. Even the crunch of booted feet making their way over heaps of debris. On Sunday mornings, the 'rubble-women' are out in their special task units. A clip and clap of bricks being tossed onto piles, the sound of shovels, but the workers' words too, all of them season Sunday's stillness.

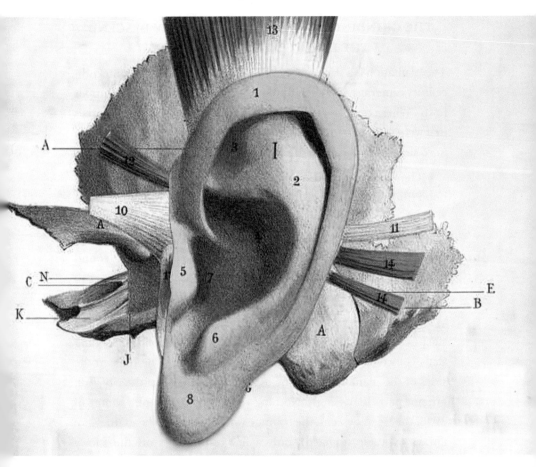

FIGURE 7

THE GRINDING SOUND OF SLEDS AS THEY DESCEND
THE HILLS OF THE PLANTATION

The plantation is a park space in Halberstadt. Laid out by eighteenth-century cameralists between the city walls and recently forming 'upper town'. Where once stood ramparts and moats, they planted the trees that were necessary for mulberry cultivation. And it was there that now were sled runs for the children in winter.

The noise level on the hills of the plantation in the early afternoon (the children are still at school or eating) is different from that at dusk. The sinking winter light sparks the sledders' spirits. The sleds make a grinding, 'muddy' sound. Above them, the children's cries. Snowfall. Cold on the cheeks and hands. A rattling sound when the sleds make their sharp turn at the base of the hill to stop before hitting the wide pavement.

For the adult eye that tries to reconstruct the scene today, the steepness of the hill which corresponds to the sound of the speeding sleds is inconceivable. As is the feeling of danger. The hills on the sides of the plantation, leaning against the remains of the city wall, are not particularly high. Nothing recalls the reality of a winter in 1938, the steep descent, the courage when a sledder's head (they are always on their stomach), only a few centimetres off the snowy ground, virtually plummets downwards. The sound I think I hear in my ears hits a nerve. The shouts of my many peers ('Alarm! Alarm!') like a cloud over it all.

THE SOUND OF THE 'ZEPPELIN OVER TOWN'

The airship itself so close, there, just above the houses. It hovers over the intersection of Kaiserstrasse and Bismarckstrasse. Inaudible. Small motors on its sides to steer. At a distance, they make no noise at all. It was only based on my eye's impression that I *thought* I perceived a whirring sound. Today I think that, due to the distance, there was no way I could have heard them. But that's not the only reason—it would also have been impossible due to the 'chattering', 'fluttering' sound of many excited people throughout the town drowning out all the others. We ran out of our houses. All the children in the neighbourhood. The adults followed. I think we were screaming. We boys excitedly shared whatever details we could see. Shouts, not informative messages. A collective excitement lying over the city like a heavy cloud.

FIGURE 8

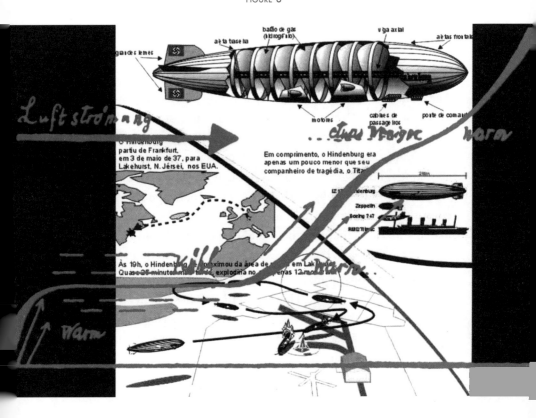

DIFFERENCES IN THE SOUND
BETWEEN WAR AND PEACE

I can pinpoint the difference between 1940 (wartime) and the spring
of 1939 (peacetime) in the sound of city traffic. At the outbreak of
the war, 95 per cent of private vehicles were confiscated or immobi-
lized in people's garages (because of the petrol quota). The gradual
'awakening of the city on an early Monday' morning as perceptible in
the growing noise of Halberstadt's vehicular traffic was absent during
the war. What was even more striking was the roar of the traffic in
Greater Berlin, which had made such an impression on me as a four-
year-old already. My grandmother was driving me to Anhalter station.
Around me a MASSIVE SOUND: the city itself. I don't believe that
the GREAT CITY NOISE of 1936 has returned to the noisy traffic
sounds of today's Berlin. Either because my child's ear exaggerates
the sound of those early days, or because the acoustic emissions of
engines today no longer achieve that same humming effect.

BOMBER FLEET OVER TOWN

The sound of bombs crashing nearby is one that cannot be reproduced by words. 'A crashing sound' is just a phrase. And it's not a
case of a sound in isolation. The intensity of the sound is connected
with a quivering of the floor; more than anything else, the ceiling
above me is no longer safe. In this sense, it is a 'bang' followed by a
'burst'. Any imitation by words, however, remains poor. The first
encounter is simply unbelievable. When I experienced something
like that up close, there was no sound in the world I could compare
it to. The sound says: the next second is not guaranteed.

The squadrons approach the city with a low hum. This is due to
the power of the engines. This sound diminishes briefly when the
bombs are dropped. The weight of the aircraft is reduced. Then,
engine power increases again. In effect, the engines are doing 'work
that has become unnecessary'. Before the pilots reduce engine
power, the noise of the bombers swells. These are all perceptions
that I did not classify as a child and witness. No, we considered the

swelling of the engine sound *after* their 'wares' were unloaded to be more dangerous than the sound *before* the bombs were dropped.

I don't know of any audio document that would accurately reproduce the sound of 'bombers in the skies over town', the 'roar of falling bombs'. The radio-archive documents I am familiar with only record the bombs' impact. And the approach of the bomber squadrons from a distance. There is a lot of material in the archives on 'bomb impacts in the distance'. They accentuate the rhythm in which the series of bombs hit the city. What is firmly anchored in my ears as an acoustic impression (and has not been repeated for the rest of my life) is different from all these documents.

A CUTTING, HISSING SOUND THAT'S IMPOSSIBLE TO CONFUSE WITH ANYTHING ELSE, ANNOUNCING THE DEPARTURE OF ONE DANGER AND THE ARRIVAL OF A NEW ONE

Once the aircraft have dropped their bombs and are moving away, a singing, buzzing sound replaces the previous engine noise that characterizes the aircraft still carrying their load in their cargo holds. The cellar occupants, however, hear a sharply pointed trickling sound, similar to the sound of masses of bricks falling to the ground from the roof of a house as it is being demolished, but more concise and, again, completely distinctive, unique. *Ripple* is too weak a word here, it does not aptly describe the sharpness of the 'tearing sound'. One could replace the word with *cutting*, but that would not capture the hissing rush. This noise, which accompanies and soon dominates the sound of the departing squadrons, doesn't come from the debris, but is the sound of the fire that breaks out in the neighbouring houses, and even in one's own house, and takes over the reign of violence. I hear that sound to this day. I have done a lot of research to explain it. I certainly didn't understand it as a 13-year-old basement dweller. Hardly any other sound in the world makes my soul more unquiet than this one.

I BELIEVE THAT THE SOUL WHISPERS
RATHER THAN SPEAKS ...

At the age of four I suffered from nightmares. My nanny found me hanging off the side of the bed, my head to the floor, screaming. Her calling out my name, her calm words did nothing to bring me back to myself. She began to whisper. I responded to whispers. When I am alone, memorizing something, speaking with myself, I do so in a whisper. As far as my attention span is concerned, the older I get, the more speaking in a normal tone becomes muddy. I believe that I have already heard, already understood what is being said, even at the moment of its saying, and my senses begin to wander. I still show interest, but I'm no longer paying attention. What comes in a whisper, however, wafts like the wind along telegraph wires, far up above and deep down below, in the subtext.

At the Munich Security Conference, in one of the interpreters' booths, I notice 26 interpreters. Speaking quietly into their machines. When rival parties get excited onstage, raise their voices, thunder against one another, the interpreters' volume automatically goes down. Almost to a whisper. The interpreters' soft tones reach the speakers through their headphones. Having said that, I have never observed an excited or downright hostile debate ever become any milder because of it.

THE SUN DOESN'T SOUND LIKE IT USED TO,
IT ROARS ...

If the roar of our sun could reach us on earth, that sound would silence all others. The moon's quieter hiss would be barely perceptible in this canon of noise. In fact, space does not transmit any sound at all. Astrophysicists and NASA, however, are able to measure the waves at the shock front of a celestial body, such as the red supergiant Betelgeuse. These frequencies are audible. The distant sound is measured as a vibration curve. This returns like a very fast, greatly aged mega-sun, tearing apart space before it, and presumably pieces of time too, as it rushes forward, unleashing a wild chaos of sound that has nothing to do with any thing we know in our lives or that a human ear can tolerate without being damaged. On NASA's playback devices, this vibration is transposed into a chirping, alternating crackling, rustling, cosy sound like the noise in a disused mine in the Harz mountains, where it drips from the ceiling. To the human ear, technical translation work, an obliging, polite wonder from afar.

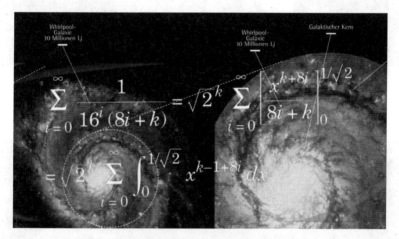

FIGURE 9 (ABOVE). Tremendous sound sources in the cosmos.
FIGURE 10 (BELOW). Spectrogram of a violent summer storm over the city.

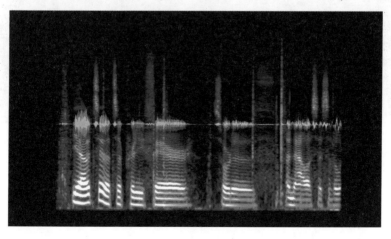

FIGURE 11 (ABOVE). Sound. 'Quacking'.
FIGURE 12 (BELOW). Ptah's ears. Hieroglyphs, 3,500 years ago.

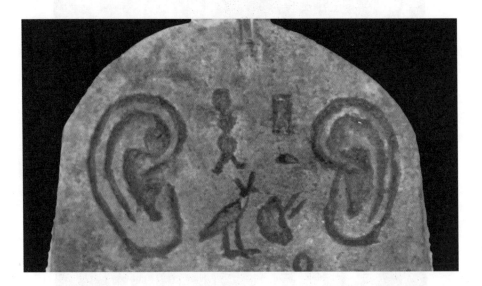

HOW DOES ONE TELL A STORY
FROM UP CLOSE?

THE REMAINS OF A DESIRE
FOR WINTER STORM TRISTAN

Two weeks ago, on 4 February, deep snow in the park, the tail ends of winter storm Tristan which hit mainly Central Germany, reached Munich. The media, focused on the ARCTIC HURRICANE approaching from the northeast that caused snowfall when it met with a moisture-swollen MEDITERRANEAN FRONT, indulged in exaggerations. In the end, there were between 30 to 50 centimetres of snow at the meteorological measuring points. In front of our house in the park, more like 20. All the same, the ice, cold, snow and snow-like slush in Holland were so powerful that our colleague Beata Wiggen slipped and broke both her legs while opening the rear of her car.

In the meantime, all the snow in the park has melted. Below a hill, a wide expanse of water has emerged. A small lake. A child in boots is splashing tirelessly in it, from shore to shore. Without stop. Enjoying the last little bit of ICESKATE-JOY transferred to the mud and water. Her stockings are probably long since wet, her shoes full of water. Soon she'll be sniffling and coughing. 'It was a pleasure.' The SUPERVISING MOTHER has enough to do getting her other three children under control. They are all hungry for exercise on the first day of the thaw. The WATER LOVER is her eldest.

INSTEAD OF A *MADELEINE*, A BISCUIT
THAT'S IMPOSSIBLE TO FIND IN HALBERSTADT

My paternal grandmother is sitting in a recliner and sleeping. Her grandson (in other words, me) is supposed to move quietly. I am not to approach the sleeping woman too closely or out of any kind of curiosity. I am not supposed to look at her narrow, white-skinned nose up close. The sleeping woman breathes gently, inaudibly. In the room, the specific smell of my grandparents. It has its origin in the furniture as well as in their bodies. Frugal citizens who think sustainably, they do not air their rooms as often as they would like, and never with fervour. The living room retained a pleasant warmth. The bedroom is cold. One does not squander the little warmth that's there in the interest of a night's sleep. The smell in the living room cannot be recalled through words. It's not *sweet*. Not *bitter*. Not *stuffy*. And definitely: not *musty*. If the word were suitable for a definition, translatable into exactness (and not merely an emotional abbreviation), I would say: *homely*. Containing something of the sour skin odour that is specific to my father's maternal side of the family. Because of it, I can recognize any room in which my grandmother has spent a considerable amount of time. Wherever she appears together with her husband, there is an additional, energetic note of cigar smoke.

Now, 86 years later, my wife and I have arrived at a similar level of comfort. All the elements—the place, kind of patience, smell, even the light—are different. My wife's back surgery. Heart fibrillation: four weeks of crisis in a large hospital. These days, I go with her to her physical therapy sessions at a rural clinic. She sleeps in a reclining chair. Parchment-like skin, shaky, unsteady gait when she gets up. When she's in her chair, she has a blanket over her legs. I can move around the room without disturbing her. The unfamiliar clinic—we are living in a more spacious room category with a view of the garden—has almost no smell at all. As for the choice of furniture, I would say 'comfortable'. It doesn't matter whether you claim the smell of the furniture is 'rural' or 'international'. Even this—measured against where my grandparents lived—'inconspicuous' smell does not pay attention to any term. It's not true that you can't smell the aseptic tint of the odours here. The position of my wife's head in her reclining chair is one of her lifelong characteristics, imprinted in my memory. Silence in the room. 'Just us old folks.' In my sleeping grandmother's room, I could not have imagined seeing her in a comparable living situation. In retrospect, the time it took me to get there turned out to be short. My memory furnishes the room and the moment. 'Time stands still.'

HOW DOES ONE TELL A STORY FROM UP CLOSE?

It snows all night and all day. The branches of the trees are covered with a forearm-thick layer of snow. My daughter hesitates to leave Munich and drive back to Berlin in this weather. We talk about the book she wants to write. She gets angry whenever my suggestions remind her of the ideas I have in mind for my own work. I concentrate on putting myself in her shoes and only giving *her* ideas narrative advice. We walk through the park seven times, taking detours.

I want to suggest that she write love stories, that is, observations about relationships. Such love stories should cover three successive generations. In other words, three women from the same family, even if they are staggered in their relationship, i.e. cousin, aunt, grandmother, mother or daughter. I notice in the first sentences that the words don't fit the closer observation of relationships or family relationships that well. Where it would be interesting to bring together many distinctions, they use a metaphorical, proverbial, even schematic word that only evokes a general idea. The words would first have to wage war with one another a while, to reforge one another. There needs to be a kind of friction between them to allow for distinctions to bubble up. What interests me is that the rules by which people approach one another or separate, that is, enter and exit the realm of intimacy, and thus the course of love stories over three or four generations, over the period from about 1914 to 2021, have fundamentally changed three times. I see cycles: a bond in 2021. It casts its shadows back to 1942. The two of us, my daughter and I, know the case. Our sentences become shorter and more rapid as we exchange observations. 'One word leads to another.'

In 2043, the bond from which a child is being born this very week will have lasted 22 years. The child from this relationship, a Corona child, will be looking at an alien world in 2043. This leads us to the conclusion—the paths of the park form figure-eights and can easily be covered several times—that a characteristic century like that from 1815 to 1945 contains different love stories than the time thereafter, as the canon of getting to know one another and the canon of separation through divorce or death are strikingly different from a story taking place between 1945 and 1989. Then another push: noticeably different pop lyrics, Schlager songs and stories in the period from 1989 to 2042. I won't be there at the end. My daughter is grappling with the fact that the cycles we're talking about are of such different lengths:

130 years – 44 years – 45 years.

What I mean, I say, is that the sequence of 'centuries of intimacy', that is, of love stories, is accelerating. I think that the cycles of economics and politics are accelerating even more. Where are the resting points? Where are the lagoons in the 'waters of love'? Where is there something flowing at a speed that suits us humans? My daughter waves away the words 'the cycles of politics and economics'. She is interested in observing relationships. We come to the keyword 'semantic fields'. To talk about them nowadays, we don't need a new grammar but countless new ways of paraphrasing. Not because love is becoming more complicated, but because the distance between the LEVEL OF TELLING STORIES and the MASSES OF FACTS OF OUR TIME is widening enormously.

FAMILIAL BONDS SEVERED BY TIME

As a child, my sister would often sit at the window for evenings on end. 'Deathly sad'. Waiting. I don't think she used the word 'deathly sad' as a child. But I am sure that she was sad to the bone without having the right word for it. She was four. Staring outside, she probably assumed that some magical power would bring the lively young woman, her mother, back through the window to envelop her. Or that the young woman would come in through the door. While she continued to look out of the window. The unexpected would step in through the door. Take her in its arms. And so she would sit there, whole gloomy afternoons long, especially on Sundays. But nothing and no one came.

That was during the time following my parents' divorce. Our mother, as a divorcee, was forbidden to visit. Later, my sister's psychologist stated that the terrible fights between daughter and mother had their basis in the 'natural antagonism between mothers and daughters that often appears'. The so-called Elektra complex. It corresponds to the 'Oedipus complex' in boys. Mother–daughter tension doesn't manifest in actions, but in endless squabbling, discussions, a mutual readiness to fight and constant disappointment.

I saw the conflict (which could not be resolved within the family) differently. A good 12 years after the phase of PRIMARY SADNESS, of the heartfelt wish that that warm-skinned mother who always spoke the right words might return, a phase followed by a phase of mourning lasting several years, the daughter—this was already after the war and from the Soviet-occupied zone—had gone to visit her mother. As soon as she entered the strange flat dominated by the new husband's furniture, my mother began to fuss with my sister's hair styled according to East German taste, which is to say: unfashionably. The daughter hated this crossing of the dividing line to her hair by this 'strange woman', the line that separated what was hers from the strange hand. Had the 'former longing been mourned'? Was it necessary to defend at all costs an independence acquired with so much pain at the border of closeness?

I think the daughter, my sister, had loved a young woman and missed her still. And yet what she found there in West Berlin wasn't the young woman whose breath had blown about her as a child, but an older woman who had become rigid in her second marriage. The person she was facing, indiscreetly correcting her hairstyle, had the same name but was definitely not the same person. A fraud. As serious as another disappointment. From that moment on, the two women never got along again.

UNDER THE SIGN OF ARIES

In the ascendant at her birth, the constellation Libra. She was an Aries. How does the ascendant Libra help? For a long time, she was good-willed. Then, suddenly, 'like a curtain tearing', she became intractable, stubborn, unruly, 'like a ram'. And so, after a protracted quarrel with her brother over trivial matters, she ran away. Took off. Her anger would shoot up as if from a subterranean chamber of ram-like energy. But in a living person, the energy is in the veins, on the skin, in the senses, in the ears which from now on no longer obey, so the word 'subterranean' is metaphorical. The surging part of her energy of departure, the break with her previous life, contin-ued to draw its strength from her resistance against our father, that is, from a much earlier time. Something inside her still raged against that tyrant. Our father had declared her his favourite. Ever since she'd lain in her crib as a cute little child, about six months old, he had sparkled at her with a delighted eye. Year after year, the helpful one, the family slave, the 'darling', controlled by her father, who was good for an order at any hour of the day. The reserve of stub-bornness she had accumulated, determined not by stars but by cir-cumstances, alternated with her anger at her brother for having once expressed himself poorly, which she saw (contrary to what he had meant) as a decisive attack on her person. And so, one day, she arbi-trarily tossed her things into a large suitcase and put a normal coat over her good one. Then she was off to the train station. Changed cities. Still full of the spirit of rebellion, just six weeks after arriving in the metropolis she was pregnant. The father-to-be: a militant from the student protest movement, which was already breaking up into groups. She'd taken him into her shared flat. She had allowed intimacy.

Some of the aspects of her newly chosen companion's style gave her pause. She pushed the impression aside. How, for example, after their car had broken down on a trip, he sat by the side of the road and had breakfast! Instead of getting his hands dirty in the necessary manual work: changing one of the old car's tyres. And she had to hurry. Their infant lying in its crate in the back seat. She could not expect this temporary accommodation for the child to last long. She wasn't trained in removing car wheels from the back of the vehicle and changing tyres. She did not feel supported by her companion. Nevertheless, she believed it was right to invest in the (socialistically defined) relationship for the sake of human progress. And so, she took her soon-to-be husband, the child's father, as he was. Repressed any doubts about the solidity of her decisions.

Eighteen years later, after years of a new kind of slavery, if different compared to her family of origin: fatigue, even gradual indifference, so-called TOUGHENING UP in the marital community. She endured it all, earning a living for the family. Her husband devoted himself to his studies, staying out late. Then one day she found out that her companion had met a young woman of means and got her pregnant. This was simply incomprehensible to her Aries instinct. That same day, she put his books, the mass of his clothes and other possessions that reminded her of him outside the door and then down the stairs and into the courtyard. For others to take. With the son from this bond, her only happiness, her property, she travelled to a new residence. This time it was the federal capital. With her medical background, she could find work anywhere in the world. Ultimately, the art of healing is needed everywhere. She was useful. She was no longer anyone's slave. And so, this character, a wall-breaking *ram*—the instruments that batter and break open the gates of foreign cities are indeed called rams—immediately opened a new chapter in her life. Throughout her life, all the rifts appeared abruptly and remained final.

EXTREME GLANCE

The doctor on night duty at the emergency department of the skin clinic treated me there. Her diagnosis: hives from neck to stomach to back. The rash that had appeared on the surface of my body could spread to the inner skins, the oesophagus, the tissues in the lungs, she explained. The result would be death by suffocation. I was put in a hospital bed with heavy doses of cortisone. At that point, I didn't realize what kind of crisis my sister was in.

I had known about her illness for two years. There were always reports, new therapies. I didn't want to lose her. I drowned out all the information with strong hope, with a positive perspective, with horizons that spread brightness at some point. 600 kilometres away from me, she was busy improvising her survival. She (a medical doctor who had worked in oncology for many years) had confided in a group of specialists, of colleagues. They had offered therapy after therapy against the cancer which, somehow escaping all precautionary measures, had taken root in organs such as the liver following a breast operation. All the therapies—she had neglected to tell any of us—had failed to reduce the dangerous nodules. There were cancerous lumps in the liver, and now new ones had formed. She knew she was going to die. My body, on the other hand, which is less of a liar than my mind, sensed that something was happening that I didn't want to see.

The body does not speak grammatically, but through eruptions. The day I'd had a shipment of chicken, honey, tinned foods, homemade fruit preserves sent to her address, my sister, having taken a spill on her way down, was sitting on the stairs in front of her flat. Which is where my daughter, who'd been sent to look out for the delivery, found her. In the ambulance, my sister said: 'Shit.' That was the moment she gave up her central hopes. She was treated for one week in a clinic specializing in urgent medical cases. Immediately after being transferred to a clinic for geriatric cases, where the hopeless cases were segregated, as she knew, she rebelled. She saw at once that the only thing on offer was palliative treatment. A young physiotherapist appeared in front of her bed—earlier that morning, she'd fallen in the bathroom—to offer exercises for her arms and legs.

This led to an outburst of anger, her last energetic expenditure. Shortly afterwards, she fell again in the bathroom, tore her forehead open, sprained her limbs. She didn't tell us any of this on the phone. We were still discussing the question of her return to her flat, her return to life. Still so many plans! How to hire Polish help for the daily services, and through which contacts one could get the address of such a helper . . .

I WAS BENT OVER MY MANUSCRIPTS, DIDN'T BELIEVE THE TEXTS . . .

I had the intuition—a wreck pumped full of cortisone, bent over my manuscripts, not believing the texts—that same afternoon that I had to fly to Berlin to see her, to comfort her. Out of the blue— 'imminent', 'a sudden turn for the worse'—the instantaneous feeling that my sister was in danger. Certain that waiting until the following day would be too late. Get out of bed, dress quickly, call a cab. I make the last flight of the day. I arrive in a taxi at the clinic in Grunewald.

'She's really gone downhill over the last five hours,' her room-mate in the two-bed room at the geriatric clinic says. I'd hardly made my way inside when my sister was moved to a single room. The reason given was that it would be easier to provide her with the individual emergency help she was sure to need during the night in a single room. The dying lay on high, moveable beds, outfitted with wheels. The machines attached to the beds just as mobile. That was how the caravan moved from room to room.

Later in the night my sister opened her eyes. 'I can't do it any more,' she said. She tried to sit up. 'I gave it a shot,' she whispered. Not because she was interested in speaking softly, but because her mouth was completely dry. Earlier that afternoon, I had spoken to her trusted doctor, the one who had treated her as an oncologist over the past number of months, while pacing back and forth at the airport. Grumbling at him for having rushed off to a conference during the week, unreachable for enquiries. I was walking along the airport's check-in desks. I asked him what we should prepare for when my sister returned to her flat. Hopefully, in the week to come. The doctor cut me off: 'You have not understood your sister's condition at all!' 'I would be surprised,' the expert continued, 'if your sister lived through the night or tomorrow.' 'You have a delusional notion of your sister's condition, dear fellow,' the doctor said. The thick growths in her liver 'had grown steadily throughout her active treatment.' Five interventions had been in vain. I was shocked. The way I was walking back and forth there at the airport, there was nothing I could do.

Now, deep in the night, in the dim light of the single room, my 'lifelong companion' was lying there, her eyes closed. Clearly exhausted, her face yellow—her blood was poisoned—lying on three thick cushions, halfway sitting up so that her lungs had room. I didn't realize that the brief fragments we were exchanging was our final conversation. I continued to be enveloped by the fog of illusion. I was no realist. But now as then, nothing about that setting struck me as real. She never would have given me permission to take her picture as she lay there with her eyes closed. I took out my iPhone.

A FAREWELL

I am acquainted with photographs from my father's family. On his mother's side. Ancestors. Even the face of my father's mother is familiar to me. That night, I had the impression that a rapid disintegration of my sister's person had taken place. This just one day after the ward nurse's testimony. But she remained unmistakable. It was the face of my sister in which the bones were beginning to dominate. Cheekbones, forehead. Across this face—sleeping? dozing?— the faces of her ancestresses passed by. One after the other. And from our father's maternal side. Over a hundred years. Like a farewell.

UP UNTIL HER LAST BREATH IN CONTACT
WITH WHAT SHE LOVED

She's stopped breathing, her son said. He was sitting next to the bed. It was true, she was no longer breathing. The rest of us hadn't noticed. Her granddaughter was playing out on the balcony. It was a bright afternoon.

Her son had arrived on time. From a flight. Held up by traffic on one of the quickest roads into Berlin from Tegel airport and on to the clinic in Grunewald. Kilometres of cars. Moving at a snail's pace. My sister had grabbed her son's (her 'child's', in the meanwhile, a grown man's) hand. As a sign that she had recognized him and was saying hello, he said, she'd added pressure with her own. That was her final sign of life. Until seven days earlier, she had been determined to hold out another year or year-and-a-half. Because of her granddaughter, who had just begun school. She had made suggestions to the team of doctors caring for her in an oncology practice for the hardest bombardment on her body in which 'the alien' was spreading. Now, 20 minutes before her last breath, she found a bit of peace. The night before already: 'no more fighting'.

SHE MADE AN ESTIMATE OF HOW MUCH
LONGER IT COULD TAKE

She watched her own death, her *death march*. An experienced physician, she recognized how the clinic was shifting from active treatment to palliative delay. This happened without the decision of a senior physician. As a doctor, she had often watched patients reach the end of their lives. She was unsurprised. She saw that there, in the geriatric clinic to which she'd been transferred the previous day from the ICU of the 'active clinic', no one was fighting for her body any more. They made her 'comfortable'. They acted as if there were still something to do. She made an estimate of how much longer it could take.

DEATH MARCH OF A FRENCH QUEEN

On the day of her execution, the dethroned and legally condemned queen woke up early. Her digestion was wrecked. She squatted. Nothing. The guards no longer thought it necessary to bring her anything to eat. A long wait. A delegate from the court appeared and read her a statement. She sat on a chair. Didn't listen. She saw from the expressions of her guards, as well as from the faces of the followers who visited her and who—at the risk of being accused themselves—were busy pestering the authorities with petitions and struggling for her life, that she had been 'abandoned'. A revolutionary, apparently of higher rank (the henchmen treated him courteously), made a drawing of her. She straightened up. 'Upright posture'. She would exercise her ability to fascinate one last time. The sketch likely survived her misery. She would have liked to ask one of her advisors to buy it and take it out of the country. To Koblenz. By courier. A sudden weakness overtook her. She refrained.

Transportation through the noisy streets. Was she visible on the ladder cart? When you saw her from a distance in the crowd, did she look like an old woman, a young woman or a child? She held a piece of her dress tightly in her hand like a knot. The skin no longer held the body, bones or soul together that well. 'Self-reassurance'.

She was helped off the cart. As if it still mattered that she did not break her legs. Maybe in the event of a broken leg or other injury, the execution would be postponed? Torture!

The surging, jeering crowd in the square awaiting the ceremony. In front of the scaffold, an unbroken line of armed horsemen. As if ready to stop a squad of the queen's followers from trying to free her at the last moment. Or as a precautionary measure on behalf of the authorities, lest the mob in the square, unwilling to see everything and excited by marching music and the shouting of slogans, stormed the stage and massacred the condemned—without ceremony and guillotine. Hatred hung heavy over the square.

If—as I have seen depicted in a Viennese morality text entitled 'The Guilty Child Murderess'—I were to be pardoned at the very last moment (the messenger hurrying through the restless crowd up the stairs to me, the guillotine still lashed at the top), the old woman says to herself, I would refuse such mercy. You can have this bag-of-bones, whatever's left of my self-confidence, my body! Her voice was full of spite when the court officer asked her if she was ready.

THE LIFE AND HOUSE
OF A RELATIVELY UNKNOWN PERSON
I DO, HOWEVER, RECOGNIZE FROM PICTURES
AND HAVE HEARD A LOT ABOUT

That person, thinner than I am today, more nervous, was a heavy smoker. With glasses and a tie. Trainees on duty were expected to wear a tie. The protest movement of 1967 with its other dress code is still a long time off. It's 1956. When I look at the person in the photograph, who has my name, it's as if I am looking at a stranger. Thinking back to my 1956 doesn't cause me to feel any draughts across my skin. Saying so would require me to lie.

If, on the other hand, I only imagine the brisk gait of my short-legged father hurrying through the November air to one of his patients in the early afternoon, I feel his (to me personally, unfamiliar) quick-pace directly in my bony framework. Obviously, my SELF allows my father to become present in me; indeed, such an exercise gives me confidence in the day, lets me feel my CURRENT SELF as 'real'. I try to do the same thing with the sluggish, somewhat dragging, rhythmically changing gait of my sister, whose soul nevertheless resides within me. Unsuccessfully. I obviously don't remember her through the gait that I see in front of me in the film. But the gait doesn't get on my nerves. In any event, it's not so much a gait as a kind of stroll. She lives, I believe, on another floor of my Self. Possibly in the 'cap of hearing'. Because the exercise of 'finding my

Self', the exact adjustment of the 'ego-radar', succeeds when I empathize with her voice. Which I always succeed in doing with the help of my brain and my imagination: her voice is present in me. I cannot imitate the way she moves.

I suspect that there are various spirits within me. My sister and my father are two among many. They haunt me on different floors and almost never at the same moment. I am quite sure that this does NOT HAVE TO DO WITH ME AT AN EARLIER TIME IN MY LIFE. Maybe I paid attention to others more than myself. When I imagine myself running through the rain at the age of six, I don't feel a thing. No doubt it's something that I did at some point. And yet I have no memory of it. On the other hand, I remember being scolded at the door, soaking wet in my clothes, coat wet, jacket and sweater wet, dripping down to my underwear, my feet freezing, prepared for catching a cold the following day. And I can feel the cool water of summer, swimming.

COMMENTARY ON THE WORD 'HOUSE'

As mentioned already, one of the zones of my Self is three-storeys tall and highly combustible. It corresponds to the little space above the attic, made of pure wood and with mighty beams supporting the pitched roof. Still at Kaiserstrasse 42 (which later became known as Hauptmann-Loeper-Strasse), a street and an attic that no longer exist. Rooms, no more than hiding places really, of little use, and yet the point of entry of the firestorm that burnt the city.

My soul's cellar, on the other hand, is incombustible. The fire crawled down a bit of the stairs, ate its way through some rubbish-strewn dust. The supply of combustible material was just enough to reach half a metre down. Then it died out on the stone. And thus, the cellar emerged from the upheaval as the SAFE SPACE it had always been.

'I COMPARE MY SO-CALLED SELF
WITH THE HOUSE I GREW UP IN'

Until I was 13, this house belonged to my daily reality. If I was away, it was in my head. If I was at home, it lived around me. Whenever I spoke about *my* and *home*, it was always a whole. A choir. Six rooms on the ground floor, eight rooms in the basement and even a stone staircase. Five rooms on the first floor, five rooms on the second floor, together with the additional attic space. And over that, another space of pure wood. I have a very clear image of me in this house, little memory. The house itself is therefore as present to me as my limbs or my skin are now. One of my few memories has to do with running through all the rooms. The draughty days of THE TWICE-YEARLY HOUSE CLEANING. A long cold, the result every time. Completely present to me now: the way from the kitchen either left across the courtyard or right over a steep stairway of stone to the courtyard entrance, past the conservatory. In other words, the way taken most often at a run between house and garden and later back inside.

And the stairwell banisters have their haptic place in my memory too, they are, so to speak, under my hands. Having said that, though I can remember the railings so well, I probably never actually touched their wood nor even leant upon them. Maybe I slid down them with my stomach half-a-floor or so to then take the curve of the stairwell on foot before going back onto my stomach. And so it was that once, in a moment of absence thanks to a clearly remembered warmth of feeling triggered by the expectation of continuing my games with the tin soldiers in the children's room, I fell from the railing onto the lower part of the staircase. Hurting my head. Brought by patients into the waiting room and then the consulting room. Given a thorough tongue-lashing, patched up and then stuck in bed for the rest of the day.

Our home's various cellars still give me, now, in 2021, a feeling of solidity and security. Although they no longer exist. Their ceilings about one metre below street level. Electrical wires fixed there with rubber retainers from which hung lightbulbs. The floor, made of concrete. At the north-eastern end, the coal cellar with its piles of coal. Every summer it would be refilled. That's when coal is cheapest. In the room next door, two large boilers. A system of tubes leads the water heated in them to all the rooms of the house, above all, however, to the conservatory. The palms and cactuses there, not to mention the glass-enclosed space itself, need a great deal of warmth.

In addition, there is a room, bordering the coal cellar, in which, at the time I was a conscious observer, the black-market goods from the canteen of the Luftwaffe's Halberstadt support centre were stored. An agreement between my father and the director there. A secret room that is always locked. Next to it, big, wide and open to all—in about the same location as my father's consulting room two floors up—the general cellar space for all the 'homemade' goods, our stocks. In multiple cabinets. And one more room, the air-raid shelter. Organized and outfitted with a special device: wooden frames for emergency cots; picks and spades in case we have to dig ourselves out.

For years, these subterranean rooms, which survived the firestorm that followed the bombings (and it was only because of this firestorm that our home was destroyed), remained a massive pile of brick and iron rods. They were only built over when the new, prefabricated postwar buildings were erected at right angles to the existing road, i.e. across the ruins of the house and part of the garden. I assume that the remains of the cellars of our old house would still be found under those of the new ones.

This is the base of the house, from which stairs lead up to the ground floor. At ground level: the well-used entrance and a solid oak entrance door, which was always open to patients, even at night. Prevented from closing by a thick leather flap. From the hallway, French doors lead to a corridor next to which is a French-style salon, silver and dark green at the back, a gold-yellow tint at the front. The wall is covered with silk wallpaper. For a long time, the piano stands here, in front of the fireplace. Later, when this piano begins to be used more often, it is moved into the so-called gentlemen's room, the smoking parlour. This so-called 'gentlemen's room' is panelled on all sides except for the window front. You can enter this wall through a door next to the gas fireplace. This room, about two metres deep, contains a safe where my father kept his cash in a wooden box.

The entrance to the house leads from the gentlemen's room to the 'dining room': a room with barrel vaults. The walls also panelled with dark wood. Lockable compartments more than one metre deep in the panelling. They house a bar, a cupboard for glasses and porcelain, a rail of compartments where the year's Christmas and birthday presents are collected, and my father's gun cabinet. Above the fireplace, opposite the drinking niche which closes the room with a broad front of blind windows, a spiral staircase. It leads to a guest bedroom on the first floor. The dining room itself opens onto a pool for goldfish, and another seating area that closes off the upper part of the conservatory and connects it via a staircase to the 'walk beneath the palms' in the conservatory proper. A glazed terrace then leads to the garden with its pond, walnut tree, chestnut and, until 1938, a large beech.

The staircase to the right of the main entrance to the house leads past a toilet—or rather, more like a toilet *facility* with ample opportunities to wash, which was modernized by my parents in 1934 (the only remodelling undertaken) and nicknamed the anti-aircraft gun stand. Another staircase leads to the first floor, starting with the waiting room, to the left of which is the consulting room, to the right of which is the treatment room. On the other side of the corridor was my father's bedroom for when he was called to patients at night and did not want to disturb my mother upon his return. Next to it, the spacious 'French bathroom' with toilet, bidet, large bathtub and a huge window overlooking the courtyard. The pear tree there has a visual effect in the bright bathroom. Adjacent to the bathroom is a dressing room, which can be closed off on both sides, and my parents' bedroom with two large built-in wardrobes and the French bed. There is also the aforementioned guest room, which can be reached via the spiral staircase from the ground floor and in which I was bedded down when I was seriously ill, accessible to my mother in the adjoining marital bedroom. A terrace no one uses faces the courtyard and is overshadowed by the pear tree.

The other floor, which is reached via two half-staircases, contains the children's room, the nanny's room, two attic rooms and the space right below the roof, which is where we store apples in autumn. This former flat for the 'caretaker', who by the time I arrived was no longer there, belongs only very indirectly to the housing of my soul. In reality, it is just the place where I sleep, the place where I put my toys, which later became shared property with my sister and the passage to an attic room where there's a map of the world hanging below a skylight. Beneath this map, my second bed, a mattress. This attic chamber is my most important domicile. The same applies to all the games with my friend Fritz Wilde and to the whole topmost floor, whose lower part is made of wood and whose upper part, again connected by a staircase, though also made of wood, has exposed beams and a pitched roof.

Though in terms of time, place and all aspects of reality I am far removed and live absolutely apart from the walls, ceilings, even the smells, proportions and inherent customs, they are present constantly within me. Which is different from the SELF.

In this respect, I still consider my soul to be three-storeyed and structured like this house. And so if someone were to ask me whether I was built of stone or wood, I would always answer: yes, of the wood of the attic and the chamber with the map of the world next to it. My skin certainly comes from the wood of the panelling on the ground floor. This means that my soul has deep, box-like interior fittings, up to two feet wide, in which provisions can be stored. One of these wooden cupboards collapsed in the hot summer of 1935.

The shelves on which the porcelain and crystal glasses were neatly placed popped off the hinges. The collapse of the upper shelves smashed what was on the lower shelves. I hear my mother's voice saying: 'Shards bring luck.' That evening, a wine punch had been scheduled for guests from the city. The guests had to drink from kitchenware. The tone that accompanied the accident still gives me a feeling of 'cheerful excitement'. The tension of an important event. For the attitude of 'equanimity' when something collapses, ataraxia, I can still make a bond with this feeling from my childhood, even though I doubt that I was even aware of the event myself at the age of three (even if I was there). So much was said about it afterwards that I cannot distinguish between memory and immediate sensation.

'COMMENTARY ON THE TEXT OF MY LIFE'

That a *curriculum vitae* is a text, I have no doubt. Not, however, a text which is ready to be pinned down in words. One would have to laboriously reconstruct it, and then it would be too long to be a commentary.

The commentary format demands short, fixed texts, texts of value which allow for the long-lasting cultivation of addendums, notes, continuations, fragments and summaries. In general, a commentary is long, the text brief. Therefore, a life, reflected by memories and dates, already contains lengthy texts which, when recounting all its delusions, its diversions, whatever remained unobserved, work against abridgement and narrative flow. If someone were to begin thoroughly recounting their life, any and all listeners would walk away.

HOW TWO LOVERS GREW CLOSER IN SPITE OF DIFFICULTIES IN THE WINTER OF 1941

He came back to the Reich from Lapland in the winter of 1941 on 10 days' home leave. The rite of Christmas was like an obstacle course between him and the woman he loved. Food, presents, visits, closed public, church visits, clearing snow, cleaning up. The pressure of love that had been running rampant in his mind and body over the year was unable to break through the pattern of the 'festive days'. What can the 'power of love' do? How powerful is the 'seriousness of war'? Both strong forces, love and war, can do nothing against the brevity of the holiday season, the persistence of the 'customs of 24 December'. The division of the holidays—including 24 December, which was a weekday—consisted of two holidays, then of Saturdays and Sundays, and the contingent around New Year's Eve and New Year's Day. The last days were already beyond his departure. Forty hours for transport and return to the front had to be deducted from his home leave. Was the shortness of time—which left no room for quiet activity, no slowly growing feeling—the sharper knife or was the 'obsessive harmony', obliging all to 'celebrate', to 'eat together', to decorate the rooms, to take ritual walks together, the worse tool, the one which severed that amorous closeness the holidaymaker so desired and that his beloved would have gladly granted him? No cuddling, no sleeping in, no 'holy fast', no dream.

On the third day, he and his beloved wife got intestinal colic. Everything inside went into flux. The abrupt transition from meagre meals to the sudden eating of fats ruined their system from the stomach, indeed from the gullet, down through the whole 'tube that divides the body' to the LOWER END. At the table, they looked into each other's eyes. Doubtingly. Escaping to a bed at daytime or meeting in a cellar alcove was impossible. Family and visitors were keeping watch. Where they lived was small. Tight quarters. Not even a last-minute escape from the round of festivities after the third day would've helped them. The sabotage of their bodily fluids and intestines (a kind of popular uprising) had decimated any erotic assets. All they could manage were weak smiles. At least there was intimacy when they helped each other to the toilet. Both felt weak. They also lent each other underwear. The underclothes were soiled so quickly that they didn't dry as quickly as they needed to be washed. In one-piece military pants, the man's sweetheart looked adorable. They both had to laugh. His body, once connoted with stateliness, looked grotesque in improvized underpants. THE RIDICULOUS IS THE ENEMY OF THE SUBLIME. And so, for the rest of the 10 days of their holiday (minus the transport to and from Lapland), they were unable to consummate the 'noble feelings' that both lovers knew and wrote letters to each other about. Not under the prevailing conditions of the holidays. Nothing wanted to succeed. The man was already packing for departure.

THE BEGINNING OF A SEMINAR ON PHILOSOPHY IN THE MIDDLE OF THE TUMULTUOUS DECEMBER OF 1968 AT FRANKFURT AM MAIN UNIVERSITY

In December 1968, the lawyer and legendary sociologist Niklas Luhmann, a direct spiritual descendant of the American Talcott Parsons, developed a POLITICAL ECONOMY OF THE INTIMATE in the seminar he was holding at Johann Wolfgang von Goethe University in place of Theodor W. Adorno while the latter was on sabbatical. The seminar was entitled Love as Passion. The plan was a reasonably accurate analysis of the ways in which, breaking out of their world of individual homes and social contexts, people allow one another to have intimate relationships. To do this, Luhmann explained, one must first understand the concept of love as a foreign word, namely, as a sign of *what I don't know*, what I must therefore produce through research—here a keyword familiar to the majority of socialist students from Chinese theory was used—that is, through collecting, sorting, relating and other forms of thinking. The first thing I have to do is produce that feeling of foreignness. Only then can I fraternize with it. The ciphers *love* and *passion*, like an ancient Egyptian hieroglyph. As an image, sign or—even better—vacuum, foreign like a hieroglyph before the discovery of the Rosetta Stone, which juxtaposed the ancient hieroglyphs with translations into demotic New Egyptian and Ancient Greek. Assume further that, apart from unacquaintance with the word in practice, there are more than 17 different forms of *loving-one-another*. Only a few of them concern the approach of the sexes and erotic attractors. Others deal with horizons of hope, an inner centre in the human being that is laid out by one's ancestors, parents or certain fantasies, but which contains a supply of fuel, namely, passion, that could be ignited with a spark. For the activist-minded students, who had broken away in small numbers from the protest spreading across campus and gathered in this seminar, there were already far too many words. I am unfamiliar with a concept, Luhmann continued, ignoring the unrest spreading through the room, unless I've gathered it first. Rather than that concept of 'love' for which one is looking, Luhmann said, that freshly created empty space in our heads is probably filled with the lyrics of pop songs, love stories and numerous figurative ideas of love and passion instead, not to mention antipathy and the pain of separation. 'I know that I know nothing' is difficult to produce.

Love is the permission one human being grants a certain other which allows them to become intimate, Luhmann resumed. Immanuel Kant speaks in somewhat 'Anglo-Saxon', abbreviated and machine-like terms of a 'contract for the mutual use of sexual organs'. This ignores a larger part of the events that only together constitute intimacy. The brevity of Kant's formulation was probably due to the desire to avoid phrases. It is a good way to test words and sentences on this difficult double subject of LOVE and PASSION. If something of these words bounces off the experience presented, perhaps another expression can be found. In any case, the imagination is 'mixed up'. Luhmann's bearing, the way he spoke and insisted with quiet intensity, created a delicate situation in the midst of the unwilling student listeners.

WHEN I THINK ABOUT CLOSENESS . . .

Our grammar school was housed in the rooms of the former Reich Youth Leadership on Heerstrasse, a government building erected during the time of the Third Reich. One morning in 1947, there was a fight. All of us were up on our desks. Fighting. I bumped my head into one of the ceiling lamps. These large-scale lamps were electrified balloons in the decorative style of the Third Reich. Their glass insides had not been opened or cleaned for more than 10 years. In my bleeding wound, a fragment of this glass, not to mention pus and germs from the pre-war and wartime period. I was taken to a British military hospital on Reichskanzlerplatz. Surgical emergency room. The wide cut in the forehead, the wound, was cleaned and stitched.

However, the cleaning was probably not effective enough against the pathogen from the past. The wound became infected the same night. The next day, I was admitted to surgery on Kurfürstendamm. Medical staff were working there who had come together in that Berlin clinic on the run. There may have been impostors among the doctors. Their papers had not been checked. These doctors opened the wound, let the pus drain out and then stitched up the opening again. I later learnt that the inflation of the left side of my head into an inflamed balloon on all sides had been life-threatening. The wound should not have been resewn. I was told that, without help, about five hours longer and I would have died.

In the crucial amount of time that remained until the inflammation would have advanced to the brain, my mother managed, in less than an hour, to reach my father by telephone in Halberstadt, 208 kilometres away from Berlin-Charlottenburg by road (through telephone cables or telegraph lines: around 250 kilometres). That was distance. The long-distance call mediated from the central office in Berlin-Mitte via Burg, Genthin, Magdeburg. Because of the description of the bandage, the wound and the now monstrously grown red head, a 'disfigurement', my father decided by phone to have the bandage torn off immediately. He was a general practitioner. He knew a thing or two about emergencies involving suppuration. He told my mother to inform the GP Dr med Fritze, a former corps brother of my father, the Borussia connection, on Lietzenburger Strasse. Above all, he told her to calm down. The corps brother appeared a quarter of an hour later. Pus shot out of the wound once the bandage was torn off and the stitches cut with scissors. The edges of the wound were a mess. Due to a duel in the distant past, about 30 years earlier, Dr Fritze's nose had been cut off and reattached, and was now scarred away from the main body of the nose.

Those hours were the last time my parents (after their divorce) were close. In fact, in the moments of the urgent phone call, the familiar tone of 1932 and 1937 (and again in Bad Gastein in 1939) had briefly 'come up'. Often, the two had not been so close. Here it was a matter of saving their first-born. Eagerness united them.

–Thank you, thank you, Ernst. (That is my father's name)

–Take care of yourself.

–I'll do the best that I can.

–Well, just take care of yourself.

–Again, thank you. I've already removed the bandage.

–Good. Now go and get Dr Fritze.

All spoken in the old, familiar tone. It had nothing to do with the words. They didn't come together out of love, but moments of need. It had been like that before too. Sudden closeness, companions needing each other. They had spent 12 years together.

The telephone connection via old networks set up in 1929, then damaged and repaired several times, with many diversions and provisional solutions, was full of disruptions. They could only interpret each other's words by guessing or anticipating their meaning.

After Dr Fritze had uncovered and treated the wound, but the high fever persisted, my mother put me in the bathtub. While I was waiting, in a daze, for the water to be let in, my muscular, energetic mother came with a large bucket of ice-cold water and unexpectedly poured it over my back. This was in accordance with the advice of my grandfather, who in turn knew this treatment method from his family's ancestors in the Owl Mountains. YOU HAVE TO FRIGHTEN THE FEVERISH BODY; THEN IT FORGETS THE FEVER. The shock of the cold caught me off guard. I actually recovered.

When I think of the word *closeness*, I think of my mother's way of acting. Closeness is when her father's advice, from distant family experience, unexpectedly hits my naked body in the hour of need.

'SELF' IN CHINESE CHARACTERS

COMMENTARY ON THE CHINESE WRITTEN CHARACTER.
AFTER ERNEST FENOLLOSA.
WITH REMARKS FROM EZRA POUND

The five forms of 'I'.

1. 'spear in the hand' = a very emphatic I. For someone who creates their own path. This I is attentive to that which surrounds it. And attentive to others as well.

2. 'five and a mouth' = a weak and defensive I, holding off a crowd by speaking. This I's facial features are a mask. It does not reveal what it feels.

3. 'an I that conceals itself' = a selfish and private I. An intensification of No. 2. No direct contact with others, to whom it does indeed belong.

4. 'self (the cocoon sign) and *a* mouth' = an egoistic I, one who takes pleasure in its own speaking. More a speaker than a self.

5. 'self' = used only when one is speaking to one's self.

FIGURE 13.1. Fenollosa refers to this character as 'to be lost in the forest'. The English scholar Morrison interprets the character as follows: 'A fire beneath what looks like a fence.' He points out, however, that the original character from which this one derives did not mean 'fire' but 'bird'. Ezra Pound interprets the character to mean 'the little bird flew off the branch'. One possesses. Now its soul has fled. It sits, deprived of its soul, in what it possesses. Beneath it, a fire. 'One is buried beneath one's possessions.' 'He has lost his way in the gardens and tunnels of his assets.'

FIGURE 13.2. Silk next to a field = negligible, weakened, insignificant. Depending on the other characters around it, this character means that 'the source of human existence is rather close to nothing and always in limbo'.

FIGURE 13.3. 'Man with outstretched arms'. 'Generous man'.

FIGURE 13.4. Character 'radical for mankind'. Through variations in the root consonant through the introduction of vowels, human qualities can be identified.

FIGURE 13.5. Character for 'assembly banner and mass' = people have gathered. They are focussed upon one action, they have the right attitude and are in the right crowd for that action. The unit of measurement is unknown in European and Arabic languages.

FIGURE 13.6. An 'I or a self assuming a bent posture'.

FIGURE 13.7. Verb 'to speak' = 'words create'. The character is comprised of 'mouth' and 'emerging from these two words and a flame'.

FIGURE 13.8. Plant with twisted root = 'difficult growth'. The piece of the character to the upper left means: 'impediment'.

FIGURE 13.9. 'Any old thing one tosses under the table' = usual, customary, unimportant, appealing to common taste.

FIGURE 13.10. 'To be divided'.

FIGURE 13.11. 'Laying aside evil' = 'self-annihilation', 'lowering the ego-barrier'.

FIGURE 13.12. The same thing with closed doors = 'family'.

EZRA POUND'S EXCERPTS FROM FENOLLOSA'S TEXT

The dominance of the verb and its power to obliterate all other parts of speech give us the model of terse, fine style. The development of the normal transitive sentence rests upon the fact that one action in nature promotes another; thus the agent and the object are secretly verbs. One of many possible examples is, 'If one reads, it teaches him how to write.' Another is, 'One who reads becomes one who writes.' But in the first condensed form a Chinese would write, READ PROMOTE WRITE.

In Chinese characters, each work accumulated this sort of energy in itself.

The true formula for thought is: The cherry tree is all that it does.

Languages today are thin and cold because we think less and less into them.

Nature herself has no grammar.

'Is' comes from the root *as* = to breathe. 'Be' from *bhu* = to grow.

In Chinese, the chief verb for 'is' not only means actively 'to have', but also shows by its derivation that it expresses something even more concrete, namely, 'to snatch from the moon with the hand . . .'

In nature, there are no negations.

A STRANGE CREATURE'S
KNOCKING AT OUR DOOR

FIGURE 14 (ABOVE)

FIGURE 15 (BELOW). Viruses under the electron microscope.

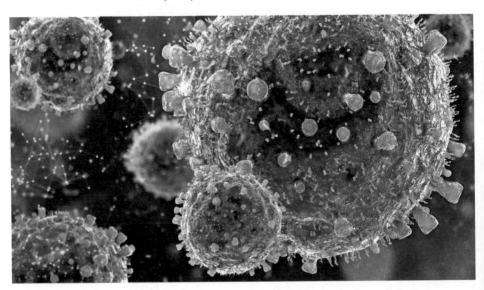

THE COLLISION OF TWO LIFEWORLDS
WITH THE ALIENS' INITIAL ONE-SIDED SUCCESS

When the aliens—billions and trillions of individuals, clumped together, not cooperating but collectively and stochastically producing errors, mathematical wonders, monsters so to speak—first encountered human lung cells, they were confused. They made more mistakes than usual, mutated faster. The ability of these small creatures to subtly deviate from millennial use depending on the location of the mutating gene in the *longue-durée* curve, biding their time in bats under survival-friendly conditions for both host and guests, made possible their 'surprising success on foreign terrain' when they met us humans. The GUESTS were no less surprised by the encounter—stunned and disoriented—than PEOPLE'S LUNG CELLS.

'DO CORONAVIRUSES HAVE INDIVIDUALITY?'

Virologist Karin Mölling answers: Presumably not! Viruses, she says, have four rather robust abilities:

BONDING

CUTTING

MUTATING

REPRODUCING

The scientist adds that they do not need other characteristics. Although they have the biomass for it, they show no inclination to become elephants. The viruses' ability to change constantly, their sense of relentless, incessant innovation that changes little in terms of their overall effect, i.e. structural properties that they have exhibited as a 'special world' for 3.5 billion years, prompted three scholarly friends at Harvard to ask themselves whether these existences from a parallel evolution possess an 'intelligence' that should be described with a term other than intelligence. The three scholars were also of the opinion that a different term was needed for the intelligence displayed in the departments of progressive American universities and that needed to fight for survival in the impoverished outskirts of Chicago.

Viruses have a precise geometric structure. They cannot form arbitrary bodies. Because they are so robust and because they follow half the laws of crystals, i.e. the hardware and the dead stone, and half the rules of life, i.e. those of reproduction, error and mutation. They form PLATONIC BODIES, of which there are five. The most complex of them resembles COVID-19.

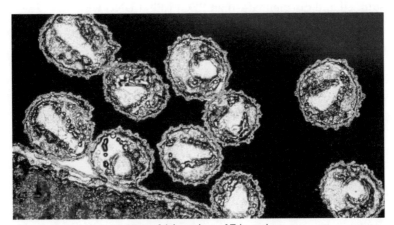

FIGURE 16 (ABOVE) AND 17 (BELOW)

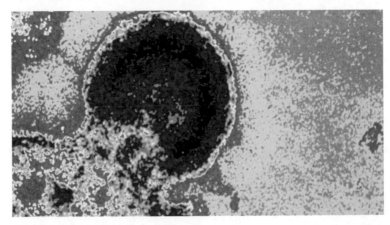

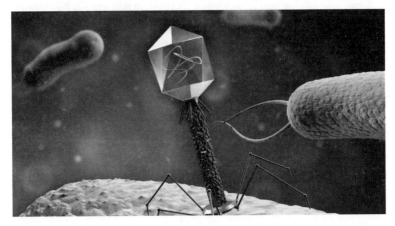

FIGURE 18 (ABOVE), 19 (CENTRE) AND 20 (BELOW)

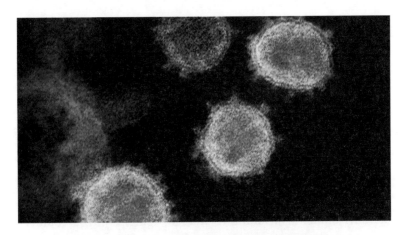

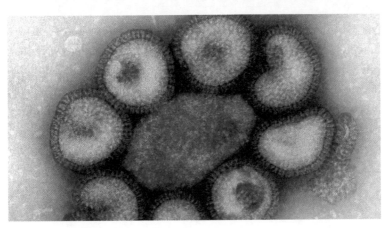

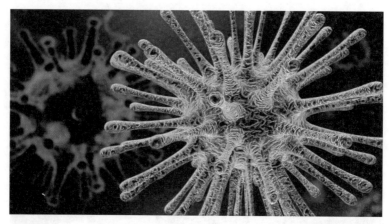

FIGURE 21

THE FACTION TO WHICH THE ENVIRONMENT
RESPONDS POSITIVELY SURVIVES

According to Karin Mölling, the 'intelligent dangerousness' of the
COVID-19 virus is due to the frequency of copying errors when these
viruses replicate. The individual errors add up to become an 'intelligent force'. The viral intelligence responds to every challenge from
the environment, including us human fighters, with a counter-
response.

This 'intelligent force' has no plan. It does not result from any
function of a 'mind'. The viruses discard their own molecules (either
when they divide due to errors in the transmission of their coding or
during their short lifetime) and replace them with foreign ones. This
is how, Mölling reports, they 'test' their environment—for example,
a human lung, a cold shower, a door handle—for a positive response
to their request, to their need for mass reproduction. The faction to
which the environment responds positively survives.

A PATHOGEN PENETRATES ALL BARRIERS AND
PARALYSES THE HEAD OF STATE

In February and March 1943, Adolf Hitler was GLOOMY. The Americans had landed in Casablanca and were on the march. The respite he had longed for in the autumn to recover his nerves had been denied him by Stalingrad. He had no hope.

That was the hour when microorganisms attacked his body. From forehead to ear: like numbness. High, even life-threatening fever for days. Viruses sense the weakness or melancholy of the host body and attack. The Führer's accompanying surgeon prescribed a complicated therapy. The idea of applying calf compresses did not occur to anyone.

The Führer's headquarters at the Wolf's Lair was protected by three security zones. At the access controls, which interrupted the strict latticework of the fences: heavily armed guards of the Führer's escort battalion. Waffen-SS. No assassin, if not identified by uniform and identification papers as a high-ranking employee, would have been able to get close to the Führer through these sluices. Having said that, Hitler's hair needed to be cut, and it had been planned for some time. Which is why a non-commissioned officer, a barber in his civilian life, was summoned to the Führer's headquarters from the neighbouring garrison of Rastenburg. This soldier, however, had contracted a HEAD COLD. The infection was still incubating. No external symptoms. But the virus was ready to be passed on to third parties.

For three weeks, this head cold paralyzed the supreme head of the German Reich. Who just pretended to rule the country for an hour every day. Feverish, dazed, he lay in bed. A mirror image of the hopeless situation at the fronts.

The source of the virus, which so quickly overcame the barrier of the headquarters and then Hitler's blood–brain barrier, was thought to have originated in a certain area of Galicia. The population of the area had been expelled and some groups of this population had been shot. The virus had spread to the conquerors, older land rifle-men of the German Wehrmacht.

According to the military doctors, the microbe was new to German nationals. The stationary population might have been adapted to the virus (and the virus to them, so that it did not have a lethal effect). The same was not true for the invaders. As a result of evolutionary chance, a receptor in the brains of the soldiers had matched exactly the attack molecule of the small creatures, a racial peculiarity. Visiting the supreme commander of Army Group South, the chief of medical services estimated that the virus had devastated three to four divisions. As far as Hitler's infection was concerned, the additional damage, he had no idea.

SHIGA-KRUSE-RUHR BACILLUS IN HALBERSTADT

Autumn 1943. In the garden, two trees have been felled. Two scaf-folds have been fashioned out of the trunks and branches. The autumn leaves have been swept up into a huge pile. It's getting cold.

There has been an outbreak of Shiga-Kruse, a dangerous bac-terial diarrhoeal disease. It is transmitted by faecal–oral route (from faeces/urine via the hand to the mouth) or by lice bite. Even small amounts of these aggressive microbes on a door handle, a poorly cleaned glass, a piece of clothing that has been touched by a hand, can trigger the disease. And in a close-knit group of people such as a soldier-, refugee- or prisoner transport, an epidemic forms.

In my father's case, this is compounded by the fact that: his wife has left him. In any case, he will be lonely. It's getting cold.

The dysentery that has attacked the city belongs to the severe form of Shigella dysentery A. The bacteria devastate the large intes-tine. They slit open the cells of the body and forcibly penetrate them. They spread toxins in their environment. One of their active substances is a nerve toxin that causes paralysis, extreme weakness and fever. Another agent causes unmanageable diarrhoea.

The disease was to be reported. After initial reports were received from the three practising doctors the city still had at its disposal during the war, however, the supreme authority decided that no more reports should be made in future and that the names 'epidemic' or 'Shiga-Kruse-Ruhr-A' were to be avoided. It was also pointed out that news of epidemics breaking out in the Reich would be a boon to enemy propaganda. Confidential communication in place of a report was recommended. On the other hand, it was inconsistent for the medical officer to send a circular to the doctors asking them not to go into the homes of the sick people without their shoes and to refrain from touching anything there. The doctor was also not to carelessly put his hand to his mouth. None of this was feasible, because it would have seemed inappropriate in relation to the sick. A doctor cannot refuse a hand extended in greeting. He cannot use rubber gloves to ring the doorbell, and he cannot refuse a schnaps proffered.

And so my father was one of the last to fall ill once the epidemic had already subsided. He lay in bed, a thin wreck, right next to the bathroom with the toilet to save him. Only he was allowed to clean it. For weeks he was so debilitated that he was unable to make a decision about separating from his wife, my mother. Was there any chance to get her to come back? Or should he drag out the process of separation in the hope that there might still be a way out? For a few weeks he could say to himself: 'I'm a vegetable.' From time to time, the chief physician of the district hospital, a surgeon, would visit him. But even he was unable to do more than counteract the dehydration with injections.

IN THE TONE OF MY BEDTIME STORIES

Mölling knows how to tell a story. And does so just the way my nanny, Magda, once did. I can see that in the way that I hang on her every word just like a four-year-old. Mölling comes from somewhere in Northern Germany. Even when she talks about her science, virology, an inflection which is also predominant in my hometown of Halberstadt follows her. It's not a dialect, but it's not standard either. I am connected to this reporting tone with my ears.

OPPORTUNISM

KLUGE: A moment ago, you used the word *opportunism* for the virus' way of working. As hunters, our forefathers were opportunists in nature too. They sought out hurt animals. They trailed behind weakened gazelles until they were tired, and then strangled them.

MÖLLING: An opportunist is someone or something who or which takes advantage of a favourable opportunity. For example, there are the herpes viruses. They are best known as opportunists. When the host is weak, these viruses come out of hiding and make us sick.

KLUGE: A person is sad, that affects the body. The cells slow down, as if they themselves were crying. How does the virus notice something like that? It sits, for example, in the ganglia at the back of the throat. Under regular conditions, it has a growth opportunity or a waiting position. But then, when certain chemical substances change—it could happen, for example, within the immune system, which is weakened, or it is too cold or it is hot, the sun can activate such a virus: Then the virus multiplies and it either goes into the eye or on the lip or causes a case of shingles . . .

MIMICRY

KLUGE: Now you've used the word *mimicry*. Mimicry is more common in nature. For example, butterflies can disguise themselves as leaves to protect themselves from predators . . .

MÖLLING: The virus must somehow find access to a host or a host cell. It pretends to be something that the cell knows and accepts.

For example, there are surface molecules in the cell, receptors, and then a virus comes along instead of a molecule, activates this receptor, but isn't a signal factor, just a virus.

KLUGE: Like an actor?

MÖLLING: Like actors or soldiers or spies who disguise themselves in war . . .

KLUGE: Odysseus did something like that consciously and with cunning. He tricked the cyclops saying: My name is 'Nobody' ('Odysseus', mumbled, sounds like the Greek word 'udeis' = nobody, nothing, no one). He deceived by means of words. He deceived by means of disguise. Similarly, the virus deceives molecularly. In its RNA-language.

IS THERE COOPERATION AND DIVISION OF LABOUR AMONG VIRUSES? EGOISM?

MÖLLING: In a society of billions of viruses, there is almost everything. But viruses have not yet formed states. Often there is an initial force and then a successor force of a different kind arrives. The first infection is via a particular receptor on a cell, and when that is conjugated, there is a second variant of the virus; this existed before in the population but is only now coming into play. If it was your turn, now it's mine in the second round, and I take another host cell.

KLUGE: But that's how cooperation begins among humans too.

MÖLLING: Yes, I see it that way as well.

KLUGE: There was a first birth among humans. The first-born gets the whole field, the inheritance. The second-born, Franz Moor in Schiller's *The Robbers*, gets nothing, not the inheritance nor the love of the woman he adored. He becomes a vengeful spirit. In modern times, in Swiss families, every third son had to go abroad as a mercenary. This is how rivalry arises, so-called emulation, competition between rivals, which can turn into cooperation, because rivals, enemies, know each other well and learn from each other.

'BONDING'

MÖLLING: With many viruses, there is a mechanism. In German, I call it: 'Zutritt verboten!' In other words, 'No entry!' If one virus is in the cell, then the second one should not get in too. Then you would have to share the resources. The first one to arrive runs away and takes building blocks from itself and the cell. Then it attaches these building blocks to the cell wall, so that a second infection cannot take place. If you like: the first to arrive is the first born . . .

KLUGE: . . . builds a wall.

MÖLLING: . . . builds a wall. That prevents a superinfection. This is a kind of building-up of the most primitive immune system. Cell material and virus build together. A virus sits in the cell and brings substances to it, which it sticks to the outside. The receptor is plastered shut, and then the next virus can no longer enter. There are more complicated processes with the same purpose. They act like a kind of immunization of the cell. If the cell has learnt how to develop an immune system in this way, then the type of virus that arrived first can no longer get into such a cell. That is the beginning of the immune system. This is called a silencer, a silencing nucleic acid. The interesting thing is that the building blocks come from viruses.

PHOENIX, A DEFECTOR FROM THE WORLD OF VIRUSES

MÖLLING: 50 per cent of our genetic material consists of former viruses. They are incorporated into our genome, patriots of our survival. And they have even been reconstructed. A risky experiment. One virus that has been brought back to life, a component of our genome, is known as PHOENIX. It entered our genome millions of years ago. Sitting in this genome, it has protected us against attacks from external viruses or bacteria. PHOENIX exists in lab rabbits. You can see it under the electron microscope.

KLUGE: The archaeal virus became a patriot within our genome? Like the French Huguenots who emigrated to Prussia. They became a kind of elite of cameralist stewards and plucky officers, the best Prussians around . . .

MÖLLING: The viruses within our genome protect us. And they dream, I would almost like to say, of viral attacks that took place a long time ago. They are fighting against viruses and bacilli which don't exist any more. They are leading imaginary battles. There's an animal in Australia where we can observe the process. The koalas. Monkeys infected them with a leukaemia-causing virus that killed them en masse. But after 10 generations, they became resistant. Thanks to 'defectors'.

KLUGE: Could some angel, in the guise of a virus from ancient times, experienced in battles against long-extinct viruses, have been sitting inside us for a long time in a crisis in which humans are fighting against a present-day virus, as an evolutionary doctor, so to speak? By chance or because a molecular password repeats itself—just through the abundance of mutations?

MÖLLING: We just can't speak with them. How are we supposed to find this angel or doctor or what-have-you within the genome? They don't know a thing about COVID-19. Theoretically, it'd be possible. What you are describing is an immune system that no longer relies on having identical sequences.

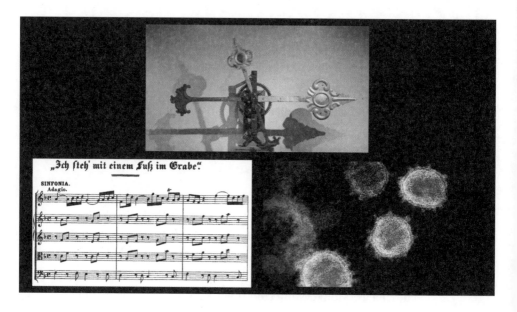

FIGURE 22 (ABOVE) AND 23 (BELOW)

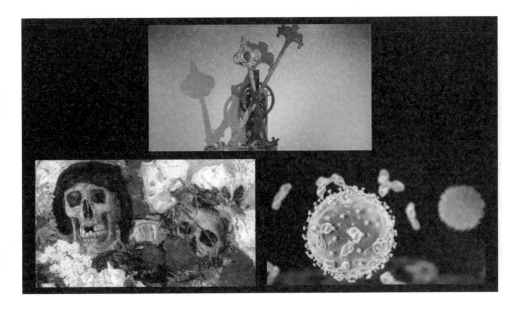

FIGURE 24 (ABOVE) AND 25 (BELOW)

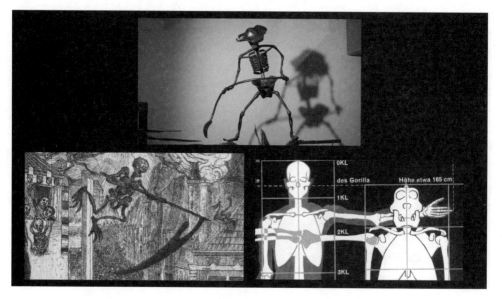

FIGURE 26 (ABOVE) AND 27 (BELOW).
Film stills from a triptych on J. S. Bach's prelude for organ 'Ich stehe mit einem Fuss im
Grab'. Here Karin Mölling plays it on her organ.

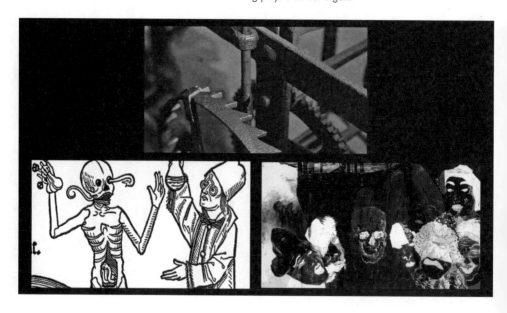

BATTLESHIP IN A QUEUE

During the very first moments of the pandemic, a French aircraft carrier, a fast, largely automated ship, sailed the seas without a port. While on a short stay in Brest, most of the crew had contracted the virus. The men lay sick in their bunks. There were deaths. The news was impossible to suppress in the cramped quarters of the ship's hull. The doctors were helpless. And so, the mighty warship sailed into the Mediterranean, past Malta, then in a great arc back into the Atlantic. Now, in Advent 2020, the ship lay in a bay, all rooms strictly disinfected: the crew needed to operate the giant was put ashore.

DEFENCE AGAINST THE FOURTH ASIAN CHOLERA EPIDEMIC

Marcel Proust's father, characterized in a text by the former as the progenitor Abraham, was a doctor and held a high position in Paris as a civil-servant hygienist. In one of the waves in which cholera reached Europe, he was responsible for the CORDON SANITAIRE: the sealing off of France and the western Mediterranean against the 'Strait of Germs'. The barrier focused on Russian ports on the Black Sea and extended across the Levant to Egypt.

In his 1883 paper on cholera, Dr Adrien Proust writes:

Of the two routes cholera follows to reach our continent from India, the land route and the water route, the first has not seemed to frighten us for some time. As I pointed out at the last meeting of the Academy on 10 October, our continued surveillance should focus on the sea route. [. . .]

But since the British occupation of Egypt, a pernicious doctrine of defending Europe's sanitary interests has taken root in Egypt, by virtue of which the British authorities in India issued a *patente nette* (a letter certifying that medical authorities had inspected the ship in her various ports of call, and found no sign of dangerous disease) to every ship coming from Bombay on the pretext that cholera was not epidemic, since only a few isolated cases had been noticed. That was a mistake, one of the most serious. And what has just happened in Damietta is the most obvious proof of it [. . .]

THE FOURTH CHOLERA EPIDEMIC
AS 'ENGLISH IMPORT'

Dr Adrien Proust's account has the following to say as well:

The International Sanitary Council of Egypt, in Alexandria, which had the duty of enforcing sanitary measures, was no more than a sham in the hands of the English government. When the measures were announced in the Council, England's representative had the meeting suspended, and on one occasion there was even the singular result of seeing three or four members voting for or against, while there were ten or twelve abstentions. I need not say under what pressure these abstentions were obtained. As a result, the International Sanitary Council of Egypt, which was only a shadow of its former self, finally disappeared and did not meet again. [. . .] If we have to go through a fourth cholera epidemic in Europe, we'll declare that this one is an English import.

FIGURE 28.
The father of Marcel Proust. A doctor and hygienist. Photo by Nadar. Given names 'Achilles' and 'Adrien'. Check out the chain in front of his stomach.

A CONTAMINATED BRITISH FLEET'S ODYSSEY
DURING THE CRIMEAN WAR

A black cloud is said to have hovered over the British fleet, bobbing in the Balchik roadstead for more than an hour this afternoon. The BRITANNIA's sailors did not believe this celestial phenomenon to be the omen but the *cause* of the deaths that so terrified them over the next two nights. The sick left puddles of water under their clothes, which could not be removed quickly enough, and vomited. Rapid onset of shock. Until then, none of the ship's passengers had any experience with cholera. There were reports from India, which can be found in brochures. The sick had hands 'like those of washer-women', cracked, dried-out skin. Faces chilly. Elsewhere it said: episodes of high fever, followed by depressive exhaustion.

The QUICK-TO-DIE did so of side effects such as kidney fail-ure. In many cases, the lungs were full. Thus, no one really knew how the disease was supposed to end on its own. Litres of fluid leaked from the anus. This was confirmed by the ship's doctors of the British fleet in the Black Sea. Like a freshly cooked rice soup with mucus flakes. The doctors thought the 'water' was poisonous. The sailors, as I said, suspected the dark cloud.

In a panic, the fleet set sail. If the ships were to remain at anchor in the roadstead (so ran the opinion of the sea officers), the greatest danger would come from the crews themselves. No discipline could be demanded of those threatened. Staying put entailed a risk of revolt. If, on the other hand, the fleet was underway, the inertia of routine would, the fleet's leadership hoped, keep the crew on task.

Under a north-easterly wind, the seven ships covered eighteen nautical miles in a south-easterly direction. That was the day before the worst outbreak of the disease occurred, beginning in the fourth hour of the night. The ships sailed along as if chased. Fifty-eight sailors were stuffed into sacks and thrown into the Black Sea. It was not known whether the devastating disease had been caused by contagion, by a curse or by the fever breath in the air that had blown in from land six days before. Watch commandos were still ready to touch the dead and clean the wide pools of diarrhoea from the decks. The preconception that a putrefaction of the air had caused the illnesses ensured temporary obedience when it came to carrying out medical services and handling the contaminated. A lot of wind. The seagoing vessels ploughed swiftly through the sea. The squadron travelled a further 32.2 nautical miles towards Asia Minor without any intention of landing on the coast. None of the officers was ill. This could be an additional point of attack if the sailors suspected that only they, the lower ones, were threatened. Those who were still alive seemed to be in a mood that precedes class struggle. Over the course of the day, 45 men died.

Surgeon Dr Rees, doctor on the flagship BRITANNIA, campaigned against the crew's belief in the dark cloud. It was not a curse, nor any kind of death-bringing cloud. To Rees, the dangerous thing about this superstition was that, in this particular case, only a bright kind of counter-cloud could bring salvation, nothing from human hand. Dr Rees, the third generation of the fleet's doctor, was committed to the maxims of the Scottish Enlightenment. He knew nothing of the paths that the vibrios took in the bodies of the afflicted. Was it a poison in the blood? Were dietary errors or slurry in the bowels of the ship, even faeces, the starting point of the affliction? The attentive doctor was in a state of self-experimentation. No laying on of hands, no touching of any of the ill had led to his infection. He refused to be perplexed.

For his own safety (and that of his two medical assistants), he had cordoned off his 'clinic' in the rear of the ship and had a guard posted outside the entrance to the hospital. How many times had the fear-inspired anger of a desperate crew turned on the healers when their art was obviously useless? More than disease, Dr Rees feared lynching. He'd witnessed such a scene during a mutiny in the Caribbean.

WHAT WE KNOW TODAY

Today we know that the vibrions, driven by flagella, biochemically inert rod-shaped bacteria, penetrate through the mouth to the stomach. There they are decimated by gastric acid and destroyed if the stomach is over-acidified. But if they overcome this barrier and penetrate the small intestine, they multiply horribly and irreversibly poison the epithelial cells of the intestinal wall. They force the vascular walls (which later benefits their collective spread but is initially detrimental to them individually) to secrete ionized liquid on a massive scale, so that the bodies die of thirst from the inside. At the time, Dr Rees had no other remedy for the epidemic than to wait for the deaths to cease and for cholera to collapse due to its successes.

A DOCTOR'S ALCHEMICAL KITCHEN

Dr Rees managed six rooms in the stern. They were below the waterline. The medicines were stored in the rearmost compartment. In the absence of a blackboard and chalk, Dr Rees had hung sheets of paper on the walls on which he recorded courses and experiences. He presented the results to the officials and his under-doctors. In the two rooms in front of this 'apothecary' (a bed, a store), the patient is placed in a hot bath (up to 44 degrees). Rubbing of the abdomen and extremities with rough cloths. Then the towels are thrown overboard. The treatment relieved the cramps and improved circulation.

Then a drachm (3.72 g) of opium tincture *per os* in flavoured water reduced the depression, which seemed to Dr Rees to be as deadly as the emaciation of the body. Then two gran (0.124 g) of Calomel as a bolus every half hour. One drachm of turpentine oil plus three ounces of plant mucilage every two hours. The latter turns the watery stool a slight green. This demonstrates 'effect', confirms the treatment.

As his alchemical experiments were having little effect on the course of events, however, Dr Rees was desperate. Nature confronted him like a robotic automaton. He did not like to acknowledge the sovereignty of the disease. At night he screamed at it, exhausted as he was. He tried to exorcize the curse by cursing it. In the fourth hour of the night, the darkest phase in which most of his patients died (he was already superstitious himself), he seriously examined whether the cloud that had passed over the fleet might have contained ghostly power. It was said to have come from Russia.

Bloodletting for severe spasms—as much a disadvantage as an advantage. Mustard plaster. If the vomited liquid reacted acidly, Dr Rees added carbonated water. Placing feet with hot water on the abdomen helped visibly. Dr Rees himself, possessed of his two forefathers' medical will to fight, had a pinched mouth. Lips always tightly closed due to an excess of energy. Not a single superfluous word, not a yawn, not a peep. Which probably saved his life, as the cholera germs could not find their way into his interior through the closure of his mouth.

Any clues as to why the officers did not fall ill?

Based on what we know today, Dr Rees' assumption came very close to the cause. Generally, he says, the officers' stomach acid was elevated by their constant schnapps intake, excessive smoking, large amounts of coffee, diet of meat and consumption of a whole barrel of pickles. Not to mention that they also failed to ever come into contact with the bilge water in the ship's hull.

COMMENTARY
ON THE SEARCH WORD 'STRANGE'

'THE APOGEE OF STRANGENESS
ARE THE TWO-WAY GODS'

Spanish soldiers step foot on Caribbean soil. They consider themselves explorers. Occupy that foreign land as if it were henceforth their own property. In their iron-girdled bellies, deep beneath the skin—between the stomach and intestinal tract—they are carrying germs that will be deadly for the island's indigenous people. Every piece of excrement, deposited in the bushes or out in the open, contains an alien, deadly, new kind of danger for them.

The natives are strangers to the Christian conquerors. Whether they are human beings has yet to be ascertained by the theologians back home in Salamanca. In any case, they are 'non-Spanish'. Armed in a unfamiliar way, unable to express themselves in a 'civilized language', unable to effectively defend their own will, their peculiarity against the foreign arrivals. The summit of strangeness is the difference between the mutual gods. The god of Jerusalem is 'fighting'— recognizable by every iron point of a Spanish sword threatening the neck of a native—the gods of the Caribbean, the spirits in the rocks, the rivers, the trees, in the animals and locals . . .

AS IF WOLVES DIDN'T HAVE ANY KIND OF LANGUAGE!

While preparing for her legendary role as a wolf's companion in the film *Wild*, actor Lilith Stangenberg observed wolves in an open-air enclosure. She reports:

> After a while, I saw that the animals who seemed to be running back and forth in their pack without any direction and not paying any attention to me were almost constantly touching one another with some part of their bodies. Nudging, jostling, brushing past. Every time, some kind of touch, and as far as I could see: each one different. And, from the way they did it, I concluded without erotic intent. They were expressing themselves differently, the touching was different, the whole ceremony was different from what I call 'the wolves talking to each other'. They live in a strict social order. The expert looking after the wolves said that there were almost no violations of their 'community order'.

First and foremost, the ranks. All sexuality, I maintain, is a one-way street with these animals.

In contrast, this stirring, groping, bumping into one another, running towards, running away from one another, is more like a kind of 'net'. You'd have to measure the distances along which they approach and then ritually move away again and make a sketch of it. Maybe then we'd have 'the language of wolves'. The longer I watched them, the more frequent the sequence of touches seemed. I probably only noticed now because I'd recognized the grid.

Whenever one of the animals changes its location, the other animals respond. The places they occupy are, so to speak, I think, their sentences, paragraphs, and the course of the day their chapters, comparable to a novel. The bumping, the passing by with its accompanying brief-nudge-of-the-flank, the swift BRUSH PAST THE OTHER'S FUR, these are the words. No mention of wolves only being able to howl at the moon at night. They have their own language, it's just not in their throats.

'THE LIONESS DID NOT RETURN HOME'

A trained lioness was released into the wild in the successor state to the former German colony of Togo by a European non-profit organization busy with repatriating colonized animals (after the keeping and showing of such wild animals had been banned in the circus). The lioness was taken there in a comfortably padded cage under veterinary supervision.

Once released, this returnee was observed by a team of experts. It turned out that the animal had not forgotten any of its training despite the (for the animal incomprehensible) change of location. She did not join the other lionesses begging from tourists. That was not part of her routine. But she often jumped when a stand of trees reminded her of the tyres she had been trained to jump through, and openly showed her sadness when such 'arts' went unrewarded. At the moment, and later too.

She did *not* join a column of unfamiliar lionesses roaming the area where she'd been abandoned. Who was she? Was she a wild animal? Was she African or European? Had the circus 'civilized' her? Did she vacillate between two identities, the one originating in the steppes and forest lands of north-eastern Togo, where her ancestors can be shown to have come from, making up only the very least of her character?

She was acting like a stranger. Behaving bizarrely. To the enjoyment of the tourists watching her through binoculars. The team of experts was confused. What does emancipation mean now? wondered the reporter covering the case for radio and TV-broadcasters NDR and WDR and the *Süddeutsche Zeitung*. What does 'reintroduction' mean for a creature that still trusted and even mourned the training which had challenged and rewarded it? For a long time, through the binoculars, the still-young lioness could be seen standing 'pensively', 'somehow passively' beneath the trees. Then hesitantly, after long days of hunger, she began to hunt. 'She didn't want to be wild.' In her jeep, the reporter, binoculars before her eyes, full of observing patience, proceeded professionally. She thought she could see the lioness 'waiting' to be released. She was expecting a 'task' from her environment. Something that deserved reward. Perhaps, the reporter concluded, the lioness could have performed without reward. But where on earth in the steppe or primeval forest would there have been an audience? Where a trainer's brief, approving, affirmative hand gesture in the wilderness of FIRST NATURE? The lioness, in the words of the reporter from Bergisch Gladbach, was restless. She was already interpreting a bush as a WHEEL OF FIRE, through which she jumped.

The news of the animal's failed emancipation (presumably you cannot simply 'repatriate' works of art, which are like living beings,

either) was not something that could be printed in the *SZ* or reproduced on NDR or WDR. The reporter had problems accounting for
her increased travel expenses. She had observed longer than·what
was deemed necessary for such unattractive reportage.

'DEPENDABILITY
IN THE UPPER ECHELONS
OF THE WORLD'S LEADERS'

DIARY, NIGHT OF 3–4 NOVEMBER 2020.
WEDNESDAY MORNING, 4 A.M.

My wife and I in front of the TV. We hardly ever get up at four in the morning to go and sit in front of the TV. We're watching CNN. Our daughter is relaying headlines from individual US states, regional programmes and the internet from her iPhone. A plethora of news is giving an indecisive image. It's possible that President Trump will manage to achieve another four years. We go back to bed. At seven in the morning, another view of the data from our TV window.

I've never felt as politically disenfranchised in my life as I do right now. We citizens of the Federal Republic don't take part in the superpower's elections. Neither the Chancellor's Office nor the bodies of the EUROPEAN PUBLIC—just as little as Africa and other continents—have any influence on a decision on which war and peace may depend, at least in the distant future.

'The almost insoluble task
is to let neither the power of others,
nor our own powerlessness
stupefy us.'

Almost insoluble. And yet soluble. Adorno's statement, in which I deeply believe (irreducible by facts), is nevertheless difficult to apply at the moment. Its validity requires the hardest work of the imagination. Would it make sense for me, my relatives, my companions with whom I work—together as a group, as it were—to enter the service of an opinion-forming foundation in Washington and thus exert our influence there without a ballot? What to do? We would have to divide our forces at the same time: one part would have to appear in China, while another would be effective in the US. I don't think that anyone would accept our services in either of the two countries. Working hard (for the world's equilibrium) in Switzerland, in Davos? Or at the Munich Security Conference? Or at meetings in Africa? I only know one thing: something (as yet undiscovered, and that we urgently need to look for) will come to strengthen and demonstrate our belief in Adorno's statement (see above).

THE NOSE

A respected man, head of a group of auditors with an overview of more than a thousand companies, had acquired an abstract, sensual relationship with the movements of the stock market: that nervous social animal. An ABILITY TO SENSE A CRISIS. A kind of sensitivity to economic weather. Whereas our earliest ancestors—and even dogs today—had their olfactory centre in their brains, this expert's head had a sensory system that made him aware of certainties, curves and, above all, economic catastrophes up to twelve days or even six weeks in advance.

That was of great value. But he was unable to exercise this gift for himself or for others. It belonged to the circle of his professional secrets. As the head of so many auditors and of a company whose business was based on the evaluation of financial statements and the use of confidential data, HIS PARTICULAR TYPE OF APPERCEPTION was of no use to him. It remained an official secret. It did, however, benefit him in that, at the time of the collapse of Lehman Brothers, his sense of foreboding led him to liquidate his shareholdings in gold. He did this on his own account and, as no US companies were among his clients, most certainly not thanks to any factual knowledge.

'WILL-O-THE-WISPS IN THE SWAMP WARN THE OBSERVER . . . '

The Armenian Church is 'autocephalous', in other words, there is no foreign authority over it, no pope. It recognizes no patriarchy except its own. And has been this way for over 2,000 years. It is said that the first Christian church was founded in Armenia shortly after the death of the son of God. Neither in Jerusalem, where the Christians were initially banished, nor Rome nor Corinth are there any older Christian sites. For a thousand years, Armenia was caught between the Parthian Empire to the east and Rome to the west. A patch of freedom with long periods of occupation.

During the First World War, it was said that the Armenians, then part of the Ottoman Empire, were in league with the Russians. A clique of Turkish officers open to incitement, the Young Turks (who occupied the most important military and civilian posts during the war), organized a bloody punitive action against them.

In the late autumn of 2020, an alliance composed of Turkey and the Islamic Republic of Azerbaijan crushed the region of Nagorno-Karabakh. These 'Black Mountains' are populated by Armenians. Tanks and artillery supplied by Russia to Armenia melted away, attacked by Turkish-Azerbaijani drones.

Armenia's strength doesn't lie in the country itself, but in the diaspora, the Armenian biotopes throughout the world's metropolises which are full of Armenian emigrants. A young postdoctoral researcher has compared the unreliable five-year ceasefire—moderated by Russia—with the short-term agreements in the Balkans between 1908 and 1914. These brief interruptions to the conflicts that eventually derailed the balance of Europe in 1914, though agreed upon to last five years, never lasted any longer than three quarters of a year.

FIGURE 29 (ABOVE) AND 30 (BELOW).

THE ROLE FANTASY PLAYS
WHEN YOU MOVE YOUR FINGER
ACROSS A MAP OF THE WORLD

The heir of a multilingual billionaire—a poetically energetic man who'd settled in a castle in Scotland which he'd had built according to his own ideas—felt committed to the whole planet. Every morning, while he feasted on his one meagre egg and a lonely mix of vitamins, a liveried servant had to appear before him and shout: 'Remember, sir, that you are not a god!' This is how this heir and poet wanted to counteract any arrogance that might arise in him.

He had had a complete mapping of all five continents made for his so-called MAP ROOM, a kind of spacious auditorium with huge tables. One for each continent. Mountains and oceanic trenches in relief which the poet could caress with his fingers as well as his palm. With the help of his fingertips, he developed a feeling for the *diversity* and *cast* of the structures.

Such an approach to reality required a great deal of imagination. The stroke of his fingers measured the tips of a chain of 6,000-metre peaks, but only the power of his imagination could give him empathy for the forced march of those sherpas, who, out of breath, arrive at them.

Up in the attic of this THINKING SEAT, additional electronics were installed to receive satellites, the optics of which together gave him the overall view of both hemispheres, down to the individual road junction, wave, path through a field or valley: the sum of that poetic technology that the military employs to move through the terrain, and that its vehicles use to determine routes in the fog, the dark or when their drivers are completely unfamiliar with their whereabouts.

While looking for objects for which he could do philanthropic work during his nocturnal explorations, there, on the day side of the earth (like an astronomer at the telescope, a stargazer uninterested in stars, but in the details of earthly reality: a mole, a foxhole, a living room, a garden wall), he often thought, impatiently, like someone waiting for a drug, about the arrival of his matitudinal saying that he should not begin to feel like a god!

THE LOOK OF DECISION MAKERS
RESPONSIBLE FOR SOLVING FUTURE CRISES

The hierarchy of the foreign policy department of the People's Republic of China was fully assembled at the Munich Security Conference. The group sat united on the podium and in the first two rows of the plenary. Only the deputy chairman spoke. He was a stocky man. In terms of his stature, he could have been from the peasant class, though he could just as easily have been from the working class.

The topic of the day, which was only addressed here in the plenary in the form of short theses, had been thoroughly discussed the day before in several corridors of the Bayerischer Hof Hotel between the Chinese, the European groups as well as the US delegation. It had become clear just how much Europe and the US mistrusted the concept of the NEW SILK ROAD. The spokesperson for the Chinese delegation insistently defended the People's Republic of China's position. He denied that the port of Djibouti was being set up for military purposes, even though he knew how vehemently all the claims that came out of his mouth were disputed by listeners in Europe and the US. He repeated his statement in a measured tone amid murmurs in the room.

The Chinese column left the hall and walked down the corridors, always led by the security guards and delegation leaders. Like a well-disciplined group of students. The delegation members left the hotel foyer through the revolving doors and hurried towards the waiting motorcade but could only take their seats once the vice-chairman—the main political figure—had sat in the front limousine. He would have to wait until the motorcade's departure. First, briefcases and people were stowed in the long line of vehicles.

Then, at last, with a quick step, somehow standing out from the hierarchy, a very young, extremely slim, almost spiritual 'spirit' walked towards the vehicles. Several supervisors or coordinators turned towards him. He was refused entry into a slightly less posh vehicle and ushered to the front of vehicle number two. In that vehicle was a table in front of the rear seat. Only after this man had been invited did the convoy start to move.

The 'young scholar' is one of the president's most trusted confidantes. Physically, he is a striking contrast to the broad-shouldered deputy chairman, who precedes him in rank, but whom he controls—interlocked with the wheels of the president. The grouping, made up of such great physical contrasts, seemed to me to be a uniformly managed organism. Unlike the rather motley US delegation, made up of individualists from different universities, who at that moment, similarly surrounded by security guards, were standing in front of the lifts that would take them to the sixth floor where new appointments awaited them.

WEDNESDAY, 6 JANUARY 2021. DIARY / 'ROBBERY OF A MAIL COACH FROM THE FUTURE'

Almost five in the afternoon, our time. We're sitting in front of the TV. In Washington it's 11 a.m. We're watching the moderators on CNN, the quickly changing guests. We can't get any other channels from the US. We'd really like to see some local news broadcasts.

Trump-bashing makes one feel helpless. We've learnt that much over the last four years. We're like children, watching what's happening at a Punch and Judy show. Punch doesn't take any danger seriously. He's wrong. He doesn't see the devil approaching from behind. We children, sitting in front of the stage, aren't in any danger. However, he, Punch, doesn't see the crocodile that we see. We call out to him to tell him what to do. In the quadrangular world of TV, these roles are reversed. At best, the expressive Trump is mistaken about what's in store for him if he continues to rile up the crowd. No devil there to threaten him, no crocodile, no grand-mother of the devil. And yet his performance has made us curious, hungry for escalation and more: this is the devil of *suspense*, a devil inside of us, eating away at reason. We, the children, here in Europe in front of the TV, are in danger. My mind is telling me: an improb-able danger. My heart something else—my wife, my daughter are unnerved as well: Even if this time things turn out OK, there can be a next time when they won't. If the superpower turns authoritarian through a coup, things in Europe and throughout the world will go bad. And we, sitting in front of the screen, with our iPhones, are powerless, there is nothing we can do to avert the danger. That would no longer be any kind of theatre.

The president is demonstrating how to be 'wrong' on TV. But the error lies elsewhere. It's a mistake to believe that whatever power of the US is contained within the lawmakers' magnificent building, the Capitol, can be conquered with human fists and feet. The power of the US has long since been digitized and has always been dis-tributed throughout the country. It cannot be housed in a Roman-style building.

The superpower's capabilities are dormant. But an attack or something like the elimination of the fleet in Pearl Harbor will rouse them. Nonetheless, a large republic needs a few months to really react. The COSPLAYING REBELS have not yet awakened it. They are smashing windows, breaking in to rooms, occupying chairs and furniture, exploring the strange castle. I don't believe for a second the rage that the scene is portraying. These are not professional actors. To believe that they have sprung from paintings dating to the early days of the US simply because they are dressed in a similar fash-ion is a misconception. They have not come from days gone by. They are unquiet in the now. Fully automated, utterly contemporary energy!

FIGURE 31

CHOIR FOR SIX PARTS, 6 JANUARY 2021

1.

In his broad, black winter coat, President Trump is standing at the lectern in front of the mass of his supporters in the park. Groups of armed soldiers and militiamen are said to be among the rowdy, almost unmanageable crowd.

Presenters at the TV stations, the reporters

2.

The attacking *rioters* were 20 minutes of chaos away—according to security—from events that would have led to catastrophe. Roughly 20

3.

The slogan 'shut down the lying press' wasn't the idea of a single person. A lot of people in the crowd had it in mind. Public relations officers collected reporters' cameras and equipment, and the lights and supplies of TV crews reporting 'up close and personal'. The loot was gathered on the Capitol steps and, at first, guarded. The equipment (including cables and microphones) was strewn about in an untidy pile. Much of it most likely no longer functional. Later, 'rebels' dressed like Americans and Indians from the founding era of the USA, some dressed as cartoon characters, tried to set ascribe the president's words as ambiguous. To many observers, it appears that he is encouraging the crowd to march with him on towards the Capitol. Just like a candidate for the office of prime minister in Italy once marched on Rome with his supporters (albeit in uniform).

Given its physical presence, it seems possible that the excited crowd in Washington will prevent Congress from sealing the handover. The president has finished his speech. He is no longer onstage. The crowd starts to move. Across the flat surface to the gates that cordon off the Capitol. A crowd of brown and black with brightly coloured spots: the anachronistic costumes. Shapes scale the outer walls of the Capitol, built according to ancient Roman design. The climbers are reminiscent of the West African fireman in Paris who climbed a facade and forcefully took a child in his arms who'd fallen and was clinging to the railings of a balcony with fading strength, all physique and good will. The similarity of the images is deceptive.

minutes of Capitol-attack-time away from the legislators and senators. Bodyguards were responsible for their protection. They tried to escort those entrusted to their care through tunnels in the building's basements which would allow the congressmen and women to be evacuated to neighbouring buildings. Only a slight acceleration in the movement of the *rioters*' attack wedge and a slight delay caused by bottlenecks holding up the fleeing stream of people's representatives and the distances between the attackers and the lawmakers would have been reduced to a few metres. At any one of these parameters, one accidental *more* would have caused the bodyguards, trained to react quickly and deliberately, to unlock their pistols and fire into the onrushing crowd. How, one of the deputy coordinators of the security services asked the following day, would the armed *rioters* have responded to such protective action? Would they have fired in return? The crisis did not come about. 'You've got to have a bit of luck to be a representative of the State nowadays.'

fire to the mountain of press recording equipment. Even when crushed and trampled, the material would not burn. Journalists and reporters stood on the sidelines. They were on guard. Unsure of any reliable exit. As one of them later testified, they were careful not to make any frantic movements that might have looked like escaping. They thought, the witness said, that this was precisely how they would have attracted pursuers.

Meanwhile, online and on TV stations, attempts are being made to 'classify' and 'comment'. As permanent speech, and in the hopes of establishing a relationship to the event, of regaining a piece of reality. One of the presenters reported that she had felt a double impulse: on the one hand, she wanted the harshness of events to increase as it would be good for the 'public interest' and would certainly attract viewers; and on the other, her obligation to 'moderate'. It will take time to find a measure in all of this. Guidance: 'time heals catastrophes.'

4.

Alarms are sounding throughout the governing agencies of the US, the deep state, but without an order from a central authority, even a regional one, not even the National Guards of Washington, DC's neighbouring states are allowed to move in with their vehicles. The fire department, however, is. The brigade responsible for the government district, if it were to leave immediately and show up in front of the Capitol with its vehicles, hoses, ladders and water trucks, would presumably be an effective cool-down, a 'presence of authority' for the *rioters*. If 80 fire trucks

5.

A major study has been underway for two years in a subdivision of the American Enterprise Institute, located down the street in Washington, where all the major non-profit foundations are concentrated. It is about the danger of coups in western democracies, especially for the central institutions of the USA. The study is being funded by Canada. Canada is not indifferent to democratic or authoritarian rule in its large neighbouring country. The first part of the study deals with the FANTASY FACTOR (novel fantasy). It says that there are few objective reasons for a coup, but that what is read, heard, found on the net and in the media, even in cartoons, can stir up subjective

6.

On 11 September, the US president was kept in motion in his presidential plane in restricted airspace. Then he was hidden in a bunkered military base. The reason being that the security authorities had no idea whether the attack on the World Trade Center was an assassination attempt, an accident or an attack by foreign powers, maybe even a superpower.

Is there even such a thing in modern times as a DECAPITATION STRIKE that puts the leadership of a superpower out of action? What is the head of the community? It is not the lawmakers alone. All foundation studies to factors such as an overwhelming fear of something undefined. The assumption of a conspiracy threatening to overthrow the USA could ignite an irresistible driving force in individual minds that, if only they could find one another, would lead a group of people to attempt a coup.

In the second part of the study, a novel by Tom Clancy is taken as a starting point. In Tom Clancy's novel, the White House is attacked by a plane. The vice-president is taken through underground passages in the cellars of the White House to a neighbouring building. The authors of the study conclude that the Capitol and the White House, as centres and symbols of power, attract such fantasies of attack. The attack on the Pentagon on 11 September was not the original goal, but a deviation from the original plan. Moving on, the investigative team points out that any coup that wants a real chance of being effective should not be directed against symbolic places, but towards occupying the real centres of power. These are consistently decentralized. They are not even in a single time zone.

this effect reliably conclude that there is no 'head' of the USA that a legislative measure could knock off. The USA's 'leadership', its 'power', is decentralized. An enemy can confuse this apparatus, the 'deep state', for a short time, but not absorb it. It would be different with a centrally controlled state. In the meantime, according to the study, in this sense Russia is no longer a centralized state as it was in 1983. The last plans for a 'main strike'—all thought exercises, 'planning games', without preparation or follow-up—referred to that point in time.

...ed of time, this could—in this sense, they are also phoning back and forth—'diffuse' the situation. On the other hand, it could also cause additional chaos. As there is no order, nothing happens.

Should private security go out and help the obviously overwhelmed authorities of the government district? That would not be permissible without permission from these authorities, without requirements. Armed persons, for whatever motivation, cannot simply approach the perimeter of the Capitol. How would lay people distinguish between armed, un-uniformed private security and those who were similarly armed and storming the Capitol? The insurgents could mistake the expedition of the private bodyguards for a reinforcement of their attack.

It is only at dawn that contingents of the Virginia National Guard arrive. They set up their makeshift camps on the floor of the Capitol foyers and settle in for the night's rest, which at the same time means NIGHT WATCH. Weapons and packs around them like a wall.

A few hours after the riot on 6 January 2021, the senators and representatives who'd been evacuated by tunnel into neighbouring buildings were brought back to their seats in the Capitol by their security details. The congressional process of confirming the transfer of power from Trump to Biden was finished around 9 p.m. Outside it had grown dark. Now that it was no longer urgently necessary, all the governmental authorities were alert, communicatively connected to one another and operational.

1954 ATTACK ON THE US CAPITOL

capitol00016   capitol00018

FIGURE 32 (FACING PAGE AND ABOVE). Four rebels, led by a pasionaria, fighting for Puerto Rico's independence from the US, fired onto the legislative floor of the House of Representatives. Five congressmen were seriously injured.

1954 Attack on the US Capitol, triptych.

6 January 2021 Attack on the US Capitol, triptych.

FIGURE 33

SEMANTIC FIELD 'DEPENDABLE'

FIGURE 34

FIGURE 35

A MEANDERING TALE ON THE KEY PHRASE
'BEYOND THE GRAVE'

The legendary runner who had brought the message of the Greeks' victory over the Persians at Marathon delivered his night's tale in a croaky voice and in fragments, not in complete sentences. Then he fell down dead ('disembodied') in front of the witnesses, his companions. He'd overdone it. Against the will of his soul, which had been demanding a break, he had run many a parasang over the passes from the north, his legs, his trained body, as if he were some kind of automaton, on a kind of autopilot. Dry-mouthed, he'd spit out the message. Already mechanical, without inner motive, devoid of all reserves of vitality, spent and dead before he fell. An irrepressible good will, a piece of perfect training, had shot him beyond the goal of his life.

Presumably, this event did not take place as here described. But was told as a kind of folk tale. That was Heiner Müller's opinion. And this tale crops up again in the ballad of 'The Horseman and the Lake of Constance'. In the war propaganda of the Third Reich, it has to do with a spooky organist, a man full of inner life who had never been taken seriously by his comrades, who, when the company is out on a reconnaissance mission and gets lost in the fog, sits down at the keyboard of the local church. Thinking him weak on his feet, his comrades had left him behind. But now there he is, pounding on the keys, making the organ pipes roar. And it is precisely this mighty sound that leads the company back to safety. In the meantime, however, enemy artillery has smashed the church and killed the musician (or here: noisemaker, alarmist). His muscles weak, untrained in lifesaving, there he lies with his upper body across the keys, his feet continuing to press the pedals down in warning, though without any subjective intention, mechanically: the weight of the dead man. It is not the harmonic tone for which the organ was built. It too is damaged.

LOYALTY AS POWER'S CURRENCY

Within a modern, civilized power structure, money does not establish a relationship of exchange. In the service of my country, I do not trade for money. If someone offers me money for my services, it is a bribe, and I will report any attempt to bribe me to my superiors and the courts. But another means of exchange, reliability, is a currency that has a behavioural impact at all levels of power projection.

An officer and six men from a Kurdish combat unit had saved the life of a US captain and his men in the Gulf War. They had literally snatched the doomed men from under the knives of an Iraqi force. The captain rose through the ranks of the US Army. By December 2019, he was a department head at the Pentagon. Still grateful, emotionally attached to his rescuers.

The legendary General Petraeus, in the meantime chair at West Point, had collaborated with the Kurds. Decisive stages of his successful career were due to the military skills and reliability of Kurdish units. The alliance of American soldiers and Kurdish fighters ranged from regular officers down to non-commissioned officers and had been proven in joint firefights. Often, later at night, the two groups would ride out the excitement of battle together. There were dinners, agreements were reached. Marriages were made between Kurds and Americans.

But now, in the so-to-speak seventh generation of such camaraderie, Kurdish forces, still focused on clearing Syria's northeast of the Islam State, were caught off guard by the American president's order. Without any preparation, without any thought, without the consent of his inner circle of collaborators, Trump had handed over the whole of northern Syria to the Turkish president. And in so doing violated the sense of loyalty—and honour—of the Kurdish front in the Pentagon. The order for all GIs to withdraw opened the way for superior Turkish armoured units to enter Kurdish territory and exposed the Kurdish units to annihilation. Senior US officials considered this an act of betrayal. The defence minister, a member of the brotherhood, resigned. Other officers followed suit.

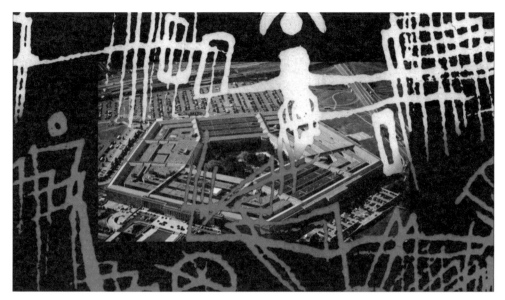

FIGURE 36 (ABOVE) AND 37 (BELOW)

THE SECRET CENTRE OF US PLANNING
IMPERVIOUS TO EAVESDROPPING

Room 2E924 in the Pentagon is known as THE TANK. The name
for this excessively sealed-off vault (windowless, the walls repeatedly
concreted and secured, where the Joint Chiefs of Staff meet to discuss top-level secrets and hash out plans) came from an earlier one
that served the same purpose of facilitating extremely hush-hush
consultations of the military core and the political leadership. That
earlier Second World War–era room was similarly sealed off and had
a tunnel-like entrance with exposed cables and pipes, reminiscent
of the entrance hatch of a tank. Hence its name: 'The Tank'.

In the new room, more spacious than the original one, furnished
with oil paintings and furniture, not to mention film projectors and
installations for PowerPoint presentations, there was nevertheless a
safe. This is where the president of the United States and the country's
military leadership met on 20 July 2017. Alongside, the Secretary of
Defence and the Secretary of Commerce. In a second row around the
military and advisers who formed the central body, a round of assistants and advisers to the advisers on folding seats or sitting around
control desks. Next to President Trump, his adviser Bannon and
White House Chief of Staff, Priebus.

A TWEET GIVES A GENERAL'S
DECISION GROUNDING

James Mattis, US Secretary of Defence, rushed to Scott Stearney's
funeral service at the Pentagon. The dead man had been his friend.
Back in his office, his mind cluttered, his press secretary showed him
a tweet that President Trump had just sent out. Looking up at the
sky, the president was addressing US GIs killed in Syria. Comforting
them, up there. For their sake, he had ordered all US troops to withdraw from Syria, to at least save those soldiers who were still alive,
though they, up there in the heavens, had already made the ultimate
sacrifice in that terrible country so far away from home. Looking at

the tweet brought Mattis back from the funeral to reality. He shed the grief of the past hour-and-a-half like a uniform. He said: 'OK.' That was the moment when he definitively decided to resign. The withdrawal of all US troops from northern Syria had left America's Kurdish allies, its comrades, the defeaters of IS, at the mercy of Turkish military supremacy. 'End of reliability.'

THE FUTURE WHIPS THE HORSE OF HISTORY INTO A GALLOP

In the hours of the funeral service for Vice Admiral Scott Stearney, Secretary of Defence General Mattis reflected on the hour of his own death. He would never have done this in a conference or crisis (or even in combat, when his life was in danger). He felt that the vast, five-sided space of the Pentagon would outlive him. He also sensed the vast rhizomatic structure of the US defence system—unlike the administration building, this root structure was invisible, but in fact the authentic reality of power. This power seemed to him to embody a life of many generations, more than 12 generations in the line of superiors he knew. As for him, he currently had a *peak time* of three years in office. The pinnacle of his career; before that, preparation, practice. He felt like a 'dwarf fish'. He compared the 90 minutes of the funeral service with those long periods of time. Before the coffin. Which did *not* contain the dead man (who was still lying in a cold chamber in Bahrain). Mattis compared that moment there, as if on a general staff map, with the clear time span since Pearl Harbor. He related that period of history to the rise of the US following the rebellion against the British-occupation army in the eighteenth century. That expanse of time made him wonder about the year 2042, by which time he would certainly no longer be in office. Why 2042 in particular? Because on 20 December 2018, planning for the consecutive and necessary responses to China's provocations, the network of deterrence, extended precisely to the planning horizon of 2042. As he sat there listening to the organ playing over the loudspeakers (the Pentagon does not employ musicians), his thoughts moved to the years immediately preceding 2042. In terms of the Pentagon's planning: the present. That future's hectic pace and gravity pressed upon his vascular walls. He found memorial services like that one, lavishly extended by the adjutants, to be a luxury when measured in terms of time poverty, when he thought of all that had to be prepared by 2042. In truth, a 'leading man' has no time to 'mourn a dead friend'.

'O rider, be clever, be bright! /
The knight never has time!'

THE PRAETORIAN PROBLEM

For four years, the president of a superpower showed himself to be an improviser, a mercurial character. He sent troops into dangerous zones of the world, before leaving them without any protection. And once he set such actions in motion, a reproachful telephone call from a foreign magnate could stun him and make him waver. Order to retreat! On one of these retreats, a large number of GIs were killed, captured by the enemy, maimed, lost. But in terms of his preferences and opportunities, he was already long focused elsewhere.

After two more presidents, one of whom was re-elected, that is, after 12 years, a left-leaning tribune came to power which changed everything. It didn't think much of the army, the navy, space warfare or aircraft. It was succeeded by a president who appreciated risks, a spy, a new child emperor, religiously hardened, driven by voters with their roots in the end-times-Christian, eschatological camp. This electorate reckoned with the end of the world; it was a matter of working towards the arrival of the Last Judgement.

This tyrant brought the superpower to the brink of war multiple times. This president was followed by a ditherer, a civilian-minded NON-DECISION-MAKER, a—as far as military circles were concerned—'wimp' who'd been elected in reaction to his predecessor's bad habits. There had been a lot of unreliability in the previous political cycles. The fact that this president avoided decisions did not stop decisions from being made. This in view of the fact that a superpower is made up of more than 10,000 PARTICULARITIES, each with a will of its own.

During this 'weak' president's 'reign', it turned out that an officer front had already been formed during the reign of the first president named. These initially small conspiracy circles had vowed 'military disobedience'. In the event of any new ill-considered steps, they would hinder him: they discussed disobeying orders, even taking away the nuclear briefcase. In the years that followed, the conspiracy spread along a longer hierarchical line between the generals and those who sat at key points in the command regime. The *conjuratio* spread through the Marine Corps, through the ranks of the computer scientists, through the military academies and into the navy, air force and certain elite army units. Within the 'covenants' based on loyalty and reliability, a faction formed and this conspiratorial, disenchanted, rebellious grouping mutated, as it were, into a STANCE OF CATEGORICAL NATURE. Finally, a president was deposed and imprisoned. Elections, professionally prepared by the media, resulted in 90 per cent approval for the coup and for the candidate put forward by the armed forces. Killing the overthrown civilian ruler—as in ancient Rome—was unnecessary. As a private citizen, he had no significant power in a world population of around 10 billion people. STRUCTURE, the accumulation of all the power that has already been created, alone can rule. A single Harvard historian, a critical man who characterized this result as the 'praetorian problem', was able to publish his book without being censored. Books are part of the FOURTH NATURE—the first is that of seasons, agriculture, cities and simple lifestyles; the second is that of systems of industry and the information society, and the third is the GOLDEN CALF OF POWER.

You can dance around this behemoth. But you cannot guide, tame or influence the direction it takes.

FIGURE 38

A MAN WHO IGNORED EVERY WARNING
HIS SOUL PROVIDED HIM

The soul is a term for the 'inner motives' that set all our actions in motion. This particular soul had been driving Vice Admiral Scott Stearney for a whole year to resign his commission. The soul had signalled its weariness. It would rather fly away than have that body, that sheath of nerves, its mask of a face, serve any longer. Then this man—in the name of all his outer walls, the outer armour of his character—took the post of commander of the US Fifth Fleet. A force of some 20,000 men who, with their ships, planes, drones and helicopters, oversee the riskiest entry point for the US Navy: the Persian Gulf, the Strait of Hormuz, the western Indian Ocean. And beyond that, the Red Sea and the Suez Canal. Areas full of the uncanny. The snake that bit him to death: the soul that did not agree with the assumption of such a risky position had been driving this vice admiral's motives and behaviour in a fatal direction for months.

HE QUICKLY BECAME A LEGEND

He had put a wall between himself and the environment. The mask he had assumed—that of a determined, concentrated officer—gave no indication of his soul's unquiet. Indeed, no one saw any 'unquiet' at all. Behind it was a second wall in the form of his efficiency, his intact nerves, his muscles, his body, his ability to react. Right after university, serving in the Navy, he became an AVIATOR. He was one of the first to fly the HORNET. Then 4,500 accident-free take-offs and landings with various types of aircraft, including over thousand landings with brake cables on aircraft carriers. Since he started wearing glasses, however, he was no longer allowed to fly.

'SCOTT STEARNEY BURNT THE MIDNIGHT OIL!'

His wife had found him in his study. He had killed himself. One of his aides, who had spoken to the navy doctors, none of whom could explain the death, thought that insomnia was the cause of the suicide. His boss had 'burnt out' the strength that a man draws from deep sleep before midnight and, if necessary, from the 'residual ability to fall asleep late at night'. Midnight Oil. That was the expression for the rest of being-for-itself that a human being needs. One of the doctors had said that sleep deprivation lasting longer than 12 weeks would by itself lead to a person's death. Guantanamo had taught that consecutive sleep deprivation over nine weeks, if completely successful, 'shatters' a person. Here, in the case of the vice admiral, the adjutant said, the soul struck 'before the body could destroy the man'.

CONCERN ABOUT AN ERROR
IN THE 'MAN MACHINE'

Pilot Scott Stearney was shaken. During a night landing on an aircraft carrier, a night with rising fog, he had not properly seen the carrier's horizontal row of landing lights. He'd seen two rows instead of one. The adaptation of the eyes to the luminous device directly in front of him in the cabin and the coordination of this data with the luminous markings outside—all this in the split second the machine touched down on the swaying body of the ship had produced images beside the facts, ghostly images. The high-ranking pilot's eyes were examined. He was ordered to wear glasses. Further flights were forbidden.

The 'lateral displacement of the impression of the eyes' had nothing to do with visual acuity, but with the way in which the impressions are put together in the brain. Glasses would not correct this. There is no such thing as 'brain glasses'. Unquiet joined the unquiet already surging inside Scott Stearney.

THE STING THAT ROBBED THE COMMANDER
OF ALL TRANQUILLITY

His job was not to supervise 20,000 men. His staff, the officers, the many different groups of non-commissioned officers were responsible for that. He could rely on the hierarchy. The scary part had more to do with his opponents' activities, their unpredictability in terms of being controlled. While sleeping, maybe new types of mines with newly developed detonators were being deposited in the waters of the Strait of Hormuz. It was possible that these explosive devices had mechanisms that removed all traces of the explosive. Tankers destroyed by a 'ghostly wind' . . .

Just like a case of inflammation spreading through a series of veins and capillaries, now, on the night Scott Stearney wanted to sleep, instead of sleep, imaginary caravans of weapons were moving through the desert belts of the Arabian Peninsula. Transports were on their way to Libya. And Stearney should have warned his peer-group colleague in charge of the US Mediterranean fleet long ago. And yet the exhausted vice admiral did not wake up, his dreams continued to frighten him. The many-sidedness of the dangers in his area of control, the fluid element of the uncanny had deprived him of any peace for months, regardless of whether he sought it in brief moments of respite during the day or night.

MAKING A BID FOR THE LARGEST ISLAND
IN THE WORLD

A cartoon shows an 11-year-old Donald Trump looking at pictures of Alaskan gold diggers. Later on, by word of mouth, he learns that the US had purchased this northern expanse of land from the Russian tsar for only $7.2 million. Any old US entrepreneur could still buy a claim of that frigid geography of foxes and water for a reasonable dollar price. 'What a wonderful thought!' the US president tweeted, possessing such a vast piece of the earth's surface, that is, a 100 square kilometres in extent. Just the thought of it was a pick-me-up.

The idea of buying Greenland came to the president by chance when a Pentagon representative considering the question of a possible Russian attack across the Arctic into Northern Canada presented him with a map of the northern part of the globe. Trump made an offer to the Danish government via Twitter. How much would the largest island in the world cost? He added a fair price for the land, compensation for the population (which he said consisted of only 57,000 indigenous people and some Danes) and a premium for the 'romance of the thought'. Greenland was close to the American continental shelf, level with Canada, but the depths that tumbled about Greenland exerted a powerful influence on New York's characteristic autumn and spring weather.

For reasons the president could not explain, the government of the Danish Kingdom refused to even negotiate the generous offer. The president's advisers talked him out of imposing sanctions on the stubborn country.

WHERE CAN WE ESCAPE TO
WHEN THE EARTH
IS DESTROYED?

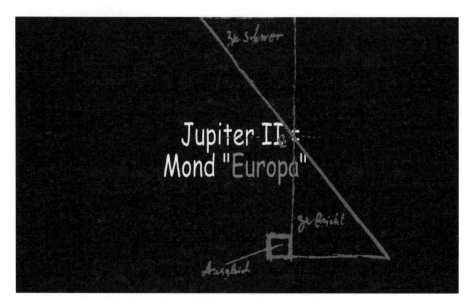

FIGURE 39

THE BIRTH OF A PROJECT FOR A NOVEL

Thanks to the Corona pandemic, but also because law enforcement had to be on the lookout for a coup, at the transfer of the presidency from Donald Trump to Joe Biden, the wide area in front of the White House where, at previous handovers, upto 200,000 people had stood, was deserted, if littered with American flags. Instead of standing people: poles.

Watching the handover ceremony on CNN, the lyrical imagination of an American poet, novelist and essayist from New York was suddenly gripped by an impression of future danger. For a moment—just as President Biden's and his wife's backs were visible, looking out from the balcony at the community not of people but of flags—he thought it entirely possible that one day the US, indeed the whole world, might not only have to have such a large public space cleared of people but abandon the planet as well.

In the sky, symbols of speed and technology (similar to flags). Masses of aircraft, capable of space travel. This, in the mind's eye of the poet, would be the evacuation of humanity. He had no idea why yet. For a moment, he didn't think it was technically possible. Then he was overcome by his narrative desire, the narrative element and a deep-rooted suspicion. None of what he imagined—there, sitting in front of the TV—was realistic, he thought. But he trusted his suspicions, the restlessness, that gripped him. What was real, what was fictional, when as a poet he 'thought' in both dimensions? By late afternoon, he'd already sketched out an idea to work on in 2021. He knew that his publisher trusted him, and that whatever he wrote would be printed.

CLEARLY A FLUKE, NOT AN ACT OF PROVIDENCE

In a single night, the poet wrote 60 pages of a draft on his sluggish computer (there was so much communication going on that night). First, a collection of material. It was less difficult for him to imagine an EXODUS OF HUMANS to an alien celestial body, a factual world with which he was unfamiliar, than to imagine the reasons that would make such emigration necessary. He began by imagining a confusion of humankind's senses. On all continents. Then he began to describe a DIGITAL DARK AGE. .

But this, narratively speaking, led him to a dead end. If all digital sources were extinguished and humanity and civilization in general forced to return to file notes, manuals, mechanical work processes, an exodus into space wouldn't be possible either, and the novel would end prematurely.

A PLOT FAILURE

Around 4 a.m., exhausted to the tips of his fingers, while trying to save what he had written the writer made a mistake. He deleted the text. But he was able to reconstruct the sequence of his thoughts from memory—the assumptions from which his first chapter could proceed.

God has removed himself from the world. This is the assumption of Kabbalah in its modern interpretation. But then God reverses his removal. An original, zealous God emerges and inflicts punishment on humanity. The prophets who communicate this are quickly discredited as adherents of a conspiracy theory. Science denies the possibility of a RETURN OF A VENGEFUL GOD.

Just such a thing was implausible. So said Prof. Dr Robert Abraham of Harvard University, the poet's fictional character in the now lost manuscript. Theologically speaking, making all the animals of evolution, the mountains, the oceans and the planet itself pay for humankind's former and present misdeeds was hardly justifiable.

The theory of God's punishment was advocated by Christological communities. End-timers from the American Midwest, but also churches from provinces in Brazil and in Kiev too. Threat number one: large celestial bodies approaching the sun at high speed from the direction of the Oort cloud. The impact of these asteroid-sized bodies would shatter the earth's crust. The communities had scientific helpers at their service. No amount of shelling, they said, could deflect or destroy the debris hurtling towards earth. Where could these celestial bodies be located? The end-timers' assumptions were fought.

In his writing, the New Yorker poet had felt strongly how difficult it was to imagine something that would correspond to the 10 plagues of Egypt in reality. He tried to include tensions between the nuclear powers of China and the US as the second greatest source of danger. But any poetic expressiveness completely disappeared when it came to the FRACTIONING OF THE EARTH'S MANTLE. 'Nuclear-contaminated sites eat their way to the earth's core.' A hitherto unprecedented PLUME, an upward chute of high-energy magma, is pushing towards the rupture of the earth's surface.

This seemed poetically conceivable, as an eruption from the earth's interior stronger than the Indonesian event of 800,000 years ago would bring winter across the entire globe due to dust in the stratosphere. The writer seemed to have already succeeded in this in his draft. Then, on page 32, he decided to leave the reasons for the exodus open. It's difficult, he'd noted, to imagine excessive dangers beyond our regular day-to-day life. Just as a person's skin is there to ward off strangers, so clothing or armour or safety suits offer protection against external danger. Not to mention the cocoon of states, armies, defensive shields, security agencies. But the strongest of these balloon-like protective skins—the 'mind's cornea'—is THE PROTECTIVE SHIELD OF ILLUSIONS which denies all dangers that we do not habitually see. This is an inheritance from magic. In this way, the poet wrote, 'every one has a shaman within'. In his project, therefore, he only wanted to hint at the danger of which he had gained an inkling from the poles on the wide expanse before the Capitol, an inkling, not a hypothesis. Writing in a blur—that, he thought, was the art of WRITING ON THE WALL.

FIGURE 40 (ABOVE) AND 41 (BELOW)

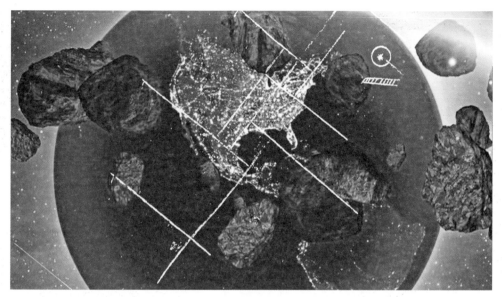

FIGURE 42 (ABOVE) AND 43 (BELOW)

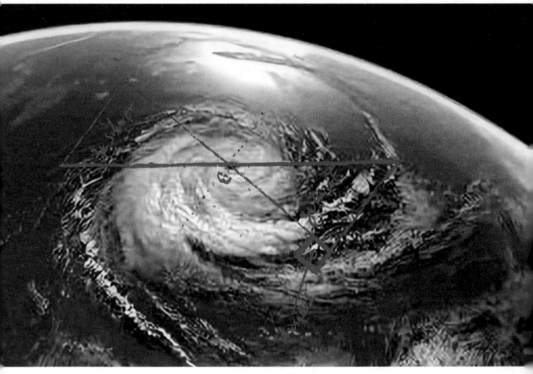

FIGURE 44

FIGURE 45 (ABOVE), 46 (CENTRE) AND 47 (BELOW)

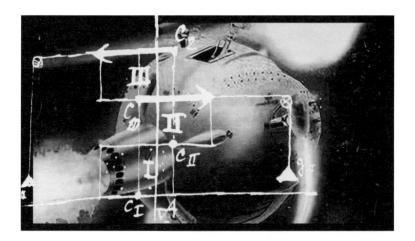

$$P = \frac{N\Theta}{V} - \frac{2\pi}{3} G\alpha^2 \bar{\rho}^2 L^2$$

ARRIVAL ON THE MOON EUROPA

To reach Jupiter's second moon—which astronomers refer to as Jupiter II Europa—the spaceships (one of which can only carry a few thousand evacuees at a time) must gain momentum by circling the sun. The gravitational pull of the massive celestial body 'the sun' gives the spaceships the necessary boost of acceleration. They need it to get into orbit around Jupiter in the limited time it takes to feed a thousand evacuees and keep them together in confined spaces. Then comes the approach to the second moon and the disembarkation of the landing ships.

So-called PROTECTIVE HUTS are to be temporary residences on the moon's icy outer crust. These structures come from tiny information containers using the 3D-printing process, which is why the materials were carried in the trailers of the spaceship and then the landing ships. In the meanwhile, they've also managed to create submarines from out of two square centimetre 'boxes' of information, again using 3D technology. These are sunk into shafts that reach from the surface of the moon to the ocean below. The challenge is to decide on the spot whether they will construct 'underwater cities' on the rocks at the bottom of the oceans or 'floating cities' halfway to the surface. 'We know too little about the core of the moon,' the planning report says. 'Nor do we know what possibilities there are for anchoring. Moreover, due to Jupiter's gravity, during orbit, the granite rock we assume to be at the core of Jupiter's moon and the water masses around that core are "rolled through" by 80 to 100 metre-high waves. Permanent pressure. As a result, the cities move—less when they are fixed to the bedrock, and more when they float in the waters themselves—like "ships constantly passing through a hurricane recurring at a fixed rhythm".'[1]

---

1 Jupiter II Europa always faces the planet on the same side. The moon, however, has a highly elliptical orbit. Consequently, it 'dances' back and forth against Jupiter's powerful gravitational pull. In this respect, the tides of Europa's ocean have different causes than the those in the relationship between the moon and the earth. The differences between the furthest and the next-closest distance between the planet and the moon 'pull' the water masses more than on the earth.

FIGURE 48

FIGURE 49 (ABOVE) AND 50 (BELOW)

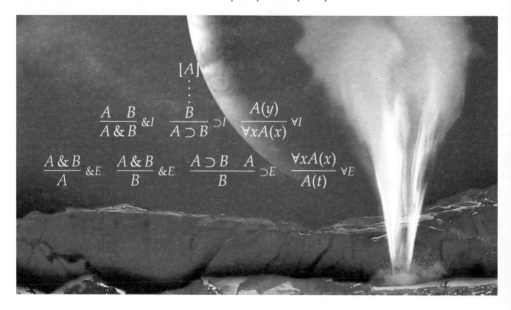

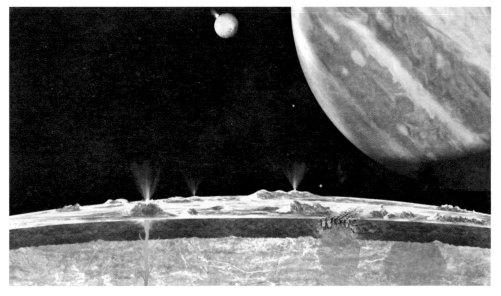

FIGURE 51 (ABOVE) AND 52 (BELOW)

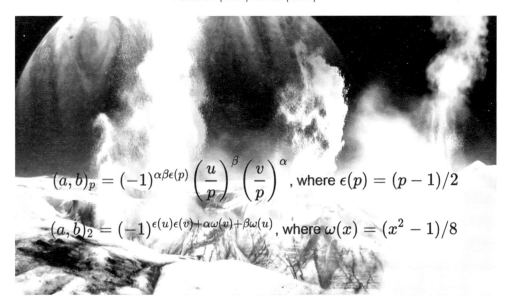

$$(a, b)_p = (-1)^{\alpha\beta\epsilon(p)} \left(\frac{u}{p}\right)^{\beta} \left(\frac{v}{p}\right)^{\alpha}, \text{ where } \epsilon(p) = (p-1)/2$$

$$(a, b)_2 = (-1)^{\epsilon(u)\epsilon(v)+\alpha\omega(v)+\beta\omega(u)}, \text{ where } \omega(x) = (x^2-1)/8$$

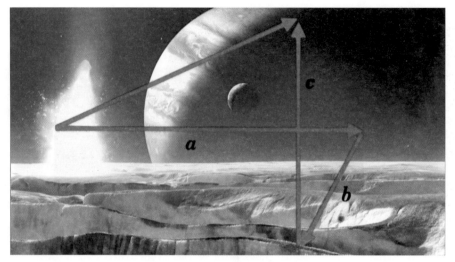

FIGURE 53

WORRYING ABOUT THE CHILDREN
IN THE SUBMARINE ON EUROPA

If only we'd discovered seaweed first! Or fish! Or something unexpected to feed us! We've been roaming this ocean to the bottom, even if we haven't discovered it yet. That is, we've managed theoretically, in our calculations, if not practically. Maybe we'll come across nodules or coral. And even though we can't eat them, we'd welcome metal nodules as a raw material.

But if our calculations are wrong—even those that assume that there is a core of rock at the bottom of this ocean that encompasses the moon—we will continue to drift into the abyss until the enormous water pressure destroys the boat.

At least we got this far. There's no way back. We've got supplies. We also have some plantations inside the boat where we grow fresh produce. And all that's enough for maybe a year. When we have children, we'll need better supplies. Until then, we have to be careful not to become cannibals. In that worst-case scenario, 'reason' will not protect us from ourselves. It will merely tell us that, if we don't feed on each other, we won't survive. We have to discover something edible. Water doesn't provide nourishment.

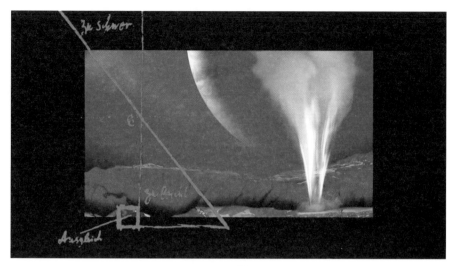

FIGURE 54

ANGELIC AID
FROM AN EXTREME TEMPORAL DISTANCE.
MESSENGERS OF THE PRIMEVAL GODS

All the astrophysicists at the Honolulu conference agreed that Kepler-444f (the sixth planet of the star Kepler-444), 117 light years away in the constellation of Lyre, was rare. The sun Kepler-444, an extremely old star, was formed 11.2 billion years ago. A rolling motion emanates from its interior. All planets orbit this sun-like (but, as I said, much older) star in less than 10 days. The orbits are much closer to the central star than those of Mercury around the sun. In this respect, the astrophysicist Monmouth estimated that the chance of finding an earth-like planet there, a possible refuge for humanity, was unlikely.

How amazed we were when we suddenly received signs from there at Planck length! Messages from a world far, far away, and separated in time. But we were able to communicate as if by magic ('nature's veins'). The foreigners were offering to cooperate with us. Whatever the signs meant, we were unable to interpret them for lack of comparative material. They seemed, however, to be an offer of

COLLABORATION. That was our interpretation. It was a desire coming from within us to find allies outside.

In any case, these unexpected signals helped us to revise our misconception that it was completely impossible for Kepler-444f to harbour life. We did not know what kind of alien intelligence had sent its message from the exoplanet. The US president commented on this new situation, saying on Twitter: 'I don't know what it means. It seems to be something new.' The aliens had put their message in mathematical symbols. We could not decipher the characters.

We could not prove to colleagues our emotionally secure assumption that these illegible characters meant positive contact. 'I myself,' Russian astrophysicist Ferdinand Smirnov said, 'assume that contact was made long ago in the long time between the sending of the message and the earthly evolution of intelligence.' But there is no documentation. 'Assuming,' he added, 'that the creatures of Kepler-444f had reached us at Planck length, the intersection of all physical constants of nature, communication between us medium-sized giants and the extra-terrestrials' fine energetic powers would probably have been impossible too.' None of these insights diminished our hope in some kind of extra-terrestrial intervention in the needs, necessities and potential horror scenarios of the European-American-Pacific conflicts to come, which we expect to come to a head by 2042 at the latest.

FIGURE 55 (ABOVE) AND 56 (BELOW)

'ON THE FRAGILITY
OF THE HUMAN BEING'

FIGURE 57. [The beginning of public opera / Monteverdi's penultimate opera:
The Return of Ulysses to his Homeland]

FIGURE 58. [Ulysses' wet nurse / NEPTUNE and the castaway ULYSSES]

FIGURE 59 (ABOVE) AND 60 (BELOW)

ON THE FRAGILITY OF THE HUMAN BEING / MONTEVERDI'S MONUMENTAL MAGNUM OPUS WITH LIFE-SIZE PUPPETS FROM SOUTH AFRICA

Ulysses is on his death bed. You can hear him breathing. It is at the same time the breath of the great Claudio Monteverdi whose opera IL RITORNO D'ULISSE IN PATRIA had its premiere in 1640. The hero remembers the end of his wandering, his landing in Ithaca, meeting his son and his wife Penelope recognizing him.

William Kentridge and Adrian Kohler have staged the drama with life-size puppets from the Handspring Puppet Company of the Republic of South Africa. As in the Bunraku theatre, the puppets are controlled by a single puppeteer and one singer. Monteverdi's opera has to do with time, luck, love and people's fragility. Especially because of the sense of alienation (people and singers controlling puppets which make breathing movements and perform actions) this baroque piece of musical theatre feels contemporary. It takes place (Ulysses in hospital, Ulysses as returnee) between the world of the gods and the world of someone dying in the intensive care unit. In the past, the gods spoke and cast threats from outside, director William Kentridge says, today they speak and threaten us from within our bodies and through the instruments of machine-medicine.

MONTEVERDI'S LAMENTO
FOR ULYSSES' DISTRAUGHT COOK

The most fragile figure in this opera is not the dying Ulysses, but his cook, Iro. He is an artist of his craft. He always faithfully served this ruler-of-the-island and his wife. But then his master went missing for 20 years, far away in the east, near Troy. The so-called suitors, a kind of occupying force—men of war fighting for the hand of Ulysses' assumed widow, Penelope—have taken over the island. Penelope continues to stall. The rivalry among her suitors keeps her from experiencing any violence directly. But this is also thanks to their daily meals, for which Iro is responsible.

The chef shows what he can do. In a sense he is working in the interest of his master Ulysses and the latter's godforsaken wife. But now Ulysses has returned, has shot all the suitors dead with his arrows. Iro, the cook, is considered a collaborator and a traitor. He is to be executed the following morning.

Monteverdi dedicated to this chef, Iro, an unforgettable scene at the beginning of the opera's final act, a LAMENTO. Iro, the master of sumptuous feasts, feels he has been misunderstood. Punishing him with death is unjust. A man is the mirror image of his skill. This skill must be allowed to show itself. Just as the feet of the maids executed on the gallows for collaboration with the 'suitors', still wriggling in death, are the centre of Homer's tale, the 'fragility of the cook Iro' is the subtext for Monteverdi's opera.

THOSE INVOLVED IMPROVISED . . .

The battered body of Ulysses had washed ashore. Naked and bloody, he lay in the sand before the king's daughter who had been playing ball with her companions. His right shoulder dislocated. Both his lower legs broken after having cracked against one of the rocky reefs, then tossed onto shore by a mighty wave. The girls tore fabric from their clothes to wrap the man's wounds. The customs of the country were not made for such incidents. Somehow, the participants compensated for one another's weaknesses (shame, pain in the limbs, ignorance of how to deal with serious fractures).

ACHILLES' WRATH

No kind of improvization helped the Trojan Hector. His opponent Achilles smashed his shield and armour. Gods without any sense of fairness intervened on his side. Or it was chance. The two heroes were equal in fighting strength. After Achilles had slain Hector, he tied the body to his chariot and dragged it through the stones and dust. Once again, it was thanks to the gods (or a miracle or a spell born of the eyes of the empaths who heard the story) that the broken body, once unbound from the chariot, transformed to its previous intact state. As young and beautiful as before the battle. Achilles did not leave this relic buried. He took the body with him and threw it to his dogs lurking beneath the dinner table. Though usually greedily snapping at any happenstance, none of them touched the hero's body.

THE FRAGILITY OF THE HUMAN BEING
WHEN ORGANIZATION BREAKS DOWN

In Ernst Jünger's *Kaukasischen Aufzeichnungen* (Notes from the Caucasus) the entry for 23 November 1942 reads: 'In the afternoon, holidaymakers awaiting their trains were stopped and sent to the front in hastily assembled marching units. It was said that the Russians had broken through north of Stalingrad.'

In 1942, none of these soldiers wear armoured waistcoats. Nor do they wear armour as in the Middle Ages. Under the thin uniform and coat, unsuitable for winter, nothing but their bare skin to protect them. But until the military organization broke down, the one that had brought them to the front, on holiday and now return, this—namely, the reliability of a troop that was well attuned to each other—formed a SECOND SKIN. They wanted to slip into it again by travelling by train on the return transport. But they have been deprived of such protection. Their new leaders are strangers. They are indifferent to the lies. They probably have not been trained for the job. They cannot rely on any of their side men. As soldiers, they have been dispossessed of their 'true skin'. Soon, as Jünger sees it, they will be deployed somewhere up north and 'burnt out'.

'OUT IN THE FIELD OF FRAGILITY'

I am not a barbarian. I am not of the 'stone age'. I am a French officer. My family can be traced back to the fifteenth century. Naturally,
it is even older (just as all humans are older than primeval times, as
primeval times also had a prehistory). But in terms of documentation, with the first honours, in the king's pay since 1420. I too
studied at the great schools. I love books.

I am serving in North Africa. I'm an interviewer. A torture specialist. It's not what I do that's spine-chilling to me, mind you, it's
my counterpart's weak points that terrify me. The methods I employ
to force confessions are straightforward. Strong characters that resist
over a long period of time break into all the tinier fragments. They
all *confess*. My art is to make sure that during questioning they do
not have any power of self-control. They must not be able to check
what it is that they have said. I must prevent them from coming up
with any kind of deceptions, exaggerations, fantasies. They must not
be allowed to gain any overview of the interrogation. I must disturb
them. And my questioning technique serves this purpose. I get to
see a mosaic; the prisoner does not. They await the crucial questions.
They more or less know where our suspicions lie. That is what they
primarily have tried to prepare for.

The crunch of a bone we break is certainly a horrible sound. I
have to concentrate on telling myself: 'That's not *my* bone.' Because
I am sensitive and nervous, I often put cotton wool in my ears. But
that is a disadvantage in interrogation because it is more difficult to
perceive the nuances of the answers to my questions. But what's
worse than the breaking of bones is the crunch of a crushed soul. In
this respect, it's not got to do with hearing. No, I 'see' such break-
downs. I see them with my INNER EYE, with that co-feeling I as an
interrogator must not turn off and that, as an individual and human
being, I *cannot* turn off. It's my 'eye'. With a dash of imagination or
better: 'imaginative faculty'. I can't do without that either if, as a specialist, I am not to become stupid. I invent new things every day. I

explore more direct paths to the evidentiary facts I know exist in the mind of the person across me. If these were to already exist in words, we experts could simply skim them off by technical means. But no, before I can record them, the one I am torturing has to communicate them. That's why those across me don't faint. And this is the art of balance! WHEN the soul collapses, I see it in the interviewee's face. The 36 muscles that keep 'the mask', a person's facial expression, under control—even when the interrogated has reached their limit—collapse like a sack, like a fluttering cloth, poetically I'd like to say: like a curtain in the theatre that I once saw in the Grand Guignol. The curtain was made of tinsel. Powerful, multicoloured projectors cast light onto the billowing, quasi-'falling' curtain. The scene was meant to express the theatre's being on fire. I call it *poetic* because at the moment one perceives a supreme manoeuvrability, the scene itself is already dead—there's no fire there at all.

What shocks me about it? Why don't I ever become used to it when I see it (how many times has it been by now)? It's always different, by the way. But the functional result of the loosened ego's COLLAPSE or CRACK is the same every time: the last statements are forced. The interrogation ends.

Now, having said that, the course of events—in the last seconds—is never the same. I am witness to this. I could chart a scale of collapses. As I said, a person's strength and completeness are related to the previous resistance. It's as if the substance of a person, like a fuel, determines the strength of the fall. I have also seen interviewees who survived the torture 'gently as a cold'. Others 'like a breaking neck'. When that happens, the experienced interrogator has to hurry. You can extract five to seven important pieces of information from the 'ruins'. After that, the person across you becomes incapable of speech.

Earlier I said 'when I *look at* the person across me'. But looking is the wrong expression. I am afraid. In the two monitors showing the video recording of the interrogation (they are subsequently deleted so that there is no proof of our methods), my eyes show horror. The horror of 'the fragility of the human being'. It's got nothing to do with the person across me. It's got to do with me. My imagination that if the balance of power were reversed, I would be the fragile one and the client an interrogator. This idea makes me uneasy. I am sure that my compassion is always for myself.

All this in the service of progress. As I said, we're not primitives, not regressives. But we must not allow rebels in the North African provinces who have nothing to do with modernity. I, scion of the great French Revolution, am not fighting a futile battle if I contribute to the elimination of the insurgency. It still is possible. But revolts mutate as well, they learn from the repression we exercise. At some point, they become resistant. If we don't hurry! If we are not strict disciples of progress!

A controller who regularly comes over from central Paris to visit our military district called me 'a barbarian from prehistoric times'. What a mistake! My techniques and knowledge, how we penetrate the weak points of an earthling sitting across from us (or bent over him when he lies before us as if dead) to access the information, is not derived from nature, from any past, but from the avant-garde of medicine. We cannot stop learning. Part of the learning process is how we keep the controllers of the centre busy, stall, deceive or point out the limits of their competence and powers. They are white-washers.

Why do we talk about 'iron realism' when we're relaxing at the bar? Our realism is not reminiscent of the brittleness of iron. Realism is elastic, pliable. In a certain sense, it's fun. But it is not true that torturing, the exercise of my office, gives me pleasure. I answer with all my heart: That's a lie! No, what gives me pleasure is the broadening of horizons, the 'fireworks of progress', the success gradually becoming apparent in Algiers, a piece of PRODUCER'S PRIDE (that engineers and planners also experience). The brothel, family, casual adventures—I don't need any of that. My sacred office is life. This is what I have firmly pledged to my comrades and my present superior.

'MY BODY, A TREACHEROUS DOG'

His whole life long he had spoilt his body. Had done good things for it. Not only veal with chanterelles, Bordeaux wines, oriental fare, rare British marmalades, fasting days, the 'good life'. He'd bathed it, cooled his airways with oxygen (in forest and park). With care. His body hadn't thanked him. An ungrateful animal. Admittedly, it often seemed that the soul rivalled this companion known as the body, treated it arrogantly, called it a 'shit'. Digestion is allowed, the body replied. This body put fat on the heart, throttled its liver function; the abdominal aorta calcified. The man was tormented by skin rashes. This was an elegant diplomat who thought himself a bon vivant. Early death. He is buried in Djibouti.

AN ARTERY'S DECEIT

An aneurysm is a bulge in the aorta. Blood circulates throughout such a bay and, when the pressure in this bifurcation, this blood sac, becomes too strong, it ruptures the vein. In a matter of minutes, the blood pours into the abdomen or, if it is the carotid artery, into the chest.

Just yesterday, the high-ranking US diplomat, based in Kabul, had his body (in which the pathological bulge of one of his main arteries had already taken hold) 'rocked' to a conference along an icy pass, in a convoy protected by armoured vehicles, shuttled back and forth in the back seat between the two doors. For six hours, he sat opposite a group of Taliban negotiators. With an ideologically hardened adversary or, on the contrary, with negotiators on the other side whom he was entitled to consider corrupt, i.e. pursuing interests, the experienced negotiator would have recognized tactics. He felt powerless in the face of the local moral laws under debate during the six-hour hearing, a debate punctuated by sudden, incomprehensible tirades of hatred, the verbose spreading of countless prejudices. It was the aimlessness of the demands (or at least of what he recognized as demands from what those opposite him were saying) that bothered him. He did not feel comfortable in body or mind. And yet some of these people seemed to be serious. Why were they talking so confusedly? Instead of the two interpreters in his delegation busy whispering the words of the Taliban negotiators to his ears, he wished he had someone who could introduce him to the meaning of what was being said, to the history of the words. As soon as he understood what the opposing side wanted, he would have found a way out.

A hundred hours later, in the plane's spacious lounge, he was already crossing Syria on his way back to the US. This, Holbrooke assumed, was the country from which his ancestors had come. Deep below him and technically inaccessible. A thin but robust outer skin separated him from the soil from which he came. The people there spoke Aramaic. Soon the luxurious service plane was high above the Mediterranean and, a little later, over the Atlantic.

Ten hours later, he was standing in front of the secretary of state. Seven aides surround Hillary Clinton's desk. He reports on his negotiations. Every detail of his report could have treacherous or postitive consequences. The diplomat tried hard, even harder than in the six-hour conference a couple of days earlier. Again, he felt a rising nausea in his body and a certain dizziness in his head. He suppressed the sensation but was already trying to speed things up. He wanted to sit down somewhere, to 'cool down', 'collect himself' in a toilet stall. But he did not feel he could simply ask for a break in the meeting with the foreign minister and her staff and leave for such a private stay behind a closed stall door. Then, from one moment to the next, he collapsed. His body fell sideways from the chair. The assistants cooled his forehead. He opened his eyes. He was lifted up and led to the lift. A helicopter was dispatched to the State Department roof. The unconscious man was strapped to a stretcher. They flew him to George Washington University Hospital. With an automated solicitude fed by thousands of medical and organizational CVs, the vast clinical machinery received him, disposed of him speedily, with foresight. Soon he was lying under the equipment and scalpels of the operation, which lasted several hours. But it was nothing compared to the unbearably long negotiations with the Taliban. The diplomat didn't notice it either. Anaesthetic had to be administered twice. His blood sac had emptied violently during that meeting and then during the early stages of the flight back. At the end of the operation, the experienced man was dead.

FIGURE 61 (ABOVE) AND 62 (BELOW)

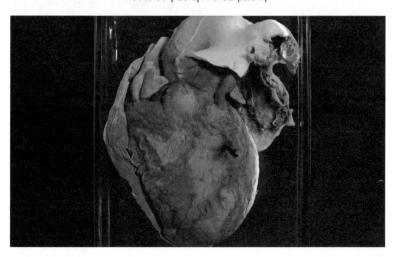

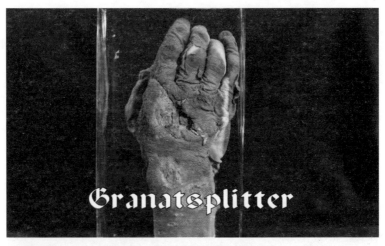

Granatsplitter

FIGURE 63 (ABOVE), 64 (CENTRE) AND 65 (BELOW)

Gasvergiftung Lunge: deutsches Gas

Erstickungsblutung: russisches Gas

Russian peace proposal
Russian radio broadcast on 28 November 1917
From: *Deutsche Geschichtskalender 1917, II, p.* [ ] – [3]
Tsarskoye Selo, 28 November [1917]

TO THE PEOPLES
OF ALL THE BELLIGERENT NATIONS!

The victorious workers' and peasants' revolution in Russia has put the question of peace at the forefront. The period of vacillation, postponement and bureaucratism has ended. Now all governments, all classes and all parties of all the belligerent nations have been called upon to answer categorically the question: whether they agree to join us in negotiating an immediate armistice and a common peace. The answer to this question depends on whether we shall escape a new winter campaign with all its horrors and miseries or whether Europe will continue to be flooded with blood.

We, the Council of People's Commissars, address this question to the governments of our allies. We ask them, before the face of their own peoples and before the face of the whole world, whether they agree to approach peace negotiations. We, the Council of People's Commissars, turn to the allied peoples, first and foremost to the working masses, to ask whether they agree to continue this senseless slaughter and blindly walk towards the ruin of European culture. We demand that the workers' parties of the allied countries immediately answer the question of opening peace negotiations. We place this question at the top.

The peace we have asked for should be a people's peace. It should be an honourable peace of understanding, which secures for each people the freedom of its economic and cultural development. The workers' and peasants' revolution has already announced its peace programme. We have published the secret treaties of the Tsar and the bourgeoisie with the allies and declared these treaties to be non-binding on the Russian people. We request that a new treaty be publicly concluded with all peoples based on understanding and cooperation. Our request has been answered by the official and semi-official representatives of the ruling classes of the allied countries refusing to recognize the government of the Councils and to enter into agreement with it on peace negotiations.

The government of the victorious revolution lacks the recognition of professional diplomacy; but we ask the peoples whether reactionary diplomacy expresses its thoughts and aspirations, and whether the peoples allow diplomacy to drop the great possibility of peace offered by the Russian revolution. The answer to this question may be given by the working masses to the capitalist governments. Down with the winter campaign! Long live peace and the fraternization of peoples!

People's Commissar for Foreign Affairs: Trotsky.
Chairman, Council of People's Commissars: (Ulyanov) Lenin.

COMMENTARY ON THE RUSSIAN RADIO BROADCAST OF 28 NOVEMBER 1917

The radio message is entitled 'To the peoples of all the belligerent nations!' It is signed 'Trotsky' and 'Ulyanov Lenin'. Being both a telegram and a radio message, it is not addressed to any one in particular but spreads itself out over the airwaves. Communicated to all the earth open to radio and radiotelegraphy.

It should be noted that the sender's address, Tsarskoye Selo, is fake. It is the name of the town near St Petersburg where the imperial residence was located. The idea of naming the sender this way was to create identification with that former centre of power which now belonged to the territory claimed by the Council of People's Commissars. In fact, the radio message and the flood of telegrams were sent from the main post office in St Petersburg.

There, Trotsky, People's Commissar for Foreign Affairs, had set himself up in a room with a field bed, a typewriter and a battery of telephones and radios. A mass of papers and documents. From there, he and his staff corresponded with the 'world'. Lenin, on the other hand, had an office in the Smolny building, a school. Trotsky's 'extended staff'—that is, those comrades who hadn't accompanied him to the main post office—had set themselves up in the corridors of the foreign ministry. From there, they controlled the traditional civil service which had led Russia into the catastrophe of the three-year war.

Few telegrams arrived at the main post office. But an immense number of them went out into the world. The core argument of the radio message of 28 November 1917 was: immediate ceasefire. No hesitation. The absolute priority of this one core point: no further winter campaign. Ceasefire and peace out of the masses' self-respect. No consideration of diplomacy.

The radio announcement was preceded by the telegraphic publication of the files of the tsarist regime: the treasonous correspondence between the Allied governments and the Russian Empire, which published the imperial intentions. At the same time, and prompted by the telegrams, the government of the Bavarian Soviet Republic in turn published the correspondence of the German Empire as well as the holdings of the Kingdom of Bavaria's archives.

The radio message takes up less than one A4 page. It contains repetitions. To me, it seems to be a text thrown down in haste, possibly dictated via the shouting of comrades. In my book, it is the text most worthy of comment. In it I sense the breath of alphabetization, of electrification, of that form of space travel which was to come. Of course, as a commentator, I know that this is not contained in the text. But who would forbid me from feeling the subtext? For me, the fact that Finland will not be occupied after its surrender in 1944 is contained in the energy of the letters of the radio message of 28 November. Imagination? DETERMINATION TO TRUST IN THE IMAGINATION. The idea of liquidating war in a robust fashion has moved me at all times of day, right up to the present.

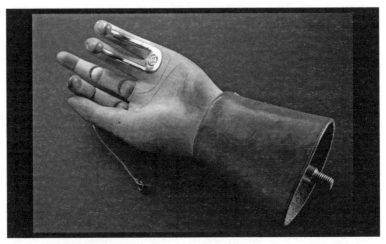

FIGURE 66 (ABOVE), 67 (CENTRE) AND 68 (BELOW)

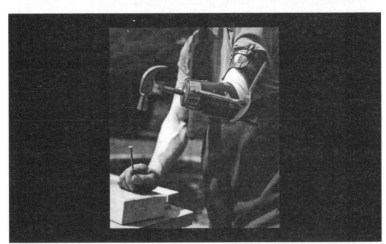

COMMENTARY ON THE STATEMENT: 'THE HUMAN ORGANISM IS A WHOLE BUNDLE OF COMPROMISES'

A RESEARCHER'S TRAGIC DIZZY SPELL IN THE HELL OF THE ARCTIC

The dog sleds rushed through the Greenland night. Driving the dogs on with poles and sharp calls, the staff sought to save the feverish polar explorer and humanitarian—their boss—who, having suffered a ruptured appendix, was wrapped up in blankets within the improvized tent placed on the sled. To stop the sleds, to erect a wall of snow against the driving snow, to set up an operating area and, by flickering light, open the doomed man's abdomen, remove the pus and then provisionally sew the abdomen back up (with what needle, what thread?)—the non-scientists leading the escort weren't about to attempt that. They were geologists. The dog handler, an Eskimo, had told them just such an operation was their only hope. The faithful sought to speed up the journey instead.

All the same, the polar explorer didn't make it. The sleds arrived at the harbour too late—some of the dogs (which would not survive all that much longer due to overstress and strain) were still panting, but it was clear that they would suffocate before the oxygen could reach their capillaries. A doctor could not immediately be found. He had to be fetched by dinghy from a neighbouring port. Even in this emergency, none of the locals or the escorts dared cut open the precious man's body, scratch his skin. The appendix—which in view of the man's size was only a tiny cul-de-sac, the appendix of the worm, the remnant of a hollow space that once served as a temporary storage space for hard-to-digest food in our ancestors' intestines, an evolutionary SURVIVOR that contributed practically nothing to life—put an end to the Artic explorer's life.

You can no longer send a man to a place far from civilization with this relic, said the representative of the Danish royal house at the funeral service. And an envoy from the USSR, which attached great importance to being represented at the funeral, reflected in his eulogy that, on future space voyages planned in his great country which covered an entire continent, owners of an appendix should not be allowed as space pilots. At that time, the Union of Soviet Republics did not yet have a space-capable vehicle, but there were plans and drawings. Only those who had already lost their appendix or had undergone an appendectomy would be considered as space pilots. The femoral neck bone and appendix are the human being's weak points. People who have these weaknesses should not be sent out into the ice of the Arctic or the deserts of the cosmos. But in the interests of internationalism and galactic socialism, sending people out into the distance, taking possession of the world in the interests of the POWER OF LABOUR, was necessary. The high-ranking delegate of the Soviet government intended to deliver a speech of consolation, to express mourning and to thank the Arctic explorer for his achievements, including the repatriation of prisoners of war on Russian soil. He was proud of the huge plans and trust that his government had placed in the future and in the robustness of humankind.

STATION 8

COMMENTARY ON
A DRAWING BY
SIGMUND FREUD

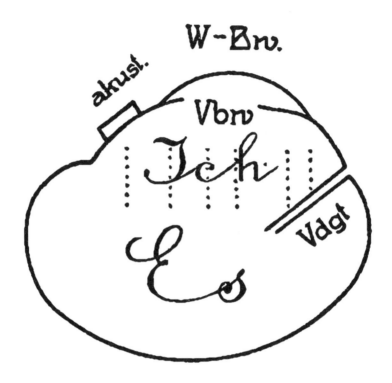

FIGURE 69. A drawing by Sigmund Freud. 'Topography of the Republic of the Ego'.
The abbreviation top left 'accoust.' Refers to the 'cap of hearing'. Sigmund Freud com-
ments: 'We might add, perhaps, that the ego wears a "cap of hearing"—on one side
only, as we learn from cerebral anatomy. It might be said to wear it awry.'
[See p. 18 of Sigmund Freud, *The Ego and the Id*
(Joan Riviere trans.) (New York: Norton, 1960)]

FREUD ON THE TERM 'CAP OF HEARING'

The 'cap of hearing' or THE THIRD EAR isn't an organ but a function; an interplay of countless physical forces or even 'something that acts on the twittering synapses between the external relations of the ego, its pasts, the lively concert of synapses and above all between all the biological activities of the brain apparatus and the influences of body, skin, intestine, heart, bile, motor activity, every-dayness, long-termness.'

THAT WHICH SITS AWRY, LIKE A 'CAP OF HEARING', IS LANGUAGE.

Those parts which, when put together, we call 'ear'—two ears and a place in the brain that connects their impressions—do not understand language individually. Only with the help of the 'cap of hearing' can communication between people be decoded. As Wolf Singer describes it: When what they are doing is made audible, the 100 trillion or so synapses that act as switching points in the human brain to connect the 100 billion neurons with one another emit sounds or a common music. It resembles the 'chirping of a great flock of birds in a park'. The neurons speak their own biological dialect. They communicate electronically and chemically. In waves and corpuscles. Never in language.

Only the 'cap of hearing', something that one who visits the brain could not see in time and place, connects the ego (though all its derivatives and sources too) with the MAGIC OF MILLIONS OF YEARS OF EXPERIENCE of both the outer and inner world in the format

CS

(consciousness)

PCS = preconscious

PCPT-CS = perception-consciousness

The bodies' and synapses' grinding noises do not yet form a psychology. And all psychology does not yet produce consciousness.

And all forms of consciousness, semi-consciousness and the raw material of perceptions do not of themselves form reason. But all reason is powerless without the productive work of the more than 12 levels below consciousness. All the way down to reception, the sensual forces, the diaphragm and again: 'the gut that thinks'. This PRINCIPLE OF FREEDOM is fixed in the language or the third ear's 'cap of hearing'. It temporarily compensates for all the weaknesses of the ego.

SIGMUND FREUD'S NOTES
ON THE CONCEPT OF THE 'EGO'

'The ego is a king without power.' 'The functional importance of the ego is manifested in the fact that normally control over the approaches to motility devolves upon it.'

'I run therefore I am.'

'I speak therefore I am, together with a second, a third or many others.'

'I love therefore I am.'

'. . . the ego is that part of the id which . . . in a sense . . . is an extension of the surface-differentiation . . .'

'For the ego, perception plays the part which in the id falls to instinct.'

'The ego corresponds to the skin of the cell.'

In its relation to the id, the ego is like 'a man on horseback who has to hold in check the superior strength of the horse; with this difference, that the rider tries to do so with his own strength while the ego uses borrowed forces.' Borrowed not only from the id, but from the diversity of all the forces of body and soul. With a rapid gain from the vacuum between all these forces. This helps to give the impression that the potencies of nothing, that is, the emptiness between the forces, contain spirit power or divine providence.

Freud's analogy goes a little further. 'Often a rider, if he is not to be parted from his horse, is obliged to guide it where it wants to go; in the same way, the ego is in the habit of transforming the id's will into action as if it were its own (p. 19).'

THE SHORT-TERM DIVISION OF SOMEONE
INTO A FORGETFUL PERSON
AND ONE MOURNING SOMETHING LOST

Today my wife briefly transformed into two people. One of them lost her big blue wallet while stepping out of the car in front of Schumann's. While still the previous person, she had rummaged through her bag, unconsciously, to find the leash for the dog, which had meanwhile jumped out of the car. The person who lost the wallet made the purchase, started the engine. Noticing the loss of the wallet when she got home, the other person—one can also refer to her as the earlier one, though she is really the later—cried bitterly. Together with her daughter, she searched the park, the pavement before the front door, the fence that led to the car park, under her bed. The moment she—quite inattentively, quite another person— had lost her BIG BLUE wallet was unavailable to her, had slipped her mind.

We, my daughter and I, were desperately on the search, trying to comfort her by saying that, when all was said and done, we would find the wallet after all. We ran to the car again, searched under the seats, as well as under the blankets for the dog on the back seat, then at the edges of the road. We thought it was possible that the wallet had fallen through the fence into one of the front gardens. We forbade ourselves to rule out any coincidence. We wanted to help.

When we returned, my wife opened the door with a happy face. Call from a finder. He had picked up the wallet at the place where it had been lost, and inside, folded, was the protocol of a cardiological examination with the doctor's address. The man had counted the money. He had found our telephone number from the telephone number on the doctor's stamp. Now the UNITED PERSONS OF MY WIFE drove to this benign finder, in a large bag a gift as a thank you.

THE DANGEROUS SPLIT BETWEEN FANTASY AND
THE OPERATION OF A TECHNICAL DEVICE

I gave up driving seven years ago after noticing an increase in the frequency of 'senior moments'. The drifting of my attention, my so-called consciousness, in the middle of traffic to something more interesting, a detail, a memory, the flash of an idea or a longer chain of fantasies, has accompanied my days since childhood. 'Daydream'. These dreams are often short and, until seven years ago, did not interfere with any of my activities that could have been potentially dangerous. But then these 'short trips' took over. Apparently, they were more exciting for that imagined central sense of ours we call the soul than my day-to-day, than real routine. At the wheel, I stopped perceiving obstacles blocking the road. Fright in my eyes when I did react. In the long term, it seemed too dangerous.

I have had my driving licence since 1949. As a guest traveller from West Berlin, as a favour for the son of Dr med Kluge, the document was easy to acquire in my hometown. In the form of a waxy leather flap, it was later renewed at my official residence in Berlin-Charlottenburg, with a very youthful passport picture, and has accompanied me thus my entire life. I do not believe that my driving skills were ever sufficient for later driving on motorways and in modern city centres. In the ambitious sixties, I bought a Citroën convertible, in direct imitation of and in rivalry with my friend and role model Edgar Reitz. He had switched from the *Opel Admiral* to a *Citroën DS*. To distinguish myself temperamentally as well, I bought a *Citroën estate car with a cargo area*. I could transport cameras, head-lights, accessories, cassettes and other technical luggage. It was the more 'business-like' format of a 'personal car'. And it was in this vehicle (which, to be honest, was too much for me) that I happened to 'touch' another vehicle when it skidded on an Austrian road in the winter of 1968. The rear of my vehicle clearly hit the rear of an oncoming vehicle. I can still hear the muffled bang now; at that point in the road, the two vehicles, skidding, could not be stopped. I couldn't register the make. By the time I brought my highly qualified French car to a stop after a thousand metres (an extremely dangerous manoeuvre on a snow-slippery road because of the vehicles behind me), it was too late to contact the other driver who might have been damaged but was obviously driving on.

Later, returning from the copying plant at Bavaria studios to the city in 1969, I found myself once again on a snow-slick road. As the heavy Citroën did not react to my 'intermittent pumping' of the brakes, in a curve I drove into a strange tin car, pushing it to the side of the road. No personal injuries. My Citroën's bonnet bent steeply upwards. The driver of the other, thanks to me, damaged vehicle and I reached an agreement without notifying the police. A towing company transported my 'wreck' back to the extensive grounds of the Bavaria copying plant.

As I said, my career as a driver ended once the 'absences', the sudden overpowering of real sensations by fantasies, took over. In fact, as far as the interior of my person was concerned, the idea of driving a car was already a phantasm. Whereas Reitz really is a 'born driver', the only place I was ever safe was on a bicycle, reflexive and 'full of attention' even when riding uphill and on associated curves. Riding in the mountains, the demands on my sense of balance when cornering and the strain on my attention precluded any sensory drift. Because this attention moved my whole body, my children later laughed at me when I leaned away from the steering wheel in the direction I had to take on the bends. To them, as a driver, I seemed like a caricature.

'THE CAP OF HEARING SITS ON THE BRAIN'

The BIG X of which Kant speaks, the 'thing-in-itself', is in truth a sound. An original sound of all differences. Moreover, the sound of planets and the Milky Way. Our ear, that trapeze artist of the POWER OF DIFFERENTIATION, and its companions in feeling, such as the fingertips, are specialized in the decoding of this sound.

The 'cap of hearing' of which Freud speaks, is not, therefore, only something one uses to hear. It is, like language, a form of nourishment. It feeds the soul with the life impulse, with rhythm and 'interest', with the ability to differentiate; in other words, with the ability to set things in motion.

WHY IS THE CAP OF HEARING'S LANGUAGE WORN AWRY?

Every time, it becomes apparent that words were invented for something other than what they are supposed to denote at the given moment. I take as an example the place specification 'at the foot of the mountain'. Of course, it is not a foot. The beginning of the ascent does not resemble a foot in any way, apart from the fact that my foot is starting this ascent. But the word or the metaphor does not indicate where exactly on the mountain I am.

'I love and I hate.' But what is that, why am I using the word *hate*? There are 4,000 rebellious demons at work here. And I'm not talking about any particular one at the moment when I think 'I hate'. In practice, however, hate is always determined. Perhaps I myself am not strong enough for hate. How then do I express my feeling of weakness? My weak vibration of aversion. The word sits on the cap of hearing awry. And this, the master of all differences, sits upon consciousness awry. And this consciousness in turn awry on reality, the vessel in which at best 'I love and I hate' can be said. The same can be repeated for 'I love'. 'You say you do, but what you feel and do,' my counterpart replies, 'is not what I would call "I love" or "you love" or "we love".' How can you settle such an argument? From the point of view of 'I love', arbitration would also be the wrong attitude. 'You're obsessive,' is what I receive in response. 'What you say when you say "I love you" is an attempt to employ an instrument of power. The attempt to use a means of power.' 'That kind of thing,' another counterpart says, 'is wasted on me.' Can one struggle for love? 'What is a ring? 'What is struggle?'

'The closer I look at a word, the further away it is when it looks back.'

In the statement 'I hate *and* I love' the word AND, oblique to so many letters, nevertheless remains the best distinction to anything else I say or do not say. That I hate and love at the same time would be a more precise definition of a feeling, among 4,000 a group of 12. It's not that the oblique is a disadvantage for 'understanding'. The cap of hearing is a master from Flanders. It is the product of a trip through time. It determines the trust we place in sounds and realities. From a zone of experience that lies far back in childhood. In this, the very crookedness of the cap of hearing and the indeterminacy of language are unmistakable. It is therefore not only a matter of consciousness but also of thought. In other words, the protocol, the observation that accompanies consciousness. The crack in the 'thing-in-itself' is what the cap of hearing specializes in: the ultimate unknown which we as persons know nothing about, but which is present in all languages.

THE BATTLE WITHIN THE DARK CLOUD
FROM WHICH THE SNOW FELL

In early 1807, a supporter (as well as poet, academic, all around curious individual and good marcher) of Johann Georg Hamann's, a Königsberg Customs official, thinker and rival of Kant's, was circling the battle of Preussisch Eylau, observing. Napoleon's army was fighting the army of the Russian tsar, led by General Bennigsen.

Just such an empirical reconnaissance mission in the middle of the onset of winter and the historical chaos of the year of upheaval was not without peril. The philosophical scout could easily have been caught by a patrol and subjected to dangerous interrogation before a court martial. How could a military guard or a court martial distinguish a philosopher from an enemy agent? A spy? If he had answered that he was exploring the excesses of reality in the service of philosophy, the exceptional state of war, that he wanted to look the demon war in the mouth, he certainly would not have been understood by either a French or a Russian interrogator (depending on which of the two parties caught him). A death sentence was foreseeable. Roaming about in wild reality for the sake of the 'love of wisdom' was no kind of professional combat status. But the impressions in daring one's ears were as follows:

The ears' impressions

The short-breathed bang of France's guns—reproduced in waves, for the guns were not firing simultaneously—was distorted into dullness by a heavy snowfall. Was more like a rumbling or humming than a bark. The Russian batteries, on the other hand, most definitely 'barked'. The guns had reached the edge of the snow and were firing blindly into it. Neither of the opposing parties could perceive the columns' positions, locations, accuracy or dispersal. The observer at the edge of his humid grove, however, had an overview. If, acoustically speaking, an overview of undulating, as far as the local terrain was concerned, imprecisely concentrated and straying sounds. No image of the imagination (and the philosophical youth was not trained professionally enough in the military to have any suitable images at all) matched—from the perspective of everyday experience—the alien soundscape. For those who were dying that minute, however, it was no backdrop at all but action. The phrase 'theatre of war' did not fit a thing in that flat northern terrain made confusing by the weather. To the ear, the broad front of Russians seemed to have strayed into a foreign land just as much as the French, recruited from far across the Rhine, must have strayed. What were they looking for in that weather? In that CONCEALMENT, in which the ears could not gather any kind of auditory perspective, even though they were prepared for localized hearing by their lateral distance from the centre of the skull?

The feet's impressions

Whenever the philosophical spy would move ahead a bit to the outermost trees at the forest edge to see and hear more, the ground—damp earth and grass islands, that is, mud and encrusted patches of snow—squished beneath his feet. That seemed unsafe. No real 'forest soil' to speak of, no soil strength. The philosopher struggled to keep his balance. His feet told him more about the chaos of battle, the disproportionate nature of all the conditions of individual events, than the impression of his eyes or his ears' continuing difficulty with orientation. His numb fingers' sense of touch had stopped anyway. He withdrew his hands into the sleeves of his thick jacket. Worrying about his next step when his one foot only touched the ground in a slippery, improvised way told him more about the frightful day than any of his other senses. Memory, 'experience', was of little use in determining the REALITY OF HIS IMPRESSIONS.

The philosophical witness and his lack of ability to formulate what he felt in any kind of text

If he'd had a pen, a hand that wasn't numb and enough paper, he might have written that the overall impression he received was 'wild' or 'disjointed'. But he lacked the words, the use and exercise of which he had not acquired on days like this, via events like this grotesque 'Battle of Preussisch Eylau'. The flow of texts he usually carried inside himself, for example on hiking trails, had completely dried up and was already frozen stiff, maybe thanks to the cold.

A dark cloud coming up from the southwest at about eleven o'clock

As it poured down, the cloud mass practically touched the ground as well as the easily recognizable black dot-like troops. Here and there, a patch of woods. The distance between the upper branches of the trees to the moss and clay below no more than two metres. The giant cloud (already moving across the emperor's cavalry) shot through with the crimson and white of powder explosions. Unceasingly dropping snow. But it wasn't snowing from the cloud to the earth, no; deceived, the eyes saw it snowing within the cloud from bottom to top. This is how it seemed to the philosophical witness. The snow crystals moved in bunches and swaths. Where it ended, the cloud left a dense wall of snow.

After a while, which the witness estimated to be about an hour, the cloud momentarily broke apart. Light fell into the gap, and it seemed that, from the direction of the church and churchyard wall of the village of Eylau, massive columns from the Russian side of the front were marching towards the centre of the French. One tumultuous column of black dots and, where visibility was worse, black smudges merging into the next. The French emperor's cavalry, in the winter light and ambiguity of the raging weather more colourful than black, cut through the columns of Russians, which then closed behind them. To the philosopher, the unresponsive advance of the Russian foot troops, easily comprised of more than a thousand limbs or rows, their immunity to the rapidity of the cavalry and its imposing appearance, seemed 'stubborn', 'intransigent' somehow. To the Kantian observer of the forest's edge, their attitude seemed to represent the ancient precept of ATARAXY. The horsemen, in reasonably disjointed formation, returned through the columns to their ranks, regrouped behind the artillery, which was now visible again, and got ready for another attack, attempting once again to break the stubbornness of the Russian soldiers that very day. One could see that it was a battle of minds, of the belligerents' power of imagination, not simple objective manoeuvring through the terrain. Then around four o'clock, offset by a few degrees in the circle of the horizon: the second black-toned (and yellow-edged) cloud, pregnant with snow from the southwest.

No benefit of knowledge from close observation

Over the course of the late afternoon, the philosophical assistant who had the good will to explore the event with his senses and to 'understand' it in the end retreated more and more into the bushes and behind the trees. Increasing numbers of scattered soldiers, the 'lost', were wandering through the landscape, some of them coming a little too close for comfort to where he was at the edge of the forest. But they also seemed distracted and, in all likelihood, uninterested in taking prisoners, much less interrogating them. The way they were stumbling about in disarray, the student of philosophy assumed that they would not even have known where to find their superiors. But, like everything else that day, that could mean either good or bad luck. The reaction of one of those cut-out-of-the-command-system's discovery of the alien observer could either mean the latter's death or, on the contrary, his good fortune in that his discovery would be of utter indifference to the desperate French or Russian soldier. The space between mercy and death the blink of an eye. Around six in the evening, the young philosopher, suffering from unprocessed impressions made up of a great amount of tension and observation, withdrew with all due caution in the direction of the forester's lodge and the village which bore the name *Freedom*.

THE COMING STORM

With my unkempt hair sticking straight up as I ran from the garden to the house, I would have been as tall as my femoral neckbone today. Over my skin, a so-called Rhabaner. With fabric up to the neck, that full-length type of swimsuit (in fashion for children at that time) was named after the company that sold it. A skin enhancer.

In my memory, wide, palm-sized drops, a so-called CLOUD-
BURST. I always say 'so-called' when I certainly would not have used
such a word on my own at the time. Unfamiliar. But the moment I
heard it used by grown-ups, I repeated it every time one of these
VIOLENT DOWNPOURS 'splashed' onto an expanse of earth.
During a downpour just a little bit north of the Harz—in Halberstadt,
in other words—the sky seems to be dumping its masses of water like
a river which, due to the rapid scudding of the clouds, has become
capable of flight. Not rain, but shreds of water.

After five metres, completely soaked. I run through the conservatory. Across the little rug and past the drinking niche, through the
dining room, into the hallway and up the stairs: the water trail.
Nannies already awaiting me with warmed towels.

What still bothers me today (I haven't come any closer to the
matter, my curiosity remains fresh): how do these summer thunderstorms usually reach Halberstadt in the evening on their long
journey from the sea and the large rivers? I used to think that these
clouds were brought by Atlantic Ocean water, but the Harz mountains would have stood in their way, slowing them down. They would
have been 'milked by the mountains'. They wouldn't have pene-
trated my town, my garden, so regularly.

Meteorologists from Potsdam who know nothing directly about
the summer thunderstorms that I experienced (and which, in this
respect, are individual) are nevertheless familiar with these weather
formations—as I am—in terms of structure and abstraction. They
tell me that there aren't a random number of laws and thus that
there couldn't be a random number of individual 'cloudbursts with
the impact of thunderstorms'. Moreover, the path of the cloud mass
would not lead directly to my city, but circle above the countryside
in great arcs of lows and sub-lows. Thus, depending on the wind and
the passage of the giant circle that makes up the weather, the cloud-
burst could just as easily come over the house and garden from
the north or east as from the west. Even if the water that so quickly

covers the ground and of which so little remains *in* the ground in such heavy rain, pushing through to the groundwater as it does, could have had its origin, its ascent into the clouds, somewhere in the northwest. The cloud towers and rainstorms coming from the direction of Magdeburg, from the Elbe, have become more violent thanks to the acceleration they experience through the storm, through their diversions to the east and their return to the west. Stormier than the thunderstorms when they come crashing down directly from the Harz mountains.

DELAYED RETURN OF A LIFE PLAN

He was a comrade. Among the rebellious student leaders. Maybe even a member of the proletariat. If you equate the origin of a soldier with the origin of a factory worker. The essential characteristic of the proletariat is 'alienation from one's own means of production'. Secretly, he knew that he was unalienated from the means of production which were characteristic of him. Seeking happiness, wandering eyes, snatching after luck when it was at the door. For him, these were primary means of production. Means for dealing with others. He did not have his own door. Luck, as it does, came and went. He didn't need to have it there, just at the threshold. Finding it was enough. How to grasp, that much he knew.

He later married five women in succession. 26 lovers. But he was not someone who counted for long. Forever naive anew. That was a generous means of production. Two-time chairmanship in a large people's party. Chancellor for several legislative periods. In France, there are piles of novels about lucky devils from the turn of the nineteenth and twentieth centuries, and in Germany in the 1920s and early 30s. Related to the hit Schlager song 'Das gibt's nur einmal, das kommt nicht wieder / das ist zu schön, um wahr zu sein'. Also related to the character of the hero in the novel *Bel-Ami*. 'Those who grab happiness.' The comrade we're talking about here repeated in shorthand these novels that the poets of his father's generation reported so assiduously. A crash course in life. Quite incidentally and during the breaks in his work of governing.

THE TRANSFER OF MY PERSON AND POSSESSIONS
TO THE SUPER-METROPOLIS OF FRANKFURT

A persistent summer like the one now, in June 2020, may have meteorological similarities to the heat in June 1954 which I experienced throughout the wide traffic areas of the Rhine-Main region. That's where I'm heading for new adventures, riding my bike next to the Autobahn. Finding paths along these kinds of main roads, next to so much asphalt, is hard. Sometimes I've got to push my bike. My clothes, books and luggage are stacked and hanging off both handlebars as well as the luggage rack above the rear wheel. Entering the city is particularly difficult where all the car lanes intersect. You've got to be on the lookout for the underpasses and small connecting tunnels.

I'm still a Halberstädter, a provincial. On loan for a few years to the University of Marburg which is in a small town. After that, a traineeship at the Regional Labour Court in Kassel. For a trainee judge, living in a cheap neighbourhood in one of the suburbs, Kassel isn't too cosmopolitan a city either. If we're feeling generous, then maybe the 'metropolis' of Wiesbaden. With persistent habit, I sit on a cheap seat in the third tier of the State Opera in the evening. The vastness of the Rheingau as a horizon for the future: in three years' time, I will be a judge in one of its small towns, state-certified for the judiciary.

At present, I am one of those bicycle commuters who visit one of the two government cities, Wiesbaden or Mainz, in the evening and return at night. Where else can you find an opera house or a cinema with the latest programme? Both cities can trace their roots back to Rome.

APPLICATION FOR FUTURE TRANSFER
TO THE METROPOLIS II

What made me give up the Rheingau, which so suits my small-town soul? Misunderstandings, scraps of misunderstood information, prejudices, the unknown, a lack of experience, the rush to make decisions . . . In addition, the 'whispering', 'seductive tone' of a colleague I considered particularly life savvy who described the super-metropolis of Frankfurt am Main to me. If I'd followed up a bit, I would have easily realized that the lure for the sake of which I applied to the presidium of the regional court to transfer me from the Wiesbaden Regional Court District to the Frankfurt Higher Regional Court District did not fit my existence all that well. I need dark, quiet rooms. As spacious and far away from people as the empty jury courtroom in the Wiesbaden District Court to which the responsible judicial officer handed me the keys every afternoon that they were not in session. At the thick wood of the judge's table, in complete silence, in the slowly changing light of late afternoon and early evening, I sit, a provincial, and fill up all my notepads. There was nothing in the super-metropolis of Frankfurt am Main that was as good for my soul and my texts. I organized my accommodation in the youth hostel across the river in Sachsenhausen. My bed in a six-person room. My 'desk' in the canteen, which was busy at all hours of the day. I only have one dark suit and two 'relative shirts'. I got the expression from a French novel. It means that of the two shirts a young man owns, he always puts on the 'relatively clean' one for the next day. I need such a relative shirt with a neat dark suit for my appearances in the offices of the judges who train me. Soon I will be transferred to trainee service in the city administration of Frankfurt. There I'll be able to wear one of my other pieces of clothing. There are not many.

If I'd applied for a transfer to the Rüdesheim district office instead of the super-metropolis (which would've been much more agreeable to my provincial soul), at some point I probably would have become a district administrator there. With a CDU back-ground.

I would have remained the native of Halberstadt that I am. Of myself, I could have said: 'In five years' time, I would be a person and an author whose well-paid position that finishes at 3.30 in the afternoon will give him plenty of time to write his stories until late at night. Perhaps he'll find a local publisher (or the printing press of a local newspaper).' I will have been a consistent (and less nervous than I am) *Heimat* author.

HEAD COLD

Winter 1954 to 1955: severe head cold. A treacherous virus through-out the Rhine-Main region. It penetrates the blood–brain barrier, which viruses rarely do. The fever sits like paralysis in the bones, heats up the skin and causes wild dreams, even during the day. It is impossible not to catch it from the crowd of people in the hostel, or from the flow of people at the court, i.e. my office. A piece of bio-logical junk, nevertheless I manage to reach the flat that my mother's brother's former lover owns (to which she lent me the keys) in Biebricher Chaussee, Wiesbaden. She herself is away. There, I lie on a wide sofa. All the blankets of the house and a carpet over me. It is a state of absence of the senses.

One of my upper canines (whose surrounding gums have been sore since the beginning of my being ill) has become infected at the root. As I don't have a dentist in Wiesbaden and don't know the prices of private dental treatment, I travel to Frankfurt, wrapped in two coats and freezing. I present myself at the university dental clinic. Emergency admission. Young assistants practise on my tooth. Then I'm back in a six-bed room at night. Eight different trainee junior doctors work on me, one after the other. In several stages (under revision, collapse of the installation and new construction, it seems to me), they manage to treat the roots and the gums. On one of the first sunny days of that winter, the winter of 1955, I feel like a new man. I have arrived in the super-metropolis.

A CASE OF EXPROPRIATION

After about 23 minutes, the bombers, that had unloaded their cargo over Halberstadt in several axis-like overflights, departed in a westerly direction. In our living room, books, furniture and unfixed objects lay buried under the glass fragments of the windows in an open jumble. My father worked his way over the crunching debris to the wooden wall in which a door had been carved that led to a safe room. From the safe, he took out one brown envelope and one with money. Disregarding the fact that splinters from the glass roof of the conservatory could kill him, he rushed through the greenhouse to the garden and saved the two items he had brought with him, the brown envelope and the one with money, by submerging them in the pond. Three hours later, the house was in flames. The following morning: burnt to the ground.

In 1969, my father came to Munich on his only trip to the West with the rescued brown envelope. The envelope contained the precious proof of the insurance policy he'd taken out in 1936. For himself, his wife and their children. Accompanied by his daughter and me, he pays a visit to the successor company of the insurance company he'd taken out the policy with in 1936. He presented the policy. The large insurance company in Munich, however, which did not dispute the legal succession, had long since excluded any liability for commitments entered into before the war. My father's policy contains more than a thousand bills paid by private patients. They correspond to his lively activity as a doctor, numerous hours of medical treatment. A good bit of my father's life is contained in the paper that has been sealed up in the brown envelope for so long. The insurance employee who listens to my father is polite but remains uninvolved in the case.

The carrier bag and the quality of the fabric of his suit identify my father as a citizen of the GDR. Yes, in addition to the general unwillingness of the insurance company to assume liability for commitments from the time before the currency reform of 1948 and from the time before the war, the lobby groups that were able to enforce at least some rights for citizens of the Federal Republic of Germany from earlier times have by no means attempted to do anything for citizens of the foreign neighbouring republic, the German Democratic Republic. The legal expert brought in by the legal department points out that my father's citizenship was a hindrance to any claim. But he had saved, invested in a security.

He had saved the document at the risk of his life in a particularly serious case. Now he was faced with a difficulty that he, as a doctor, could not solve. How peace-loving is my father? He would not have hesitated, in the heat of the moment, in the moment of his justified claim's rejection, to set fire to the insurance company's building. But the plinths of this UNBELIEVABLE ORGANIZATION's new building were not made of wood but carved out of stone.

As a skilled doctor, you could soak a piece of cotton in a bowl of alcohol, light it with a match, use that to make a piece of paper begin to glow and use that to start a fire. None of those things were available, while my father, on my sister's arm, climbed the endless stairs to the huge entrance portal. Unfaithful house. Unfaithful palace.

HOW ONE SELF DIFFERENTIATES ITSELF
FROM A COMPLETELY DIFFERENT SELF
IN ONE AND THE SAME LIFE

The me wandering around Frankfurt/Main on a February day in 1955 and the me sitting here in June 2020—the green of the trees in the park in front of my house before my eyes—at the large round wooden table, the 'cradle of texts', with my pencil out, are two incompatibly different people. We do, however, have the same fingernails.

My daughter has similar fingernails. They are more akin to my father's hand than to my mother's or to my maternal grandmother's.

Otherwise, everything else, the sense of balance, the speed with which the nerves spark, the feeling of the skin between hot and cold, the memories (which form great streams of primary things and then experience influxes of secondary things that mutate into primary things), the plans, the imagination of what I will have been in two years' time—all this is the crown property of two different people.

But as soon as I 'think' as much, that is, gather the image within me, I notice that these COUNTER-SELVES enjoy abundant kinships, commonalities from earlier years. I believe that the thirteen-year-old and the seven-year-old within me are no different from who I am at present.

READING INSTRUCTIONS

Turn the word around in your mouth, turn it around on all sides and flip it over. Examine the words with your eyes, compare the word with the greater area of its neighbouring words. Then read the text again. Now the word stands within the circle of the other words. In fact, only now has it really become a word. It has context. One may now begin reading the text again.

My advice (for my books) is this: as a rule, the stories in a chapter have an inner context that cannot be determined from the headings or otherwise externally. They have a subtext. So, if the reader has made friends with a word (they have noticed it, have anchored it in their memory), they should have that word in mind when reading one of the surrounding stories. The word changes, as do the stories read with that foreign word in mind.

THE LIFEWORLD OF WORDS

The rough, the raw: the lifeworld of words contains heterogeneity and opposition, cross-mapping too, but no seamless accuracy of fit. I wish one could temporarily delete the permanent mediating activity of grammar, which serves informative communication, the reader's voluntary consent to the texts, and lay the words next to one another like splinters, like pebbles, like a surface of foundling stones and granite. In the lead voice in a polyphonic piece of music, this often rough, 'abutting' hardness is called the 'counterpoint' (from the Latin *punctum contra punctum*, literally, 'note against note').

HABERMAS /
COMMENTARY

WEDNESDAY, 7 AUGUST 2013, ELMAU. DIARY

After fierce storms last night, lightning over the whole Wetterstein mountain chain, today it is cool. The mind and body need it.

Jürgen Habermas is back from Athens. He is interested in 'civilization's transition points' (especially the two axial ages 3000 BCE and 500 BCE). That is what he is working on. 'This is probably my last book,' he says.

WEDNESDAY, 15 JULY 2020. DIARY

The finished book, *This Too A History of Philosophy*, astonishes me. Above all, the first volume: *The Occidental Constellation of Faith and Knowledge*. Work on this book cost Habermas more than seven years of his life. Its form does not include stories and there are no images.

The project contains a stimulation of all the author's forces; these, of course, do *not* concern me at all but they revitalize me. 'Vigour invigorates.'

JURGEN HABERMAS, *THIS TOO A HISTORY OF PHILOSOPHY*, VOL. 1, P. 483

'In the Mediterranean region, the geographical point of origin of the future Occident, a unique constellation arose during the first century CE. Here, in the porous ideological milieu of Hellenism, which had been advancing since Alexander, and within the political framework of the Roman Empire, two doctrines, Christianity and Platonism, collided [. . .]'

IBID., P. 177

'The name "Axial Period" or "Axial Age" comes from the fact that Karl Jaspers imagined the year 500 BCE to be the axis around which the rotation of world history accelerated, as it were [. . .]'

FROM KARL JASPERS' *ON THE ORIGIN AND GOAL OF HISTORY* (TRANSLATED BY MICHAEL BULLOCK), P. 27

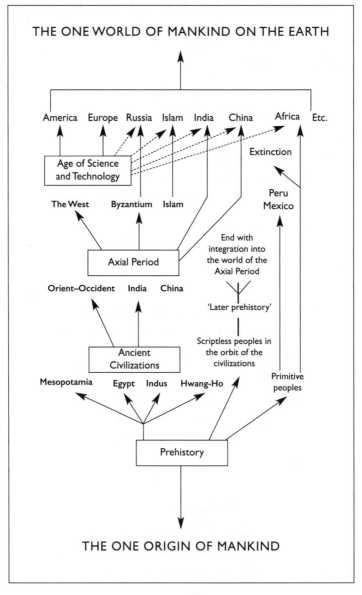

FIGURE 70

IS THE PHENOMENON OF THE AXIAL AGE BASED ON THE RADIATION OF AN UNKNOWN SISTER-SUN TO OUR MOTHER STAR?

A scientifically unidentified chronicler on the internet (who was also considered a conspiracy theorist), Arnulf-Bock-Haucke.com, pushed the idea that an X-ray pulsar—'a collapsed star', rotating excessively fast—had grazed the solar system and thus the planet Earth for a relatively short period of time with an incredible intensity of radiation. This expert or charlatan estimates the path that the radiation took on our planet to be 600 square kilometres in space. And, in terms of time, up to eight revolutions of the earth. What's puzzling, the site says, is the precision with which the coincidental meeting of earth and the radiation of the distant star repeats at very long intervals. It may not only have happened in the 'Axial Age'; it may also recur every 1,500 years. This kind of radiation might also affect the human brain. If the TRANSVERSE MODE OF ELECTRO-MAGNETIC RADIATION also influences genetic material, it would have striking consequences for at least three generations, that is, for about a century. Stress. A surprising, innovative, explosive increase in qualities of mind and/or confusion at the same time.

GERHARD RICHTER, *ATLAS*, COLOGNE, 2006
NR 222, 250, 484, 489: ROOMS

FIGURE 71

FIGURE 72

FIGURE 73

FIGURE 74

MONDAY, 12 APRIL 2021, MUNICH. DIARY

Gerhard Richter has sent me a copy of his *Atlas* for the Habermas commentary. With marks on certain pages. His 'Commentary on the Commentary' has to do with ROOMS. There are THOUGHT-HORIZONS which move as far as language and writing reach. There are perspectives of TIME. Where language finds its boundaries, perspectives of time can be illustrated by mathematical symbols. A philosopher such as Diogenes does not express himself verbally: instead, through his DEMEANOUR, through the place he happens to be, through a certain kind of disrespectful jab to his answers. Richter does not argue in words either.

During a previous phone conversation, we talked about the round table at the Waldhaus Hotel in Sils Maria. The early evening light through the large windows changing from minute to minute. Ute and Jürgen Habermas, Richter and I. What connects me to Richter is that he was born 9 February 1932 and I on the 14th of that same year. We are 'contemporaries'. Habermas, born in 1929, is always three years ahead of us.

WHERE JÜRGEN HABERMAS WROTE HIS BOOK

The house on a steep slope in Starnberg is a modern construction. The central living room is split into two levels, up above a table and entrance to the kitchen. That is the dining room. In the same unit of space below—like an arena—the place for receiving guests and for debate. On the right side of this central area, stairs lead up to Habermas' bureau. There you'll find space for a computer and a lot of room for all kinds of paperwork. *Saint Jerome in His Study*.

Unlike in illustrations of Jerome, however, no books are stored here; they are arranged in long rows in the larger living space below. The bookshelves connect the upper and lower floors.

Habermas' new book, *This Too a History of Philosophy*, opens the horizons, measured against the traditional 'fortress of enlightenment', laid out in the seventeenth and eighteenth centuries. The broadening of horizons covers around 2,300 years of history.

Similar to how, in the early industrialization phase of the cities of Central Europe, city walls were transformed from defensive annexes into monuments, and the terrain which previously blocked access to the city with walls and ditches was transformed into farmland, Habermas opens up perspectives for public thinking and the reconstruction of traditions of thought all the way back to Heraclitus, Buddha, Confucius and Zarathustra.

REGARDING PAGE 666ff.
OF THE FIRST VOLUME OF THE BOOK
BY JÜRGEN HABERMAS

The format of the commentaries and the SCHOOL OF COMMEN-TATORS is born in the context of the foundation of the University of Bologna, one of Europe's first universities. The COMMENTA-TORS are the successors of the so-called GLOSSATORS. This school of knowledgeable jurists endeavoured to intelligently receive the Codex Justinianus, the DIGEST, a collection of the opinions, reports and debates on Roman law. The GLOSSATORS confined themselves to annotations and explanations. The COMMENTATORS were concerned with creating new contexts.

Justinian had entrusted a commission and a jurist he trusted with the imperial task of codifying the most important opinions on civil law, together with debates, justifications and notes, in a central collection. Ever since Augustus, a Roman emperor had three ways of demonstrating his EXCELLENCE: by building roads, by preventing civil war and by issuing legal opinions. The sum of the legal experience gained from individual cases up to 533 CE was given the force of law by imperial authority. These digests are 'classified'. A canon. A 'ship full of knowledge'. Justinian forbade further commentary.

The twelfth-century commentators in Bologna and then in Paris and elsewhere 'liquefy' the traditional body of law: commentaries rejuvenate rigid law. At the same time, the commentators attempt to bring the law, which had become abstract in the Code, into line with prevailing practice and to apply it to the customary law of the municipalities, the courts, currents of trade and practical legal transactions. The legal grounds begin to speak among themselves. This gives rise to the commentaries on civil law. Canon law competes. The format of the commentaries spreads to theology. In the Jewish theological tradition, commentaries were always a relevant format anyway.

At the end of the development, science, through the authority of its commentaries, is powerful enough to decide on the appointment and deposition of popes at the councils, for example, in Constance. SCIENTIA, science, never again had a higher rank than in the heyday of the commentators. The actual influence of science may be higher in the twentieth century, but not its rank. The science of nuclear physics can destroy metropolises, but science *cannot* authorize the dropping of bombs.

WHERE I USED TO WRITE IN 1956

During the day, the large meeting room in Frankfurt University's student house on Jügelstrasse is empty. Werner Sörgel has given me the key. My books are spread across the 1950s-style oval glass tables. Documents, files for my dissertation. I work on my manuscript at one of the other tables, all of which have been designed as low surfaces. Writing means leaning forward deeply from my chair. My young back allows me to keep this physiologically absurd position for hours. The furniture here in the room is not at all in the style of the future university building director, Ferdi Kramer, who in a few years' time will have renewed the university's inventory.

Column after column of letters. By hand. I was ill for a long time. Am still pale. But already curious again. Flammable from my findings in all the thick monographs. I can go from table to table, make extracts. Then write again. For me, reading and writing mean COLLECTING. That remains true even today. It stands in contrast to the postulate that an author creates what they write from within themselves. Following the author's inner voice, I write sentences that come from me. What truly inflames me, however, is my discovery of THE ALREADY SAID. Amazing finds. For me, what I think inside would be too 'repetitive'. The findings inflame me, me, the one who has just awakened from a dangerous head cold and remain in the recovery phase.

We do not live in first nature, the nature of the fields, the nature of the seasons, the ordered decades, not in the sphere of WHAT'S BEEN GRASPED THROUGH THE ALREADY SAID. I fervently believe: just about everything has already been said, but THE ALREADY SAID is only binding in the fullness of SECOND NATURE when it comes together to form new constellations. There the quotation becomes the tool and material of the amalgamation. The SECOND NATURE in which we live is disconnected from the natural world, the world that existed prior to industry, the commodity fetish, the Anthropocene and digitality. This calls for a public sphere paved with quotes that irresistibly jump out at me. I seek and find them in my work for my dissertation on academic self-government. Universities have their roots in early twelfth-century scholasticism: Bologna, Paris, Oxford. The sources dealing with this 'awakening of the intelligentsia', the first attempt at self-government, moved me. It's a question of cooperative intelligence, not personal originality. Compared to what I have read, the latter seems like a 'stumbling stone on a bad road'.

Naturally, I am writing this now, in 2021. Because of subsequent experience. Back in March 1956, the second of the first sunny days dawns outside, bathing the stones of the university grounds in yellow.

UNIVERSITIES' NEWFOUND FREEDOM
IN THE TWELFTH AND THIRTEENTH CENTURIES

My soul is inflamed by the pathos of the Parisian university crisis of 1229 to 1231. A riot between students and the forces of order leads to institutional conflict. There are deaths. The king's authority and the local jurisdiction of the clergy try to suppress the burgeoning rebellion of scholars and magisters by means of violence. Thereupon: closure of the university. Exodus of teachers and students. The *Parens scientiarum* bull of the pope, himself a scholastic of the University of Paris in his civilian life, ends the crisis. But the pope not only publishes his arbitration ruling, his canonical opinion in the dispute between the institutions, he also adds a constitutional edict that is to apply generally to academic high schools in future. The core of this constitution is the right to rebellion. The right of magisters and scholars to exodus if their freedom is threatened.

The authority of universities to become arbiters at councils was not the pope's concern. But he contributes to this authority when in his document he speaks of the University of Paris as the 'rose of the world'. He and his scribes and formulators, all *milites scientiarum*, lapse into poetic forms of expression when it comes to the political, innovative concern of standing up to the regional church regime and the ignorant royalty that relied on its mercenaries and knights. The pope's bull was not intended to diminish the power of the pontificate. It did, however, apply this power to establish the equal status of science vis-à-vis the Church and royal power. Science is GOD'S THIRD EAR. It belongs to the realm of the Holy Spirit.

Is KNOWLEDGE under threat? Then it is justified to 'go out of the land of Egypt and seek a new place'. This establishes a system of equilibrium. Naturally, emigrating is a loss for the magisters—it means giving up their well-paid positions and going into uncertainty without any guarantee of an equally secure position in the new place. But that is the price of university freedom. Conversely, this weapon of guaranteed emigration (similar to Mao Zedong's exodus from Central China to Yenan) proved to be an effective weapon against almost every power in the twelfth and thirteenth centuries.

THE LILY'S THREE PETALS

Under the influence of the flourishing of the early sciences at the first great universities of the twelfth and thirteenth centuries, the scholar Alexander von Roes formulated his theory of the THREE FORCES. The petals of the lily, which is the symbol of power in France, also represent the precise scholastic sequence of argumentation: *videtur* (*'it seems that . . .'*) / *respondeo* (*'I answer . . .'*) / *concludo* (*'I arrive at the conclusion . . .'*) This sequence establishes an equilibrium whenever not one or two but three principles, powers or authorities enter in to an exchange. The world, Alexander von Roes says, is governed by:

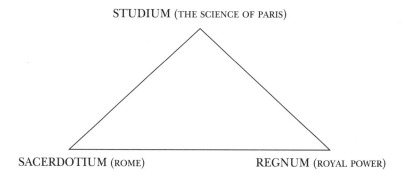

STUDIUM (THE SCIENCE OF PARIS)

SACERDOTIUM (ROME)   REGNUM (ROYAL POWER)

The triangle, which is actually a circle or a sphere, can also be described as follows:

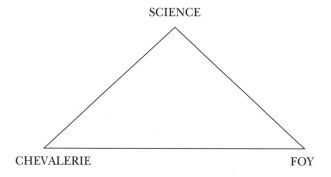

SCIENCE

CHEVALERIE   FOY

Locally this derivative of the Trinity corresponds to:

PARIS

(UNIVERSITY OF PARIS, BUT ALSO BOLOGNA, SALERNO, OXFORD)

AACHEN   ROME

(TEUTONIC CONTRIBUTION: EMPIRE)   (JERUSALEM, ANTIOCH, ALEXANDRIA,

VATICAN)

At the Council of Constance, a cardinal presides. In the absence of the emperor, however, the rule is that he, the cardinal, is the first to take the floor. At the same time, he is flanked by two university rectors and an outstandingly qualified Master of Theology. The lily's three petals thus show the balance of power in the presidency of the Council. When the rector of the University of Prague, Jan Hus, was condemned there, one of the two scientific assessors refused to take part in the respected magister's condemnation to death by fire. In this respect, the death sentence was considered 'corrupt' in scholarly circles.

LITERACY AND STUDY WITH THE AIM
OF SELF-ASSURANCE, STOCKTAKING

Otto of Freising, feudal lord and uncle of Frederick Barbarossa, rides to Central France with 200 knights. In return for a sizeable payment, the mob settles down for two years in a costly school near Paris. They learn to speak Latin from scratch. Afterwards, the crowd, thirsty for knowledge, attends a cathedral school for another two years. This school later became the core of the University of Paris, the earliest of the universities founded in the twelfth century. After his studies, Otto saw himself in a position to write world history. 'Self-assurance'. The goal of his studies? Taking possession of reality.

The author developed the time scales that were appropriate for his family's property relations, their conquests—of the Baben-bergs, Waiblings and Staufers. Nothing was looted in a short period of time, but over a long one, from Babylon to the present, including biblical dates. Thus 'possessions were acquired with God's help'. In this period, history still consists of talk, of what one has heard from another, of what one generation has inaccurately handed down to another. Events older than 30 years form the horizon. This includes the period of 'acquisitive prescription': the acquisition of a possession under customary law in perpetuity, without the possibility of asking for legal reasons. But such a tradition is insufficient in explaining the quasi-'immeasurable' wealth of the families of the high nobility. In the absence of a world history in which the course of proper acqui-sition was documented, they would appear to be usurpers. The chronicle of Otto of Freising goes back far enough in time. 'Self-assurance is like taking land.'

'26-VOLUME COMMENTARY ON A 17-LINE-LONG FRAGMENT OF ARISTOTLES!'

A scholastic from one of the early cathedral schools of the twelfth century, one of the STUDIA that preceded the founding of the University of Paris, received a shipment of manuscripts from Cordoba. Transported on donkeys. The sender was an Arab scholar who specialized in commenting on the writings of Aristotle. Among the fragments, all well packed and indexed, was a copy of 17 lines from Book I of Aristotle's *Nicomachean Ethics*. The fragment contained gaps. It was a copy from a papyrus.

On these 17 lines, practically a sacred text, the scholar wrote 26 volumes of commentary. The words of the IMMORTAL ARIS-TOTELES (the term 'immortal' was not theologically well-founded, as the biblical tradition does not recognize immortality in human beings) were reason enough for the scholar to link all the experience and orientation known to him, including what he could quote from irrefutable foreign texts, with individual words from these fragments. Thus, through commentary, a worldview of the year 1226 was created. For a long time, the 26 volumes remained unharmed. But then—in the meantime the volumes had been acquired by a Templar banking house—they were censured and publicly burnt by a zealot cathedral clergyman who was briefly in power.

FIGURE 75. [Aristotle's moles . . . / . . . resurface from the 13th century . . . /
. . . as mathematicians in Göttingen . . .]

FIGURE 76

ESTEEMED LADIES AND GENTLEMEN—

During the burning of the library of Alexandria (thanks to a victorious and imperial Christianity, one of its patriarchs having called on Alexandrians to set fire to the library, the stronghold of paganism), one of Sophocles' tragedies fell victim to the flames. It concerned the 'Death of Ulysses'. All that has survived are fragments, two half-sentences and a mutilated sentence, quoted in other plays.

What to do? We have to recreate this work. If not as individual authors, then as many. GREAT WORKS cannot be definitively destroyed by fire. They themselves consist of fire. This is their character and why they are therefore immune to merely being set alight by a mob. I know this 'because I wish it'. From the three fragments in foreign texts alone, we cannot reconstruct the drama of Sophocles. We can only imagine the circumstances under which 'the life of Odysseus ended'.

The hero has aged. Penelope is long dead. A son he fathered with the goddess Circe (who was born after Odysseus fled from Circe's island and about whom the ancient hero knows nothing) has set off by ship with his companions. Across the Mediterranean, he arrives at the beach of Ithaca. Like his father on the return journey from Troy conducting raids on various coasts, the son lives by stealing cattle and plundering.

The oracle has told Odysseus that he will die by his 'bodily son'. As a result, Odysseus banished his firstborn son Telemachus, who could have protected him against the predatory horde that has landed in Ithaca. And so, now, the old man, whose armour has become too big for his slender body, must face the YOUNG ENEMY alone. Minutes later he lies there slain. Retold in the spirit of the year 2021, the drama is transformed into an OVERVIEW.

In a first draft, our collective of authors succeeded in reproducing the narrative, which presumably constituted the main content of Sophocles' tragedy, already in the first scene. No more than eight minutes are needed for this. The prose text of this first scene was set to music by the composer Mark Andre. The following scenes (and we call on other authors and artists to accompany and enrich the 'Rise of the Phoenix' convolute with their own counter-designs) are without music.

A reversal of Sophocles' tragedy is contained in a Celtic myth: in a narrow alpine valley allowing for no escape, the aged hero Hildebrand—Dietrich of Ravenna's (mutilated in the *Nibelungenlied* to: 'Bern') master-of-arms—meets his son Hadubrand on his return home. This son is searching for his legendary father. He last saw his father when he was four years old. When Hildebrand mentions his name and claims to be his father, the son declares him a charlatan, an impostor. According to Hadubrand, his father was young, fit and strong, not a decrepit old man. The two get into a heated fight. Hadubrand underestimates his opponent's refinement: Hildebrand's SKILL in the use of weapons, guile, physical control and knowledge of his opponent's weak points. Some time later, Hadubrand lies dead in the mountain meadow. Nothing is more dismal for Hildebrand than this result of his return home.

The myth reflects a long, dark history. Fathers kill their sons. Sons kill their fathers. Brothers unite for patricide. Already in Scene 3 of the cooperatively developed recreation of Sophocles' lost tragedy, our team's draft contains an overview of 66 similar cases. A digression deals with the MYTHIC SIDELINE of the 'sacrifice of the firstborn'. This part of the draft drama is multifaceted and interrupted by films. Only the angel who prevents Abraham from sacrificing his firstborn to God shows that the original form of a social contract, the FAMILIAL CONTRACT, interrupts murder. The mythical narrative follows the actual event. For several millennia, it seems, this family contract is constantly being reinvented and concluded. Then it is broken and forgotten again, concluded once more, until it finally more or less endures. The death of Odysseus and the—in a reverse constellation (father kills son)—story of the death of Hadubrand are outliers at the end of the tragic series.

For the preliminary conclusion of the draft, we are missing six more scenes. For one of them, we have drafts sketched out in diary form by the dramatist Heiner Müller. Müller is moved by the observation that the pact, sealed with much blood, that in the future fathers will not kill their sons and sons will not kill their fathers, fathers will not kill their first-born daughters (as Agamemnon did with Iphigenia), children will not kill their mothers, and mothers will not kill their children—the FAMILIAL CONTRACT, which is the prerequisite for the later SOCIAL CONTRACT—is the cause of the fact that in the future murderousness will turn outwards. It is now a question of killing others instead of one's own. According to Müller's resigned assertion, aggression does not end with any of these treaties.

Only the SEVENTH contract—after the familial contract, the social contract and 'five further constitutions of the human race'— foresees, instead of the killing of people, the smashing of large masses of porcelain to satisfy our ever self-renewing outbursts of anger. At the end of SOPHOCLES 2021 a chorus sings 'the difficulty of taming the human race'. According to Müller's formulation, the hope for the seven contracts lies far beyond all periods of NATIONALISM.

LADIES AND GENTLEMEN—

I don't believe that the portraits of Thomas Aquinas or William of Ockham as they have come down to us, painted in capital letters from manuscripts, are true to reality. They belong to the realm of iconography, attributions in pictorial form. Thus, the image of Thomas portrays the recognition he enjoys: BROAD-SHOULDERED AND ALTOGETHER FEISTY, FULL OF THE FLAB OF EVERYONE'S ESTEEM. But I'd wager that Thomas wasn't much of an eater, that he kept trim up until old age. It was only the girth of his growing fame that caused his inordinately large abdominal area.

The iconographic mark (powerful body) is not repeated for the late scholastic William of Ockham. All the pictures of him show a delicate, thin, 'spiritualized' body. A cook would want to nurse the man. Fish oil. Pastries. Some alcohol. Just to keep him alive! But what the picture really means, regardless of whether he was fat or thin: he represents a minority. He lacks public approval. That is why, I say as an expert on twelfth-century iconography, he is not painted boldly like a Luther, but narrowly, like a 'forerunner': the forerunner John the Baptist. What he can do: he objectifies the 'scholarly gaze'. No mixture of hopes, wishes, quotations, observations. By appropriating things, my studies, *I* 'objectify'.

And then—as Habermas continues the observation—I will also objectify inwards, towards my subjectivity. I become 'a thing that thinks'.

This is the beginning of 'artificial intelligence'.

FIGURE 77. 'Aristotle's mole'

FIGURE 78. Letter from a manuscript with a portrait of William of Ockham ('Brother Ockham').

ESTEEMED LADIES AND GENTLEMEN—

A commentary is like a spring. There are those that run quite deep, that are connected to other springs by means of tunnels deep below the earth. In the deserts of the Sahara, Fernand Braudel writes, such underground water veins cover enormous distances and connect oases. Braudel compares them to the 'rivers of the unconscious' in us humans.

In the deserts of the ego, he says, in its monotony, in the organized indifference of objectivity, such waters are the veins of life. But springs are also verbs, their active thrust: they too 'tunnel'. Subtexts flow 'with power and influence' up to seven metres below the words making their way along the surface . . .

ONE WHO IS STILL CAREFULLY PREPARING
FOR HIS ROLE AS A PROJECTIONIST
(AND THUS PUBLIC-SPHERE GENERATOR) . . .

In its defensive struggle against the powerful current of Protestantism in Central Germany, which is, after all, an 'idealistic aberration', the German Democratic Republic developed the institution of the PARTY-EDUCATED SPEAKER. People were allowed to choose between a pastor, an ecclesiastical shepherd of the soul and an oratorically-materialistically trained comrade who would deliver a suitable speech at deaths, weddings or the entry of young people into a party organization, i.e. on solemn occasions in life. One such speaker was Fred Tacke of Quedlinburg.

After the fall of communism, he found himself dismissed and unemployed, with no pension to tide him over. He was 23 years old at the time. In the meanwhile, another 14 years have passed. He now has solid training as an adult educator in Halle. And it was in this context that he came across Habermas in general and his *Strukturwandel der Öffentlichkeit* (*The Structural Transformation of the Public Sphere*) in particular, a book that's been out on loan from the district library since 1992, a book which rekindled Tacke's still 'glowing' interest in the legacy of socialism (though socialism is not specifically dealt with between its covers), that is, Tacke's 'interest in the rhetorical', and provided him with what he himself calls a 'valuable toolbox of reliable concepts'. Tacke earns his money as a projectionist in former cinemas, now meeting places for young people who come to socialize, have a drink and watch films. They are no longer feature films like they used to be. Tacke has designed short speeches to introduce the film series that he selects for his screens from the range offered by an internet company—the distributor supplies the city, district and state libraries with digital material. They serve to get people in the mood and are intended to draw them away from the beer at the playback stand and towards the monitors on which the films are shown. Public speaking as a 'confidence-building measure'. Tacke could open his speeches with: 'Dear people!' Often he would like to shout informally to the assembled: 'Come on over, comrades!' Instead, he begins formally with 'Ladies and gentlemen . . .' You can see that there are no 'ladies' and no 'gentlemen' waiting to watch any films here, so those who are there have already moved closer to the screens, have become curious. Tacke refers to himself as 'a poet'. Sometimes he refers to what he does for a living as being a 'public-sphere generator'. In practice, however, no one asks him what he calls his profession.

FIGURE 79

THE MEETING IN DAVOS:
SCHOLASTICISM'S LAST DEBATE

In 1929, a sensational debate took place in Davos. The venue was the Grand Hotel Belvédère. Witnesses refer to it as SCHOLASTI-CISM'S LAST GREAT DEBATE. The rooms, furnishings and elements for Thomas Mann's novel *The Magic Mountain* were taken from this hotel. The meeting was between the philosopher Ernst Cassirer, a worldly man, and the younger Martin Heidegger, who, it is said, spent the day walking around in ski clothes and was described by witnesses as both 'inhibited' and 'offensive'.

The dispute was about categories such as being, time, 'the world of grounded reasons', the 'role of spatiality, language and death'. It concerned the question: what is 'neo-Kantianism'? The *mundus intelligibilis*, the concept of FREEDOM, the 'index of finitude', of the 'in-between', the 'finitude of ethics', its role as the 'guardian of reason', which could not take refuge in an absolute, but belonged to the world of things, the 'piety of thinking' and (polemically) 'philosophical erudition'. At times the debate was hostile, several times 'purposeful', then 'icy' once more. It took place between 11 a.m. and noon. There were minute takers. The lead-up to the confrontation had consisted of several rather amicable meetings between Cassirer and Heidegger. One of which took place at Cassirer's hospital bed, where he was laid up with a high fever. A contemporary French witness described the dispute as a 'Locarno of the mind'.

'THE UNTRANSLATABILITY OF GEWORFENHEIT'

Beginning with Kant, Heidegger explained his 'concept of *Dasein*' at the Davos debate. This concept does not have the secure ground of the logos. The heart of the concept, rather, is 'groundlessness', or more precisely: *Geworfenheit* (thrownness). The 'basic character of philosophizing' had to do justice to such *Abgründigkeit* (bottomlessness). Heidegger explained: *Dasein* is not merely consciousness, but concerns the 'relatedness of a human being which to a certain extent has been fettered in a body, and which, in the fetteredness, stands in a particular condition of being bound up with things [. . .] in the sense that Dasein, thrown into the midst of beings, carries out as free an incursion into entities, an incursion that is always historical and, in the ultimate sense, contingent' [Quoted in and translated by Peter E. Gordon, *Continental Divide*: *Heidegger, Cassirer, Davos* (Cambridge, MA: Harvard University Press, 2010).]

Accordingly, Heidegger sought to demonstrate (with increasingly vehement words) that there was no such thing as a 'bridge from individual to individual'. Just as two drowning people prevent each other from getting to the surface and breathing air, the philosophizer is left to their own devices, radically separated from every other philosophizer. In this respect, it requires a 'will to dissent'. To this the worldly Cassirer responded with a reference to language, which was not individual, but which, even if Heidegger spoke in dialect, possessed a common consistency in which cooperation beyond the foreign, 'dialogue', proved possible. Cassirer spoke of a BRIDGE OF MEDIATION. In his stubborn way, Heidegger made an impression on his student listeners by showing himself uninterested in the historical ideal of objectivity. As one witness reported: Heidegger was out for victory, not understanding.

WILLIAM OF OCKHAM, THE NOMINALISTS AND THE GÖTTINGEN SCHOOL OF MATHEMATICS

Ancestor of Protestantism and the RATIO of the bourgeois age—if without any direct genealogy to late scholasticism, simply due to the 'mind's mole-like lust'—the 'nominalist revolution' which critically curtailed the excesses of scholastic frenzy has its most consistent successor in the Göttingen school of mathematics. Carl Friedrich Gauss, Bernhard Riemann, Richard Dedekind, David Hilbert, Emmy Noether. Theologian, mathematician and logician Gottlob Frege also belongs to this circle.

FIGURE 80

Cassirer stopped short of consolidating the thinking horizon of this 'Göttingen School' in philosophy. Concepts, he says, are an object of investigation and a tool. On the examination table, the traditional ('naive') elaboration of a concept shows that it is defined 'by reference to the real substance of the world': the concept is oriented towards recognizing the similarity of real things 'and at the same time defines itself by abstracting from their particularities'.

Cassirer contrasts this 'realism' of concept formation with his 'concept of function'. This is the beginning of the algorithms of Silicon Valley; at the same time, it is the COUNTERALGORITHM to all algorithms in the world. Ette, the literary scholar of Chemnitz, puts it thus: 'After the thirteenth fairy in the fairytale of Sleeping Beauty (or "Little Briar Rose") is banished from the castle, Cassirer comes along as her advocate and demands—so that the castle will not fall into a thousand-year sleep—that this thirteenth of the wise women be given her ancestral place in the middle of the castle: a ban on exclusion!'

SUBSTANCE AND FUNCTION
IN ERNST CASSIRER

Cassirer's work of this name appeared in 1910. William Curtis Swabey and Marie Taylor Swabey's English translation of 1923 says the following:

> The genuine concept does not disregard the peculiarities and particularities which it holds under it, but seeks to show the necessity of the occurrence and connection of just these particularities. What it gives is a universal rule for the connections of the particulars themselves [. . .] and this determination can only be expressed by a synthetic act of definition, and not by a simple sensuous intuition. [*Substance and Function, and Einstein's Theory of Relativity* (William Curtis & Marie Taylor Swabey trans) (Chicago: The Open Court Publishing Company, 1923)]

As in poetics, mere abstraction is confronted with its own act of thinking, a FREE PRODUCTION OF RELATIONSHIPS: an ARTEFACT. Best expressed, according to Cassirer, in mathematical language. As alien to everyday conversation as mathematical modes of expression.

FIGURE 81 (ABOVE) AND 82 (BELOW)

$$4\arctan\left(\frac{\sqrt{2}}{5}\right) - \frac{\pi}{3} = 0,0553736$$

FIGURE 83 (ABOVE). A 'mathematical animal'.
FIGURE 84 (BELOW).

'FRUITFUL' AND 'PROFOUND'

In the mathematicians' language, the words in question denote the quality of a mathematical work. Such work is *fruitful* in the Old Testament (and evolutionary) sense if it begets many generations of follow-up work, if it is 'consequential'. *Profound*, according to the consensus of the MATHEMATICAL WORLD REPUBLIC, means that the work is desirable and necessary for the solution of a relevant problem.

BAKHTIN ON THE RELATIONSHIP
BETWEEN THE NOVEL AND THE CONCEPT

Russian literary scholar Bakhtin created the theory of the grotesque and the irresistible tickle of laughter. He compares 'concept' and 'narrative' as forms of literary expression on the one hand and, on the other, the resistance of marginalized, rebellious ways of speaking in the slums, which do not care about literature but could be its roots, with a LINGUA FRANCA that subordinates itself to the practicability of familiar information. Terms are complex poetic artefacts, the most powerful tools of the human race. They are always forged from two sides: bottom up from plebeian intelligence, and top down from the learned. What is the hammer and the anvil changes by the minute. A 'spiritual hammer' or a 'spiritual antipole of the hammer (in other words, an anvil)', is not a physical object but a powerful tool in a parallel world. Thus all narration, all language, consists of a series of parallel worlds, which only as a whole, by constantly translating and transforming themselves into one another, resemble a CONCEPT OF TRUTH. Any realism or materialism that excludes this polyphony, that is, REALISM AS A CREATOR OF UNITY, blocks human access to both narrative and civilization.

A GEOGRAPHER'S OBSERVATION
ON 'THE WORLD OF CONCEPTS'

For Ortwin Romanov, from the research centre in Akademgorodok, near Novosibirsk, CONCEPTS are a subordination of cartography, of topologies—they are maps. At a ratio of 1:1, the description of a country is true. At a ratio of 1:300,000 or at other scales of mapping, the description is an 'intelligible abstraction', a tool, an abbreviation, an artefact. CONCEPTS ARE WORKS OF ART.

Every deviation from the 1:1 spatial ratio, which corresponds to the gaze of a hiker or a scout from orbit, implies that the observer is moving in a strictly alien, non-mimetic world, that they are moving 'anti-realistically'. If they stick with this, a reasonable geographer could talk to them about the relationships between location and paths on the blue planet. If, with their tyrannical gaze (i.e. as an abstractor, as a 'possessor'), they imagine themselves to be dealing with the particularities and details of the world, they will find themselves further away from the knowledge of objects than if they'd recognized the distance between their gaze and the objects themselves right from the start. Either things and thought each have their own FREEDOM, or they tyrannize each other. The geographer explicitly relied on 20 lines in the main work of William of Ockham.

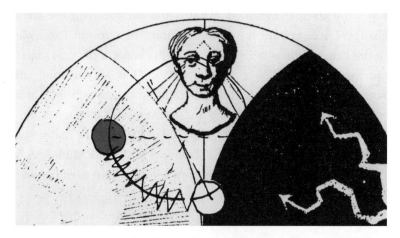

FIGURE 85 (ABOVE) AND 86 (BELOW)

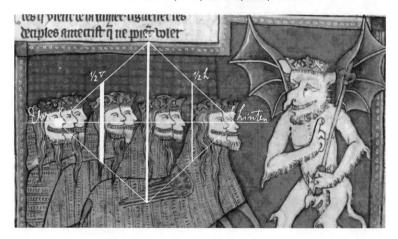

THE CONFESSION OF AN ANONYMOUS DEVOTEE
OF JÜRGEN HABERMAS' THEORY OF COMMUNICATION

I don't have any exams. Nothing in the slightest is keeping me from being happy. Any chance of furthering my education has been blocked: after two unsuccessful attempts at getting my *Abitur*.

My partner tells me I'm hungry to learn. Indeed, what I eat at night is of little interest to me compared to the books I devour. Where does all my 'fluent speech', my rabid desire to write, come from? I listen to others. And carefully! A word that flies towards me, an observation that charms me into conversation, a quotation that I read: all of this gets stored inside me for the long-term.

I usually tear books to shreds, marking any places that captivate me in colour pencil before ripping the page out. These I attach to other findings of mine with a paper clip. They're often annotated. My flat is full of these piles of paper. My personal bastion against the 'ignorance that shakes the world'.

I came across Jürgen Habermas on the internet. I have the two, several-thousand-page volumes, printed in a practical way, with my annotations and notes. The author never answered my phone calls: answering machine! Well, he may have answered once, I heard a low, grumbling voice, slurred speech. That's when I hung up. My respect was too great. I can't spontaneously (and uneducatedly) have a telephone conversation with an authority on an informal 'you' level, although I appreciate dialogue and yearn for lively 'intellectual exchange'. I do, however, respect the division of labour. This author writes thousand-page books. I collect. In the meantime, I have become a language specialist. On pages 173 and 174 of *This Too a History of Philosophy*, Volume 1, it says:

> For this animal (*personal note*: humankind) has emerged from the natural evolution of the mammals and the great apes. From these it has inherited affective endowment, intelligence and certain dispositions for social coexistence: a

'consciousness' which—together with changes in the organism, above all the growth of the size of the brain—has been transformed in all its components since the mode of socialization changed through the *conversion of communication to language* and a corresponding readiness to cooperate.

I copied this text by hand, annotated it and filed it with a bundle of about 80 pages of good citations (all the way back to Epictetus). This bundle is on top of the pile and is marked with the note: 'to be pursued'. In my consideration of languages, it occurred to me that the human ear, though equipped for the perception of balance, music and language, is *not* open to a few particular TYPES of language which humankind has at its disposal:

- The language of mathematics
(Careful! Letters here have a different meaning
than in the alphabet!)

- The language of notes in music
(Only real when they are hummed, played,
whispered or sung!)

- The oral way of speaking we grow up with

- The language of 'marginalized groups' (Bakhtin)

- The language of academia

- The language of the suburbs and slums

I grew up speaking in dialect. In addition, I speak six foreign languages (including mathematics). Moreover, without ever having taken an exam, I am able to communicate—with misunderstandings—in the ruling language of English in which the globe travels. Without getting tangled up! On the internet, mistakes are smoothed out, remain unconsidered. They are cleared up in an average understanding. That helps me. And though I express myself precisely and in a differentiated manner, I never quite feel reflected by the LINGUA FRANCA.

Essentially: rhymes are insufficient for philosophy. The leading of errors and unrhymed statements to a middle sense, to one of COINCIDENCE (a word which, basically, I collect and is hostelled in my 1,000-page bundle of paper clips), is on the other hand 'fresh land ready to be developed by the mind'. My 'eagerness for expression' is oriented to the term DISCURSIVE (740 elements in my collection). I need up to 300 pages or a stretch of up to three-hours speaking time whenever I set out to reproduce even three minutes of a 'real event' in a montage of words or pictures. The real, consisting as it does of detail and particularity, is treacherous. It needs a 'concentrate of expression'. The expression must be full of particularity and singularity while also 'logical' and 'general'. I apologize again for insufficient understanding. But what have I got besides that, what's at my disposal? Courage. And that's got to be enough affectively and in terms of ideas. Otherwise, I would be unable to express myself.

In this respect, the title of one of my favourite volumes (1,166 pages), *Ideals in Algebraic Bodies*, is one of my FAVOURITE CHIL-DREN. I am unaware of any thing as lyrical, as beautiful as this expression—'ideals in algebraic bodies' (which, mind you, I don't understand)—in everyday language. And I've never come across it in any books of poetry. I've got a library card from the county library. IN AND OF ITSELF this expression, which I happened to come across while reading, is of no practical use to me—I'm on welfare. But I want to find out what Kant means by the concept THING-IN-ITSELF: namely, that which cannot be outlined by any sensual or intellectual forces. I want to understand the unknown (and I'm afraid that Habermas disapproves of my approach). This has led to a bundle of 740 pieces of paper with the inscription THING-IN-ITSELF. And yet this pile is such a heated attractor of my interest that I nurture this expression 'IN AND OF ITSELF' like a newborn. Yesterday I held my grandchild in my arms. How small such a crea-ture is at the beginning! I was amazed. Tiny as it is, it slept. In my arms.

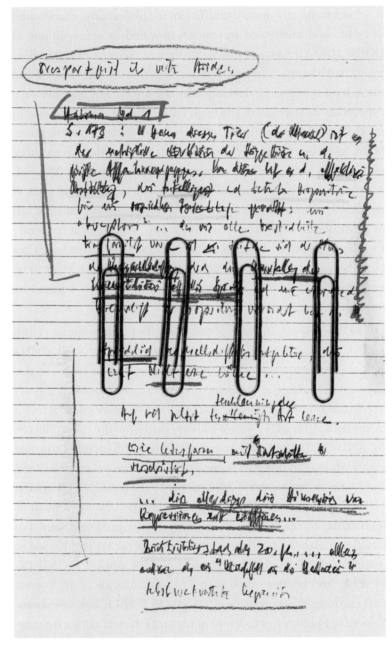

FIGURE 87. An example of the 'bundle with paper clips' in the collections of the 'patriot of knowledge', referred to by his partner as 'hungry to learn'.

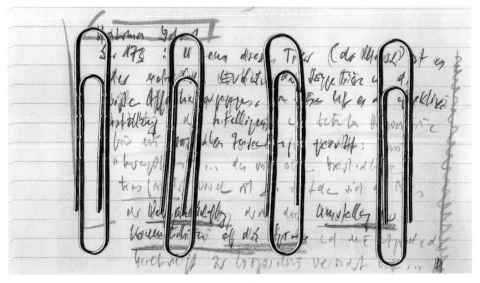

FIGURE 88

GERHARD RICHTER, *ATLAS*

NR 234, 243: ROOMS

FIGURE 89

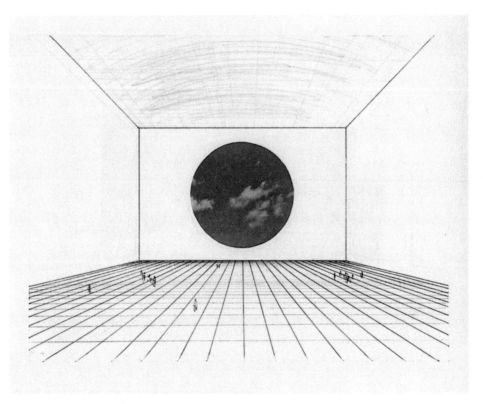

FIGURE 90

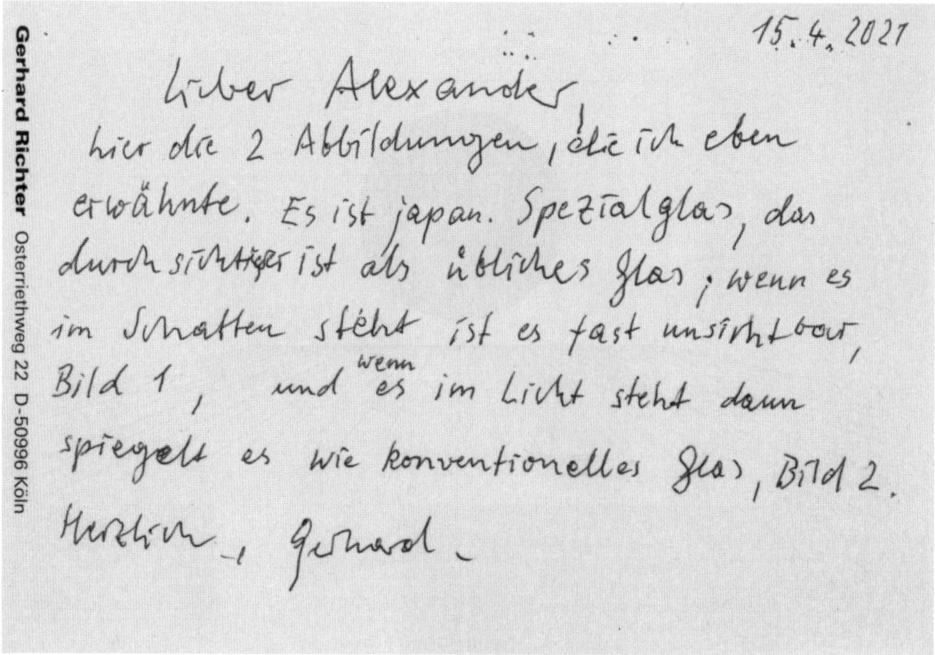

Gerhard Richter Osterriethweg 22 D-50996 Köln

15.4.2021

Lieber Alexander,
hier die 2 Abbildungen, die ich eben erwähnte. Es ist japan. Spezialglas, das durchsichtiger ist als übliches Glas; wenn es im Schatten steht ist es fast unsichtbar, Bild 1, und wenn es im Licht steht dann spiegelt es wie konventionelles Glas, Bild 2.
Herzlich, Gerhard.

FIGURE 91. 'Dear Alexander, here are the 2 images I was just speaking about. It is japan. A special kind of glass that is more transparent than regular glass, when in shadow, it is almost invisible, Image 1, and when in light it reflects just like conventional glass, Image 2. Fondly, Gerhard.'

FIGURE 92

FIGURE 93

PERMEABILITY /
TRANSPARENCY

IS THE TELESCOPE OR THE TEARDROP THE BETTER

AMPLIFICATION OF THE EYE?

OUR MOTHER STAR IS A COOL SUN

RHUBARB LEAF NEAR OSCHERSLEBEN

LIGHT MEETS GLASS AND THEY TALK TO EACH OTHER

WITHOUT ANY HUMAN MESSENGER

DUNS SCOTUS:
'ABSOLUTE NOTHING IS NOT THINKABLE'

The late scholastic Duns Scotus, who was not appreciated by all circles of the Church, distinguished between the relative nothing from
which God created the earth, animals and humans, and ABSOLUTE
NOTHING. From the perspective of its opposite pole, reality, this
ABSOLUTE NOTHING—due to the way such a powerful substance
as nothing would bend truth—is NOT THINKABLE. There can be

FIGURE 94

no such nothing in the world. Nor in any other. Neither as an eclipse nor as a 'completely transparent brightness'. Duns Scotus proved this from the 'silent truculence of all elements of being'. He writes that not all entities (which support nothingness like a gigantic cave) can be active at the same time. So the cave always collapses miserably, as God alone can force an all-round agreement of the elements to obedience; in ABSOLUTE NOTHING, however, He must be thought of as absent. No matter what the masters of the Orient say, Duns Scotus literally says (news reached him from India and he read texts of the rabbis of Babylon): Nothingness is not a safe 'cave without false belief' into which the believer can go in search of purity. Not, the theologian added, because he would not feel the impulse in his heart to remove himself from the arid world: the fact that this longing was directed towards something impossible prevented him from even looking for the entrance to the cave of refuge.

THE VOLUME OF A STRUCTURE
COMMONLY CALLED 'NOTHING'

It caused some confusion when an astrophysicist recently strayed into the annual meeting of researchers of the high period of scholasticism at a congress in Hawaii. Although evidence made it clear that he had come through the wrong door, he nevertheless presented his prepared manuscript. The complicated journey had been too long to stop now. The volume of what is commonly called 'nothing', he told the congregation, was physically defined as a state in which all elementary particles (and their substructures) had an energy amount of zero. But it is precisely this state that can be ruled out in the cosmos (from its beginnings up through the Planck length). It is possible neither in closed nor in open spaces, nor outside of space, i.e. in nirvana. The properties of the quanta are good for all kinds of things, for improbabilities of an unbelievable kind, but they can never agree on consistently uniform behaviour. Some would always be forced to rebel.

At a measurable energy level of zero, they form virtual particles, he explained. This is how his father recorded it in his diary during the German retreat in the Balkans in 1944: wherever there is a heavy concentration of occupying forces, partisan hideouts increase. The vacuum—and here, having already returned to the main road of astrophysical knowledge of the present, the guest indulged in a bit of lyricism—he spoke of 'sourdough', the 'primordial source' and the 'alchemist's kitchen of matter'. This is, so to speak, the state of newness, of the not-yet and the no-longer-but-immediately-once-again. He had exchanged ideas about this with physicists in India. The high scholastic community was enthusiastic.

STAGES OF PERMEABILITY

FIGURE 95

'THE SINKING OF THE COLOURS'

Twelfth-century church window from St Burchardi monastery in Halberstadt. As the church was unused, for 200 years the glass was stored in cellars. The colour has sunk to the bottom. The lower parts of the coloured windows show a denser light. This sinking of the colours, as Magdeburg curators confirm, was not due to gravitation.

Gravity does not pull colours down. Rather, the effect follows from the rise of impurities from the bottom upwards. Microbial 'disturbances' make colours vivid.

PROFESSIONAL GLASS

Sunglasses, indispensable for the secret service officers who guard the president. They have to keep away from the vicissitudes of sunlight, the glare.

A DELICATE CREATION MADE BY HUMAN HANDS

The ingenious transparency of the four lenses on the digital recording devices of the probe that crashed on the comet Churi is not having a positive effect at the moment because all the optics are pointed at the wall of a cave. The grains of the comet's substance, often only a thousandth of a millimetre in size, would be clearly visible if any light at all could penetrate the cavity in which the probe is stuck. It is hoped that in June of the coming comet year, a spark of light will reach us down here for the purpose of research.

ALPINE ARCHITECTURE

At a distance of 25 kilometres from Montblanc, Bruno Taut would have liked to have equipped—as if with a kind of DIAPHONOUS LENS—a mountain dome with a series of different plates of glass shining in all of day's different colours. Looking from the nearest mountain to the north, towards the Rhone, the series of eight glass surfaces would appear to be 'more transparent than air' as well as 'treasure troves of light'. For someone who wouldn't be able to see it for themselves, the effect would be difficult to describe. No enlargement! No addition of any thing at all: ABSOLUTE LIGHT. But to achieve this, Taut would need the address of the workshop which produced the glass for the Toyoshima project.

ONLY BECAUSE NEW DESOLATION
HAD COME OVER GREECE

Pasolini took issue with the claim that there was such a thing as absolutely silent suffering. On the contrary: the rebellious forces of the
will come out of their hiding places, where they have so far survived
every Hun battle, at moments of deepest shock. They begin to disturb the suffering to such an extent that it expresses itself once more.
How to irritate an aching eye until it tears when it does not want to
cry. But, Pasolini adds, it takes a long time for suffering to flow out
through such a window (the blurring of the gaze). Niobe's tears at
'Weeping Rock' could still be seen in 1941 by a German captain of
a reserve unit from Jüterbog, a senior civilian director of the military. They showed no intention (as indeed they had to do with the
mourning of her children killed by cruel gods) of stopping after
more than 2,000 years.

THE DIFFICULTY OF BECOMING 'NOTHING'
RADICAL PERMEABILITY AS THE IDEAL OF
INTERPRETERS IN PEACE NEGOTIATIONS

DIPLOMATIC EXCHANGE
LIKE INSURMOUNTABLE MOUNTAINS

At the Geneva Conference on Indochina in June 1954, the People's
Republic of China had only existed for five years. No one in China's
leadership team had any negotiating experience on international
terrain. The best negotiators, like Chou En-lai, knew how to conduct
negotiations between factions of the party, debate with dissenters,
lead capitulation talks with Kuomintang negotiators—village conversations, in other words. Against the skilled knife-throwers of
France, graduates of the great schools of Paris, who found or changed
their common rhythm in seconds, they could only improvise. On
the last day of negotiations before the expiry of the ultimatum that
Pierre Mendès-France, the French leader, had clearly set himself,

there were still plenty of unanswered questions to be resolved. So many unanswered questions that there was little hope of success.

A 'mountain of unanswered questions' could not be translated literally into Chinese, as, according to Chinese understanding, unanswered questions do not form mountains but gorges or hollows. 'A nothing awaiting an answer.' Even such trivialities of communication demand communicative attention and time. The translators, a collective of both sides that had grown together in four weeks of negotiation, were 'drunk with fervour'. It meant: MAKING THEMSELVES PERMEABLE.

Nothing of a statement's sharpness was allowed to remain untransmitted if the translated message was to reach one of the 'long-noses' or (vice versa) one of the 'yellows'. In the end, it was not clarity that led to agreement but a series of massive errors about the course of streams, river mouths and borders which they were attempting to negotiate: by means of such confusions, and not their exact intentions, both sides found a kind of 'mean' which remained acceptable to all.

At midnight, they set the clock back 20 minutes. In those final minutes outside of world-time, peace was achieved, a BLITZ-PEACE AGAINST ALL ODDS. The willingness to surrender, which manifested itself in the ability of the translators on both sides to forget themselves, should have made that *peace* in Vietnam last longer than it actually did. The very word 'peace' for the conclusion of the treaty contained difficulties. In the Chinese version, it was 'a ceasefire with prospects', not peace, which was not to be expected with the class enemy. The word-games and metaphors of both sides were 'insurmountable', and no negotiation can do without them. The difficulty at a certain stage of the debate was to distinguish between the terms 'open water', 'swamp', 'absolute barrier', 'red line' and 'permeability'. Had the French translators compared obstacles to negotiation with climbing over a mountain, their counterparts would have spoken of walking through a desert. Only because they refrained from all these linguistic chasms did they succeed—as if on a bender, as if in a trance—in communicating in the last 20 minutes. In the end, it looked as if the documents, draft agreements, maps, and presidential documents on the negotiating tables were speaking directly to one another, without the participation of anyone present.

'TILL EULENSPIEGEL WAS NEVER IN PRAGUE'

Following the debate, cult figure and peasant trickster Till Eulenspiegel is said to have led the teaching staff of the University of Prague—42 people with numerous assistants and companions (witnesses)—out of the city in the direction of the Bohemian Woods. On a peninsula surrounded by thickets and a marshy flood plain, bounded by trees, no one in the long train of people could get away from him that easily. The whole troupe had to turn around and only then could they flow back towards the city. Nor could they pursue or punish him, the fool, who escaped across the water on a bridge of branches or trees as if he were copying God's son. Prior to the TUMULT which concluded the DEMONSTRATIO, that strange Germanic spirit had asked the learned to turn their gaze to heaven. With arms outstretched he'd shown them the 'window to heaven' up above, between the treetops. That was precisely where—he measured it with measuring tapes upon the ground (analogously, so to speak)— Mary sat at God's side. Some of the witnesses who'd accompanied him claimed to have seen a crescent moon in the section of the sky.

But none of those who'd been pushed back to the stone rooms of the university in Prague had actually looked at the square Eulenspiegel had drawn, a kind of cathedral made of high trunks, branches and a piece of the colour of the sky. They were all distracted by trying to seize the seat of the divine with their scientific eyes. The enormous wilderness, the evening sky changing from minute to minute, did not touch them at all.

"EULE der MINERVA"
(Die Philosophie)

FIGURE 96 (ABOVE). ['Owl of Minerva' (Philosophy)]
FIGURE 97 (BELOW). In the lower image: Till Eulenspiegel.
In his left hand a mirror, in his right the owl.

FIGURE 98. [' . . . the owl of Minerva spreads its wings only with the coming of the dusk.']

FIGURE 99

FIGURE 100

WEDNESDAY, 21 APRIL 2021. DIARY

What a socially artificial product the modern individual is! Traversed by so many other forces than just the ego. Sociology must, Habermas says (we are talking ourselves into a lengthy pre-Christmas conversation), be completely reconstructed from its very foundations. It's a question of the architecture of society as the art of building. It'd have to be a subject at the Bauhaus. It needs the precision of urban planning. It is not in the main an issue of sorting the outside world, of sorting SOCIAL REALITY. It's got just as much to do with people's INTERIOR CONFIGURATIONS. What belongs to the knowledge of the architecture of the subject? This subject is permeated by its own self, but this self cannot be distinguished from the foreign contained within it, indeed, it is based on a 'societal unconscious' that is both 'its own' and 'foreign' at one and the same time. Habermas hesitates to accept the expression 'societal unconscious' (but there is none better on hand in the late afternoon). But if it is a matter of both foreign and individual flows in the subject, then the art of cognition that deals with it (the 'sociological eye') is related to the art of eighteenth-century pond building, to the knowledge of how to build canals, drain swamps. Preparation for a better ciphered, sorted, 'constructed' subject. If the coarse, abandoned human being can barely separate its liquid forms from its solid forms (that would be swamp) outside the process of summarizing production (as the industrial structure becomes unstable), then there can indeed be places within the subject where canal construction reigns: fortified banks, lively flow in the middle of the canals and streams as well as dry earth awaiting rain and building. This pre-Christmas evening we sing a song of mourning to New Year's Eve 1799 when so much future still seemed possible.

LUMINOSITY OF THE CONATUS,
AN UNDERRATED CONCEPT IN THE WORK OF SPINOZA

The thinking for which the philosopher provides instructions encompasses a peculiarity of the human race: namely, that it accompanies its actions with consciousness, a kind of cash register and book-keeping, a topography, a mapping of places and times, in other words, with NAVIGATORY COMPETENCE. The connection of motive or the centre of power and orientation, what is today known as personal identity, is what Spinoza calls the

CONATUS

Our innate self-precision, the directional arrow of the Tom Thumb-like 'I' embedded in the state of fate (*deus sive natura*), the hand out of which the tiny one cannot fall, exercises a kind of magic known as the ANTHROPOMORPHIC WORLD OF IMAGINATION which 'incorporates' the cosmos. The CONATUS' MOMENTUM, which is repeated in plants' and animals' robust will-to-survive, in all the elements of the earth's circle as well as 'children in the womb', not to mention the robustness of those souls which have not yet found a body and are circling the plane of Saturn before swinging around the sun, picking up speed through its gravitation and finding their housing on Earth. This conatus is just as present in the unborn, who nevertheless still desire to be born, as in the living. And likewise, the conatus of the long dead continues to nourish the dead's living followers, their heirs.

In other words, it's not—as Heiner Müller comments—the judgement of the dead, the preponderance of the dead over the number of the presently living which is responsible for keeping balance on earth. Rather, it's the other way round: as long as unborn life designs its programmes, desires to be born and carried into the world, as long as the future exercises its CONATUS, then 'humanity's self-inflicted downfall' will be postponed thanks to a kind of writing, a GLOBAL CONSTITUTION.

This conatus documents itself anew in the spherical position of the birth bubble in every mother's womb. The mutation rate of our large mammalian bodies, with human elephant souls, is so low that we hardly notice—even over the course of centuries—how the mutation rate of the forces of the soul as contained in the conatus (the 'co-born' and hyper-dimensionally different from the mutation rate in a viral species) is gradually accelerating. This means that, with the help of our conatus, we humans are already responding to dangers that will only threaten us in 40 years' time with psychological variance. This ability in the human race could save us. Is *conatus* another word for 'lucky star'? Do children carry such lucky stars inside themselves?

Here I am relating a piece of the philosophy of my sister, a practising physician, psychologist, greenhouse operator in the plantings of my own patrimony. When they describe the key of the soul's mood in contradiction to every scientific page, the fragments mean that there is a topography, a gravitative and a gravitationally dissimilar but similarly attracting 'system of the living' in which we humans are not imperators. It's what the philosophers call a 'reflection of truth'. A light source of 0.9991 per cent luminosity. The other 99.0009 per cent do not give any illumination. The decimals, as in any explanation, are imprecise.

LEIBNIZ COMMENTS ON THE APPEARANCE OF FULLY FORMED, INTELLIGENT IMAGES IN THE MORNING RIGHT BEFORE WAKING

Leibniz was known for going to bed early and for sleeping up to 12 hours. Upon waking, he reports that—no longer asleep though not quite awake—he often saw letters and numbers when gazing into the 'cap of his skull', even the finished form of arguments, proofs, 'ideal constellations.' These were 'intelligent images', the message of which he would not have been able to put into words. But he always saw something whole, interrelated. Something that was not deducible from a single line of thought or axiom. This is the way the lively interplay—in the form of a great structure of Jacob's ladders— between GOD'S GENERAL HARMONY and the blind but nevertheless clever work of MONADS came to him as an image before he was able to reconstruct the vision in words. The initial image, richer than the text to come, was there even if it didn't reveal the individual steps it had taken to appear to his inner eye. 'They also decayed rapidly with increasing wakefulness as soon as the limbs of my body stirred.' The prerequisite for such a phenomenon, Leibniz comments, was obviously that the body was still at rest, that it did not disturb the animal. 'A fine web.'

LEIBNIZ'S MILL (1714)
('perception and that which depends upon it are inexplicable on mechanical grounds')

'. . . And supposing there were a machine, so constructed as to think, feel, and have perception, it might be conceived as increased in size, while keeping the same proportions, so that one might go into it as into a mill. That being so, we should, on examining its interior, find only parts which work one upon another, and never anything by which to explain a perception. Thus it is in a simple substance, and not in a compound or in a machine, that perception must be sought for. Further, nothing but this (namely, perceptions and their changes) can be found in a simple substance . . .' [Gottfried Wilhelm Leibniz, 'The Monadology' and Other Philosophical Writings (Robert Latta trans.) (Oxford: Oxford University Press, 1898).]

A COMMENT OF HEINRICH VON KLEIST'S ON THAT PART OF THE ALLEGORY OF THE MILL: 'THUS IT IS IN A SIMPLE SUBSTANCE . . . '

'I compare the FLOW OF PERCEPTION to a stream of water. The voices of all the people we love (as well as songs of hate if we do not succeed in removing them from our ears, which is difficult because we cannot grasp sounds and voices there) affect this fast-flowing stream. Part of this often hastily flowing groundwater is the inner and outer connection in which every being is connected to the rest of the universe. And thus the raw material from which thinking is made is also in every animal, worm and medusa when, at night, in the sea, seeking light, they strive to reach the surface.' *Esse est percipi* ('I am because I am perceived.') = I AM BECAUSE I PERCEIVE . . .

SATURDAY, 12 DECEMBER 2020. DIARY

Habermas has watched my film *The Owls of Minerva*. Our call turns towards the project 'The European Public Sphere'. Habermas sends me a link to a book by Eckart Conze, a historian from Marburg, *Schatten des Kaiserreichs* (Shadows of the Empire). I should read it. The battle of Königgrätz and the founding of the German Reich in 1871 are 'drag-marks of the world spirit'. The balances destroyed in Europe at that time have now been superimposed, but subversive ones are still effective. To observe such historical processes first-hand, we both realize, a life would have to span five generations, that is, 150 years.

THE TRAFFIC FLOW OF CONTEMPORARY IMPRESSIONS OF A BUMPY PUBLIC SPHERE

Twenty-one years before my father's death, scenes took place in contemporary history that excited that level-headed doctor even as a 48-year-old man. On his way to visit a patient, at a newsstand he had bought a bulk product of the Scherl group for 80 pfennigs. A piece of propaganda from the Greater German Reich. The mass-distributed print product had been published on the occasion of France's capitulation in 1940 as an 'experience report', that is, with a yellow emblem on the top left of the front page. It described the approach of a train to the city of Aachen and its subsequent passage through the main station and onward to Schloss Wilhelmshöhe in Kassel, where, not too far away, there was a railway yard. The report referred to the year 1870. According to the text, the train was pulled by a modern locomotive. It included a coal car, a salon car and a Third Class car for the guards.

In the salon car, without the possibility of closing the window blinds, sat the Emperor of the French. Visible to curious onlookers at all the stations and all the closed bars, the train passed. Together in the form of patriotic choirs, veterans' associations and individuals and families too, the Germans who watched it pass through Aachen (the train had already reduced its speed before entering the station and passed the platforms at a slow walking pace in order to resume its higher speed afterwards, out in the open) sang the WACHT AM RHEIN, the 'unofficial national anthem of the Germans'.

Over the Christmas days of 1940, my father—who read the propagandistic work with an interest that was clearly distinct from the journalistic interest of the editors of the large publishing house—studied the text several times. The first time round with a roll, a bit of lard and some hard cheese in his hand, plus six beers and two Nordhäuser Doppelkorn schnapps. On the second day of Christmas, already taking notes at a desk and beginning to sketch the emperor's route on a prescription pad, he read the text entirely from the perspective of his father, who as a 13-year-old boy from Halberstadt must have witnessed that day. In this way of reading, the story—a cheap bit of propaganda only a few pages long—remained emphatic, gripping and developed an imaginative power for which 600 pages would have been appropriate. The emperor, forcibly removed from office and transported in a salon car, was hunched over. That is how my father saw it in his mind's eye. Just a few weeks beforehand, Napoleon III could have decided on the course of borders, the composition of large bodies of troops, even the construction of future roads and railway networks. He had been banished to Wilhelmshöhe Castle in a sardonic allusion to the fact that a close relative had once ruled West Germany there for a few years as King Jérôme of Westphalia.

The building still has British-style furniture. The mortar in the walls is the same. Over the course of the day, the staff had knocked dust out of the wool-covered furniture and aired the rooms. At the main railway station in Hanover, many residents were already on the tracks leading to the platforms. And there were visitors from the Hanseatic city of Hamburg, which had been a French department in the years of the Emperor Napoleon I, with all the rights and duties of the revolutionary and imperial periods. Many a dark-eyed child has lived in the city ever since.

The emperor of the French in his 'shame box' of a salon wagon, drawn by considerable horsepower which would have been enough for 10 or 20 wagons. Over the tracks to the south, towards the Weser. How different the situation would have been if the fortune of battle had seen an immense number of French trains send some of its enemy's (i.e. Germany's) army corps off in a curve via Aachen, Hanover and then branching off to the south towards Göttingen and Kassel, as far as Frankfurt. Austro-Hungarian units would have advanced towards their French ally. All German troops to the west of this encirclement would have been surrounded.

The tract reinforced the experience of that day in 1940, the capitulation of Marshal Pétain, in wide circles who read it upon publication. In relation to this, my father's ideas were based on individual observations from a life that had lasted 48 years, at least 43 of them with conscious perception, its individual excerpts often confusing when measured against the images of today. And strongly supplemented and—as if by gravitational force—reinforced by stories about the days of the birth of the German Reich, days my father did not experience firsthand.

'ON THE THEOLOGICAL RELATIONSHIP BETWEEN
COURAGE AND INTELLIGENCE'

FIGURE 101 (ABOVE).
FIGURE 102 (BELOW). Hares on damaged Jewish gravestones.
Film still from *Yesterday Girl*, scenes 173–181.

Der wehrhafte Hase

FIGURE 103 (ABOVE). The hare which is able to defend itself.
Twelfth-century book illustration. Aluminium print. 2020.

FIGURE 104 (BELOW). Artificial hare with metal in its stomach. Aluminium print. 2020.

FIGURE 105 (ABOVE). Hare with a snail on its hand (instead of a falcon), riding knight-like upon a dog. Book illustration. Aluminium print. 2020.

FIGURE 106 (BELOW). Hare upon a dog.
Twelfth-century book illustration. Aluminium print. 2020.

FIGURE 107 (ABOVE). Hare with bow and arrow. Aluminium print. 2020.
FIGURE 109 (BELOW). Twelfth-century script. Aluminium print. 2020.

FIGURE 109. Hare with sword. Aluminium print. 2020.

Film-triptych *There Is No Right Life in the Wrong Hare*.
Text and music by Eva Jantschtsch ('Gustav'), Vienna.

Wortfeld zu Mut

Deutsches Wörterbuch von Jacob und Wilhelm Grimm, Band 12:

*... mut bezeichnet das innere eines menschen
nach allen seinen verschiedenen seiten hin, aber
stets auf dem deutlichen grunde des bewegten
gefühlsleben, im gegensatz zum bloszen walten
des verstandes oder der erinnerung.*

*„Mammäa führt zwei pauken, die regen blut
und mut"*
Friedrich von Logau

„als sitz des mutes *wird das herz ...* **MUT**

Wagemut   „hoher Mut"

Kühnheit

Hochmut

Mißmut

Tollkühnheit

Gegenpol zu Mut:
Feigheit, Zaudern, Zögern, Ängstlichkeit, Zweifel,
Unsicherheit
**„ein Gefühl, den Boden unter den Füßen zu verlieren",
„im Sumpf"**

FIGURE 110. [Semantic field 'Courage'.]

STABILITY

'It is our habit to think outdoors—walking, leaping, climbing, dancing, preferably on lonely mountains or near the sea where even the trails become thoughtful.' Friedrich Nietzsche [Ecce Homo (Walter Kaufmann trans.) (New York: Random House, 1967).]

'Where is the seat of resolve?' (In the stomach, in the solar plexus, in the rest of the heart, in the breath, the front of the forehead, between the upper end of the spine and the beginnings of the brain, beneath the feet determinedly seeking their way).

'To take a piece of amber and electrically charge the word *courage* and then the word *intelligence* and then the theological term *pietas*.'

OUR HERALDIC ANIMALS OF THE ENGLIGHTMENT

The heraldic animal of the Enlightenment is the bat, but also the mole (which burrows underground and has amazingly human-like hand-shovels), the rabbit, the hedgehog and the weasel. As far as the cooperative context is concerned, Bonaparte's bee is also a dialectically thinking animal. And I cannot fail to mention the deep droning sounds of elephants nor the children of gorillas.

None of these metaphors in animal form, however, correspond to the nature of these animals. They are animals from our subjective narrative world.

Owl of Minerva.
Philosophy. Triptych. Full screen, 8 min 15 sec.

Sidreal Time / Axial Age / The Present. **2 min 55 sec.**

Axial Age. **After Sigmar Polke. 4 min 9 sec.**

'The Library of Alexandria Is in Flames'. **Triptych. 2 min 1 sec.**

Words from the Zohar (after G. Scholem). **3 min.**

'The Revolution Is a Being That Is Full of Surprises'

'Lamento on the Death of a Mole'

STATION 10

A LONG LINE OF
CLEVER GREEKS

'CORINTHIAN ORE'

Until well into the Middle Ages, among Mediterranean traders, CORINTHIAN ORE had a special reputation. Coins struck from this metal were considered more valuable than other money of the same weight and were kept separately in the merchant houses.

Roman legions had besieged Corinth. In a fire that raged through the city for a whole week, the gold of the temples and the metal of the iron weapons melted into one single alloy. Bronze, parts of silver too. The legionaries of the consul Lucius Mummius collected the solidified molten mass and shipped it, hand-packed on carts, to Rome, from where the metal that would later become so sought-after was introduced into the flow of the markets. At first, it was cheap, it could be had at knock-down prices, but later it became more and more expensive. When coins were struck from this amalgam, no one could know exactly how much gold the money contained. The acquisition of just such a coin was considered a kind of bet.

Years before his death, the dramatist Heiner Müller compiled a collection of sketches, drafts and poems. *History Takes Place through Diversions*. Müller meant that barbarism, suffering and guilt trigger circular movements in history—like 'whirlpools in time'. Müller's notes range from the fall of Troy to the founding of Rome and the burning of Corinth. In the beginning, the Greeks burnt Troy, Müller explains. When the leader of the Trojan rearguard, the hero Aeneas, fled, the misfortune of Troy clung to the soles of his feet. The beautiful queen of Carthage, Dido, died because of it. Aeneas then founded the ill-fated empire of ROME, and with the Romans burning the Greek city of Corinth, the circle was complete: 'so that the Greeks would get a taste of what their deeds in Troy were worth'.

But, in fact, as one of the notes and scribbled beer mats in Müller's collection says, 'the cycle I observe is neither a circle nor a spherical shape, but a spiral that continues to work onwards through the ages'.

An Alexandrian sect of moneylenders specialized in the cultivation of Corinthian ore in the High Middle Ages. The Fuggers mixed Corinthian ore with gold from Venezuela. Even with this mixture, it was impossible to guess what amount of gold could be contained in the individual coins. No ruler could successfully reduce the value of the currency by cutting its edges. This money which had sprung from 'original doom' or, as Müller puts it: 'THE MELTING OF TWO CITIES' (Troy, Corinth), captivated people's imagination. This is how Troy's misfortune, according to Müller, 'bred offspring'.

THE THOUGHTS
OF RESERVE MAJOR ALFONS KÜNNECKE,
IN CIVILIAN LIFE A SCHOOL PRINCIPAL

Now we have occupied this country with weapons in our hands. Conquered it in April 1941 with motorbikes and tanks. Machine guns in front of the mayors' offices. But above all, ADMINISTRATIVE COMPETENCE. I have been in charge of the military administrative district of Thebes since the beginning of May.[2] I often search this small city, its alleyways and streets leading out of town, for clues about the princess Antigone. Wander about looking for the fields where its first humans once arose.

'Night (nyx) spreads its black wings
So that they will become pregnant with wind'

Early man arose somewhere around here out of the will of the gods and chunks of earth, though today it is all bisected by a road. In the days before the outbreak of the first Peloponnesian War—which

---

2 Not for long. We'll soon be handing it over to the Italians. I find it to be a 'betrayal of the Greeks'. The citizens of Thebes have no idea that we plan to deliver them to their archenemy. Here in the south all powers are enemies of one another.

then didn't want to end—here, in Thebes, there was a performance of the tragedy *Medea*. What a contrast between the thoughts of an old philologist like myself and the reality of this little town. It's not even called Thebes any longer. I do not mean to be presumptuous. But I would refer to this conquered city as 'Slavically degenerate'. Fully aware of all my prejudices! So do not take me by my word. Consider my powers of discernment instead. Uncollected rubbish in all the alleyways! The little town's stature: rural. In this respect, I believe that I am using the wrong expressions, but not that my eye and my general 'impression' deceive me. I can read the text of this dilapidated city. Once again, I refer to it as 'Balkan'. I take the inhabitants to be immigrant Albanians.

I am saying all this because I miss what I longed for in my soul, ancient Greece, so much. What do I imagine that to mean? It's funny, but I never asked myself that question before. But now, as the city's administrator and commander, I am. A few buildings on the outskirts of town feature twentieth-century architecture. There are not many nouveau riche here. The bits of antiquity present in the local supply here and there do not stand up to scrutiny. All that is authentic and interesting are individual pieces and they are Turkish.

So, in the meantime, my thoughts go forward to the years following our ultimate victory. In my estimation, this period of rebuilding will fall in the years after 1952. My point of orientation is the planning sites that connect us down here in our exile with the large-scale planning of the Greater German Reich. The four-year plans. The next but one is scheduled from 1948 to 1952. The figures, experience values, reports and cost budgets always refer to the accounts of the previous four years, which are subject to auditing, and extend four years into the third-next future (1952 to 1956). Therefore, we commanders—and I as a chronicler—live in multi-annual cycles, while 100-year cycles govern the destiny of our nation, Europe and the world. And cycles in such centenary steps, added up to millennia, are the TRUE REALITY in which our cells, nerves, thinking abilities and, yes, the powers of a chronicler too, as I am one, move.

ZEUS' PARALYSIS / RECOVERY OF INNATE
FREEDOM (KÜNNECKE'S SECOND NOTE)

Typhon is not a dragon. It is a giant with a snake's body, hence the confusion with a dragon in the reports. Several of Gaia's heirs have serpent bodies, as do the giants, 'Mother Earth's' first-born sons.

The gods fled the primeval monster Typhon and, in Egypt, transformed themselves into animal forms. This is how Apollonius of Rhodes tells the story. Then, Zeus beat the monster back to Mount Hazzi in Syria.

In the scuffle with Typhon, however, he lost his sickle-sword, HARPE. With this tool, Typhon removed the TENDONS from the great god's hands and feet. Imprisoned the motionless man in a cave. But Hermes managed to steal these sinews from the giant, which the latter was keeping in a box in a neighbouring cave, and returned them into Zeus' body. With lightning and thunder and renewed strength, the god descended from the heavens on his winged chariot and pursued Typhon beyond Thrace to Sicily, where he buried the monster in Etna.

KÜNNECKE'S ADDENDUM TO HESIOD'S REPORT
ON ZEUS' PARALYSIS

There is, Künnecke notes, a 'primal affinity between mythical stories'. The report of the loss of Zeus' sinews corresponds to the tale of the blacksmith Wayland in the Edda. As a result of his longing for his beloved—who comes to him from time to time as a swan—this black-smith is *self-forgetful* and distracted when it comes to his self-defence. A certain Nidad, king of the Nidungs, takes advantage of this, over-powering the longing man and slicing through his tendons. Unable to move any more, Wayland the Smith sits before his workbench.

He forges swords, jewellery and armour for the criminal king. A second 'Hephaestus in Vesuvius'. But then this 'northern hero', a heterotope of the titans, forges a pair of wings for himself. Here, Künnicke notes, we find a mythical tale of wandering, and it is specific to such a revisiting of motifs from faraway places that the accents are reversed. The longings are not reinserted into the 'hero Wayland'. Instead, the paralysed one has made himself wings. He flies past the palace of the tyrannical king and on towards the south.

Künnecke's commentary was edited by literary scholar Dr Irene Baumann. She places fragment against fragment, mosaic against mosaic. A structure emerges. Dr Baumann says: Like a prophecy! She didn't want to say what she concluded from the similarities in myths that have been handed down so separately. She says only this much: If there was such an event back then, 'sinews are removed from the body of a ruler or worker, re-procured and re-inserted . . .' then it is told in different places of the globe. And if it happened once, it will happen again today. All we have to do is decipher: what is yearning? What bodies are involved? Who is competent enough to find the hidden 'elements of mobility' and how do you operate them back into the paralysed bodies? Her desire was to reconstruct this 'work process', as she calls it, and then comment. She called her research project, which remains subsidized for two more years, a 'contribution to the concept of freedom'.

KÜNNECKE'S THIRD NOTE

The word 'punishment' must be omitted entirely in relation to ancient myth.

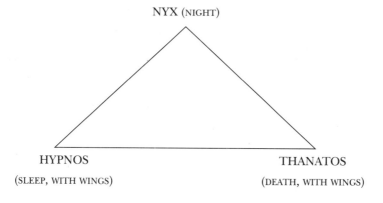

The birth of Athena. From the head of her father Zeus. Who had previously devoured the Titan Metis, Athena's mother. Then the labourer god Hephaestus was summoned and opened Zeus' skull with a double-headed axe. The obstetrician present (Eileithyia) immediately wrapped the newborn in swaddling clothes.

This is an example of violence from the National Socialist point of view as well. One simply does not devour the bride with whom one conceives a child. Even if a newborn is born as a result of the violent act, it remains violent, as well as politically inappropriate, to split open the skull of the worshipped god with a double-headed axe just to be able to reach in and lift the virgin Athena to the light. Wherever this extension of violence takes place, there must, according to National Socialist understanding, also be counter-violence, a tempered violence. And consequently, a process of returning the owl of Minerva or the rebellious Athena (when she becomes precocious and gives the wrong advice) to the great god's skull.

THE LAST WAY OUT FOR KÜNNECKE'S NOTES

With a heavy lantern in its belly, in the autumn of 1944, a fishing boat leaves a small harbour in the Peloponnese with the stormy north wind of Greece, Boreas, at its back. It is loaded with tons of gold from the German Reichsbank. The man who has rented the boat is Hans Laschke, an employee of the Deutsche Reichsbank in Athens. One of the last to leave the country before the German withdrawal. He uses the gold to rescue Künnecke's manuscripts from holy Greece. His boat lands briefly in Ithaca, then follows the autumn current to Venice. He and his goods are unloaded. With the help of rubber dinghies, the HEAVY GOODS (alongside the indeed light weight of the manuscripts) are removed from the belly of the boat, brought ashore and loaded onto a freight train; they also reach the imperial border and final destination. There the manuscripts, which are taken to the Bavarian State Archives, are separated from the gold which is barricaded in one of the deep caves in the southern foothills of the Harz.

BUILDING A BRIDGE TO THE RENAISSANCE

The Christian and physician Philipparchos emigrated to Venice with three sons and three daughters in the year before the Ottomans took the city of Byzantium. All of them spoke classical Greek in addition to three urban dialects of Byzantium and were now learning the Italian dialects spoken in Venice and Tuscany. The three tutors became respected grammarians who later taught bankers' sons in Florence, and then married. The sons: two doctors and a jurist. This 'vanguard of the 1453 exodus' was, in terms of spirit and prescience, a co-founder of the Renaissance. These Greeks introduced their Italian pupils from the agricultural valleys (where their minds were atrophying) to the life of antiquity. Because they had it in their heads that they could no longer do anything with it in Byzantium, and came to know the value of what they carried in their heads to the extent that their new fatherland fed on it.

A GREEK ALEXANDRIAN HELPS THE EMPEROR
SAVE THE WORLD

At the court of Emperor Rudolf II in Prague, there was an Alexandrian Greek, an alchemist who had studied the Arabic and European laboratories of his profession—all rather particular cabinets of curiosities, WUNDERKAMMERN. Emperor Rudolf II, the grandson of Charles V, had an outstanding interest in the swirling and mixing of elements, a more-than-thousand-year-old tradition. Instead of the two worlds his grandfather had ruled in reality, he ruled over seven spirit realms. At night, he prowled the laboratories and cellars of his castle. Out of a certain caution and full of avarice and mistrust, many of his treasures he hid.

Although whole wagonloads were later removed from his castle and *Wunderkammer* by the Swedish occupiers of Prague during the Thirty Years' War, RARITIES can still be found within its walls and in deep, carefully sealed, walled-over and whitewashed cellars, including alchemical equipment and the results of experiments by the emperor and the Greek who worked for him stored in tins and boxes. Some of the characteristics of the alchemical material found in these two places are inexplicable to science.

The Greek or Hellene and the emperor—in some cases, with the help of Dr Robert Fludd of Oxford—held séances. To avert dangers to the empire and to the person of the imperial prince. Above all, it was a matter of warding off the emperor's power-hungry brother, who Rudolf assumed was after his life, or at the very least his reign. The Greek, with his superior magic powers and distillates, kept the emperor's arch-enemy, his brother-duke, at bay. He built a wall measuring seven German miles around Prague. Invisible to travellers and no obstacle to them, the partition brought every steel column that approached, especially the brother's, to a determined halt. The riders came up against a spiritual wall they could not see, but one which stopped them like thick glass. Mercenaries fell off their horses. The brother, having slipped from the saddle, was exposed to the kicks of his troubled animal. And so, for some time, the arrivals who wanted to ride to Prague lay in the autumn leaves as if struck by a blow. They could not move their limbs. The horses with broken legs, 'battered heaps'.

Not with grammar or eloquence did the emperor seek to block universal war—which, following his death, broke out into what we now refer to as the Thirty Years' War—but with a cloudy brew, clouds of elemental substances from his laboratory. From all the ovens of his alchemical kitchen, he let atmospheric combinations of substances blow to the north and northwest, spiritual powers from the glass flasks. Many an equivalent of a silver fleet (of which, according to a treaty between the Spanish and Viennese branches of the Habsburg dynasty, every seventeenth belonged to him) was lost during the course of this performance, this cultivation of an effective dark world. The emperor often rose at 4 a.m. He would pass the morning among the subterranean foundations of his castle, having supplies for the spiritual salvation of the world made and preserved.

It would be a mistake to believe that the salvation of the world could consist of statecraft.

FIGURE 111. [TURBA = pile, horde / MONS = mountain, raw material /
HORTUS = 'Alchemist's kitchen']

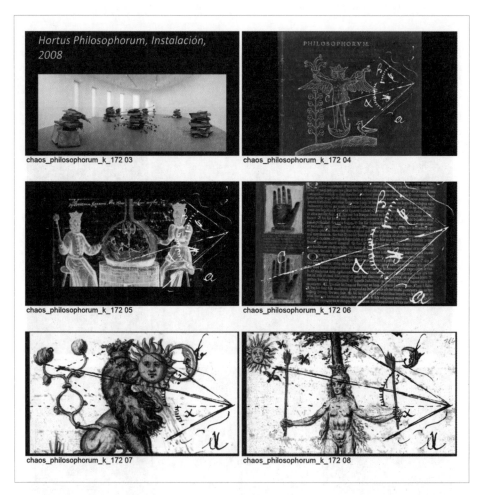

FIGURE 112.1

FIGURE 112.2

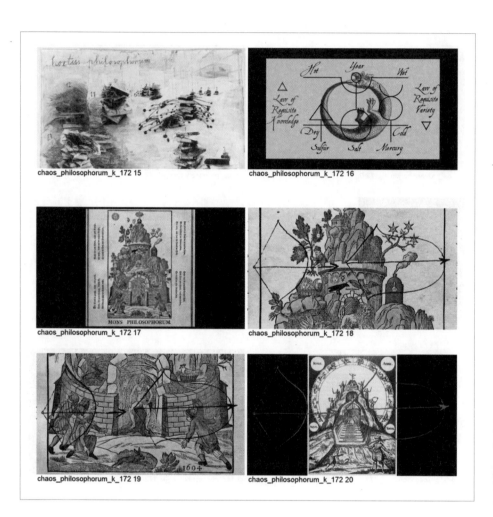

chaos_philosophorum_k_172 15

chaos_philosophorum_k_172 16

chaos_philosophorum_k_172 17

chaos_philosophorum_k_172 18

chaos_philosophorum_k_172 19

chaos_philosophorum_k_172 20

FIGURE 113

DANGER LEVELS ONE THROUGH NINE
FOR DENSELY POPULATED AREAS

There is a Greek architect in Istanbul who traces his ancestors back to the time of Emperor Justinian. With skill, these ancestors survived the conquest of Byzantium by the Ottomans in 1453. Only two years after the occupation, they were available once again to the Ottomans in their old offices, in aristocratic rank, for new services. Even though they do not belong to him, the architect is emotionally attached to the buildings being erected on the Bosporus under his planning and guidance. He feels that he has been propagated by his children and his children's children, but by his buildings too. He is keen to draw public attention to the fact that the city of millions and its buildings have been endangered by being in an earthquake zone since the time of Emperor Justinian. In geological terms, this zone has existed 'for only a short time' at the point of rupture where two continental faults—violently rubbing against each other—push past one another. If one of the subterranean parts of a mountain or other kind of rock formation gets caught on the other, i.e. if they are stopped from FLOWING PAST EACH OTHER, then the violence accumulates until it is discharged in the form of an earthquake, accompanied by a tsunami at this meeting point of the seas. The investors paying for the buildings don't tend to spend money on avoiding future dangers. They don't derive any income from that kind of future. And when they build, they do not do so with an eye on individual rent payments. By the time the future arrives, they have long since sorted out the buildings, put them into packages and sold them off to pension funds. Danger from the belly-of-the-whale-called-the-future simply doesn't affect them.

The architect—careful by nature, prepared for long-term observation by the long line of clever Greeks from which he descends (sometimes he thinks that his most distant ancestors did not come from Alexandria or Syria, as available documents indicate, but from one of the suburbs of ancient Athens)—has his assistant continuously check the earthquake measurements put out by the Institute of

Geosciences at the University of Potsdam. They refer to the depth of the earth's crust, from Anatolia to the Sea of Marmara. He is conducting research on the 'wedging' of the inexorably advancing geological masses, an upheaval of the telluric element. Maybe the Titans are not dead. The longer the wedging lasts—sometimes it is blown up and the free flow of rock breaks away—the more violent the eruption. The diligent assistant, who travels to Potsdam himself and recently obtained information from the geoscientific institute in Akademgorodok, always provides static material alone, probability data. The Greek remains uneasy. With a probability coefficient, as the institutes report, the disaster can happen in 12 weeks' time or in 8 years. You shouldn't build a city of 25 million people near a dangerous geological jam of two rubbing faults.

The investors rule like frivolous pashas administering a province they don't like from the centre, i.e. like overlords who do not care about the territory and would just as soon get rid of it (and as quickly as possible). But what could be the counterproposals? At the last architecture biennial, the Greek consulted with contemporary architects like David Chipperfield. Today's architecture must be compatible with the structure and construction of the stock exchange, banks and markets. This sets limits to suggestions for improvement.

The best thing would be to take the metropolis, which has not been the capital since 1918, and decentralize it. Happiness for the entire Balkans could result if the population and economy were not clustered in a hothouse-like manner on the Bosporus but spread across the whole of the Balkan peninsula, all the way to Vienna, in cheap and low buildings. What if Vienna were to be 'conquered' again this way, but creatively this time, creatively and with all the riches of the Orient? Another option would be a flexible building method, or brick instead of concrete. Which constellation of the building mass would be elastic enough to withstand earthquakes? Japanese architects have a lot to contribute to the question but are hardly ever active on the Bosporus.

THE ANKARA FILES

One of the last 'victories of the GDR on the battle front of the people's ambassadors in the service of internationalism' was its success, in the spring of 1989, in getting a perspective agent, i.e. a comrade, to work as deputy head of the archives of the Turkish Ministry of Foreign Affairs in Ankara. A perspective agent isn't trained nor used to spy on state secrets. No, they are trained to be AGENTS OF INFLUENCE. They are to occupy key positions in foreign countries and, in the event the fatherland of the working people requires it, introduce power or knowledge: a rich harvest for a lot of waiting. The waiting is the training. Waiting is needed to bring the agent to the desired position. And then there is a long wait for the services of the agent to be needed at all.

This particular young agent, born in Radebeul near Dresden, the second generation of illegitimate birth, found himself abandoned by his employer shortly after infiltrating his new office in Ankara. The GDR ceased to exist at the end of 1990, but the perspective agent still felt like a 'spy of the Revolution of 1917'. The group in the Ministry of State Security to which he had to report in case of an assignment was called 'Dzerzhinsky'. This spy, whose real name was Bernhard Zache, but who worked there under a Turkish name, was loyal. In his secure position, he had attracted a confidant. The two spies formed a lonely republic.

The two had access to vast sources of files. The Turkish Ministry of Foreign Affairs keeps the files of the Ottoman Empire. In addition, it has the enormous source material of the Eastern Roman Empire, which was transferred to the Ottomans' administration when they came to power. They are stored in the office's cellars and in rented storehouses near Ankara, as well as in military stables and ammunition barracks. The wait times the perspective agent looks back on are short compared to the long amount of time this 'collected world experience of Eastern Mediterranean politics' has waited to be discovered and poetically processed. The two republic-less agents spend a lot of time reading and making excerpts. From week to week, their SPY-LIKE GAZE becomes more and more interested. It's all about exploration and retelling. The new 'fatherland of knowledge' they have devoted themselves to covers a time span of more than 1,400 years.

Often our perspective agent wonders with whom he could share his industrious spying and collecting activity, his KNOWLEDGE. Both scouts have sworn allegiance—though currently addressless—to socialism. They have not given up hope that at some point a head office, a community, will become visible to which they can hand over their volumes, results and experiences.

A total of 6,000 files relate to the struggle of Young Turk officers against the Italian attack on the province of Libya, which belonged to the Ottoman Empire until 1912. Over the weekend, they excerpted the two files on the shelling of the Ottoman port of Beirut by the Italian fleet. The officials at the centre of Ottoman diplomacy, according to Zache, 'were excellent storytellers'. They can trace how the crudeness of Italy's attack was taken as a model among those Balkan insurgents rebelling against Ottoman rule. The Turkish occupying forces had barely been driven out when the newly founded Balkan states began to wage wars against one another. The search for traces in the files shows how events on the Libyan coast in 1912 were the direct precondition for the outbreak of the First World War in June 1914. Diversions, bifurcations, wild changes in the intelligence services, clusters of coincidence. Poisonous paths and—visible to the poetically inclined as well—the trace of potential antidotes. Many afternoons and nights are spent working on the material. The only thing missing is an addressee.

IPHIGENIA, THE FORGETFUL

The descendants of Tantalus committed crime after crime. Until the murder of Agamemnon and his murderess Clytemnestra, who was beaten to death by her son, fate and doom ruled the family.

Agamemnon wanted to slaughter his daughter Iphigenia to obtain a favourable wind for the journey to Troy. The gods cast a cloud of mist over the scene of the sacrilege. Then they rescued the young woman and brought her to the Crimea. There Iphigenia proved to be a bit of a scatterbrain. The hereditary information which condemned her to being murdered had slipped her memory. Fortunately, evil requires the exertion of great force. Something is good when it ends the series of evil. In praise of forgetfulness.

THE REVERSAL OF TIME'S ARROW

A STRANGE REPERCUSSION OF A RUSSIAN RULER'S WISH ON THE COURSE OF HISTORY

A wish of Tsarina Catherine had a long-distance effect for more than a thousand years. It swept causal chains out of place. Regrouped prehistory around its axis. The ruler's wish was not just a whim. It was Protestant–Anhalt-Zerbstian granite (if you can compare human tempers to biologically formed stone). The tsarina understood Greek. She'd already had good teachers in the castles at home in Germany. In ancient Greek, there is the optative mode, a grammatical mode which expresses a wish or hope regarding a particular action ('I wish', 'you wish', 'he / she wishes'. . .). According to such grammar, a Russian tsarina can command the arrow of time.

The tsarina's explicit wish was that Sophocles' tragedy *Antigone* would not end with the titular character being walled up and killed. Instead, the composer of the opera based on this material, Tommaso Traetta, was to recompose his play in such a way that, at the end, the son of the tyrant of Thebes, Antigone's betrothed Haimon, would force her father to change his severe mind by threatening to kill himself, the knife already against his vein. Antigone and Haimon appear before the audience. The chorus explains that Antigone's act of burying one of her brothers beaten to death by the other— the burial of one forbidden by the state, the other the recipient of a state funeral—is to be forgiven.

With the tsarina's wish, however, the historical course on which the tragic story was based had subsequently changed direction. Antigone, who after Creon's death had five children by her former lover, now King Haimon, ruled the city of Thebes until her death. Descendants of the legendary figure reached as far as the Crimea. There, after the expulsion of the Ottoman administration, the family clan, which had in the meantime died out, was recruited by Prince Potemkin for Russia. Two mathematicians, two philologists, a musician and a philosopher from the Antigone family came to the academy in St Petersburg. They survived the tsarina, a devotee of the Enlightenment, and after 1815 corresponded in the interest of French-Russian international understanding. One of the two mathematicians and the philosopher advised Georg Wilhelm Friedrich Hegel in writing his *Phenomenology of Spirit*, which deals centrally with the myth of Antigone. At the end of Traetta's opera (*Antigona* in Italian) Haimon and Antigone are seen sitting in a bathtub. There, still stunned by the happy turn of events, they whisper, sing and tell each other what happened.

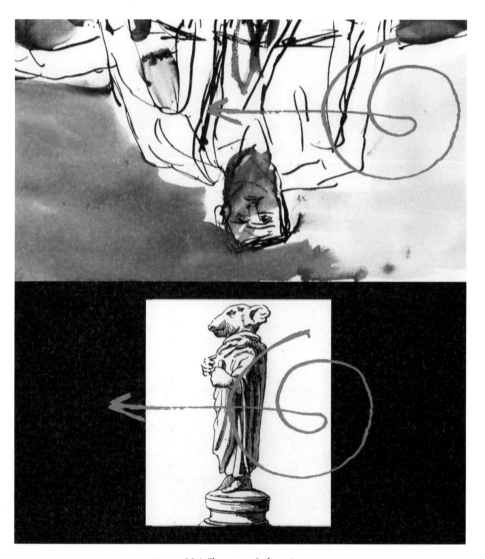

FIGURE 114. The reversal of time's arrow.

IN THE LAMP OF THE SOUL'S
FLICKERING LIGHT:
INTELLIGENCE

$$\left(\text{A.}\right)$$

TRANSFER OF EXPERIENCE ACROSS
MULTIPLE GENERATIONS

NARRATIVE STRETCHED OVER 90 YEARS / NAVIGATION

Experience, narrative and intelligence organize themselves in LIVES and GENERATIONS. Statistics calculate a generation at 30 years. A narrative (and the transmission of experience) from grandparent to parent to children comprises three generations = 90 years. A huge mass of experience. As music, language, the arts, refined tools and thus 'modern' intelligence emerged in Central Europe some 40,000 years ago, there have been around 440 such 90-year stretches. The time between Barbarossa's baptism (the first 'stories' about him and the first 'stories' he heard as an infant) and 2022 contains 10 such 90-year stretches.

'A MATTER OF SECONDS'

In the calcified veins of a learned astronomer and mathematician, blood clots clung to the walls of the blood vessels for SECONDS. Some of these tiny plaques later detached themselves from their 'banks'. It can take a whole night for a particle like that to start moving. A few of these treacherous particles formed in the abdominal vein. The calcified neck veins almost didn't let the particle through. This process (of trial and error) was a process of weeks and days. Then, at some point, one of the blood clots crossed the blood–brain barrier and caused the stroke. The mathematician woke up at five in the morning. He still thought he had to hurry to the toilet. By then, one side of his face was limp. After months of training, only partial control of his facial features was possible again! As I said, the assassination attempt on the brain of this highly gifted man lasted only a FRACTION OF A SECOND.

Unusual times and unheard-of events
for which 90-year narrative stretches just seem grotesque . . .

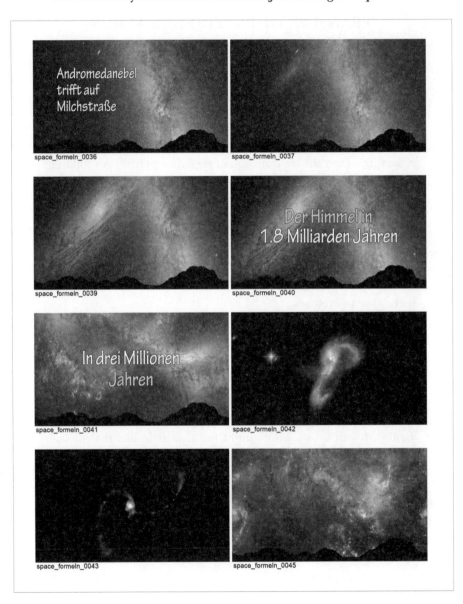

FIGURE 115

FIGURE 116 (ABOVE) AND 117 (BELOW)

FIGURE 118. [In six billion years, all of our nights will be bright . . .]

'41 YEARS = AN EXAMPLE OF HALF A 90-YEAR NARRATIVE STRETCH'

This is a story of father and son. And of two world wars. In the year 1898, the influential British government official Joseph Chamberlain (1836–1914), father of Neville Chamberlain (1869–1940), proposed making an alliance with the German Reich. This was done in informal talks with the German ambassador. Such a proposal was unusual, as it had been British policy since the middle of the century not to bind itself firmly to any particular alliance on the continent. The changing majorities in Parliament would have made such a commitment difficult. Chamberlain was confident that he could win over the Germans and solve the problem with Parliament. He was wrong on both counts.

During a pause in a TV conversation I was having with the historian Christopher Clark on his book *The Sleepwalkers* (dealing with the outbreak of war in 1914), I asked him about this incident. He confirmed that the German Empire's brusque rejection of the offer became one of the 40 reasons for the outbreak of war in 1914. Chamberlain the elder sought peace. But he had misjudged his opponent.

41 years later, his son Neville Chamberlain—after attempting to reach an understanding with the German Empire and losing part of his political authority in disappointment—also deviated from England's diplomatic tradition of not committing itself definitively to any continent and signed a treaty with Poland in March 1939. The treaty made inevitable England's entry into the war in September, something Chamberlain had wanted to avoid. Both men, father and son, were 'peace-minded people'. Their policies are considered refuted. The opposite of what they had hoped to achieve. The experiential content of their deeds, however, will not be overcome by the prejudice that 'all APPEASEMENT POLICY is obsolete now and in the future'.

TEMPERAMENTS OF INTELLIGENCE

AN 88-YEAR-OLD ANSWERS THE PHONE
7 DAYS BEFORE HIS 89TH BIRTHDAY

Two years ago, he suffered a brain haemorrhage. Since then, his reactions have been slowed. When spoken to in a friendly manner, however, his replies still sound sharp.

But he could no longer keep a sudden sensory impression, a surprising message, in his head for long. Immediately after the impulse in the synapses of his brain, these 'beacons of knowledge' lost their power, were quickly forgotten, emptied their energy into a never-never land. The old man interrupted the phone call. He was interested in what he'd heard. 'I've got to stop,' he said. 'I have to speak to my co-worker immediately, tell her what I just promised you. Tell her to record it, otherwise I'll have forgotten it.'

WHY DO JELLYFISH CONTINUE
TO RISE TO THE SURFACE OF THE SEA
SO PERSISTENTLY AFTER MILLIONS OF YEARS?

At night in the southern oceans, jellyfish approach the surface of the sea. As if they were moving towards the shimmering of the stars (as well as the broad face of the moon). Yet marine scientists—including jellyfish specialists—know that these ancient creatures are made entirely of outer skin. Devoted to their environment. They have no head. Nor eyes with which to 'see' the glimmer of stars. For them, EYE WORK would also be evolutionarily useless as they have no jaws to snatch whatever it is their eyes might spy. It must be something other than the sight of the sky or a sea surface bathed in light that prompts the medusae to make their nocturnal and irresistible ascent towards the surface.

THE JELLYFISH RESEARCHER SVERDLOV'S THEORY

Russian jellyfish researcher Dimiter Theodorovich Sverdlov—who is familiar with his research objects only from the pools of Akademgorodok, that massive 'academic city' in Siberia, and who has never visited the sea where the originals live, thanks to the fact that the authorities have always refused to grant him a passport—considers the JELLYFISH SPECIES to be 'representative of humanity'. Once humanity is extinct, or causes itself to be extinct, he teaches his post-doctoral students, these 'outsiders', 'creatures-made-entirely-of-skin', 'creatures-in-total-contact-with-nature', these HEADLESS ones will be ready to replace it. Full of perceptiveness, full of life.

From such a side tract of evolution (one could also say, such an early preliminary stage of later intelligence), Sverdlov explained, mankind's ancestors also arose. As tiny sea creatures. A trace of this origin remains: tears. A watery solution that removes salt from the body—a function that only exists in marine animals and that only developed in them. And then our ancestors' ancestors developed skeletal structure and that in turn paved the way to the spine, skull and cerebrum. The former precursors of this development (the jellyfish within us and the jellyfish themselves) remain rulers who neither know the word *rule* nor ever learn how to exercise it. LIFE HOSTS OF SENSIBILITY.

THE HEAD'S VICTORY OVER THE BODY:
SEMA / SOMA. 'LOSING ONE'S HEAD'

In addition to the creatures she was looking for, a Japanese researcher found tiny mussels in a layer of mud that had been prepared with laboratory precision. Beneath her microscopes, she observed that the head of these unsightly, blackish-coloured small animals separated; she saw how in each and every case the head began a life of its own. The bodies—with their hearts, digestive systems, protein stores, skin—lived for a long time after the separation of the head, which contained an essential part of the body. They greedily took in the food the researcher offered. They responded to being poked with tweezers. Then, after a few weeks, they died. The severed heads, on the other hand, compacted—autonomously—the skin above the dividing line. Without a heart, they steadily took in food with their tiny mouths. Later, a heart arose. Internal organs according to the construction plan of the original snail. The head created a body for itself. It may be, the researcher surmised, that, by freeing themselves from the body, these sophisticated creatures opened up a chance to hear. Perhaps, the researcher thought, they were saving their future from a horde of parasites that would otherwise have taken up residence in their bodies. But it could also be a kind of 'rejuvenation'. The head triumphing over the sluggish old body. The phenomenon was only observed in young snails. Older age classes did not separate from their head. The juvenile age class was easily recognized in this species by its faster, more 'eloquent' movements.

THE SOUL'S TRUE WEIGHT /
AN OPERA FROM THE YEAR 1600

Two years after the first opera of which only fragments have survived—Jacopo Peri's LA DAFNE (1598)—Emilio de' Cavalierei's opera LA RAPPRESENTATIONE DI ANIMA, ET DI CORPO was premiered. As this took place in a church, the official history of opera does not really begin until Monteverdi's ORFEO (1607), an opera which was performed in a municipal theatre. It concerns the characters of CLEVERNESS, the BODY, the SOUL and LUST. All the characters deal with the tension between heaven and hell. Of primary importance is the tender and aggressive dialogue between BODY (corpo) and SOUL (anima).

'ON THE WINGS OF HIS LONGING . . . '

In 1943, every evening around 8 p.m., the flight instructor and fighter pilot Wolfgang Wilhelmsen took off from Halberstadt air-field—a training centre for extreme pilots and paratroopers during the war, a billet of the daring—in an experimental Me 109. Full of longing for his beloved in Stuttgart. His plane flew 200 kilometres-per-hour faster than any other Seiren-produced aircraft. Comrades hid the rare piece for him in a hangar outside town. And at about six o'clock in the morning, this pilot, body and clothes still soaked with the smell of his night-time companion, would set off for Halberstadt to report for duty. This went on until his fuel consumption revealed his nocturnal holidays. Disciplinary proceedings.

But they couldn't do without this 'daredevil', holder of a Knight's Cross with Oak Leaves, though not in this war in which the overwhelming power of the enemy was consuming all their forces on all fronts. No, they needed him to train young pilots. So he was sentenced, immediately pardoned and reassigned. No orders, no threats of punishment could keep him from longing for his only beloved who lived in a radio station near Stuttgart. Sometimes the lover's night flight crossed the approach of Allied bomb squadrons to the same region, but he zipped through their attack formation like a shadow. He did not shoot at them; they did not shoot at him. Ghostly separate, two alien worlds (placed on the same planet, but separated by their respective reasons for existence and warlike intentions).

WHAT GOOD IS THINKING IN THE AGE OF UPHEAVAL?

Horst Böhlitz, a Kantian contrarian from Braunschweig, who'd set his mind on visiting the disintegrating German Democratic Republic in the late summer and early autumn of 1990 to witness the formation of a new republic, had taken up residence in a state-owned HO inn in the Uckermark region. The founding of a republic is the hour of philosophy, of 'scientific amity'. He also had it in mind to map the historical days, at least in the form of notes.

Thoughtful steps beneath the beech trees of Uckermarck.

While he was busy equilibrating his thinking with contemporary history, however, elsewhere, especially in the industrial parts of the worn-out republic, economic emissaries from the West and people of action were breaking up companies, dividing them up, sorting plants into 'effective' and 'ineffective', tearing valuable individual items out of businesses and appropriating them in the form of general partnerships, limited liability companies or even individual property. That was acting and not thinking.

In one of the factories in the chemically blackened sector of the Buna chemical works near Halle, in previous decades, the foremen and engineers had been happy to restart production in 187 repair cases. Now, as a result of DISRPUTION, the organizational-economic ground on which this industry was based collapsed. In a way that was similar to how, during an earthquake, an abyss opens up and swallows a piece of the upper world, accounting funnels emerged (on the highly organized ground of second, accounting-based nature). In safes, on inventories and balance sheets. This ground wasn't laid down in the language of land registers, but in the accounting language of socialist economics, in a form of slang or, as far as Western markets were concerned, oddly articulated expressions.

AN ODD COUNTER-IMAGE TO THE GARDEN
OF EDEN DEEP IN EASTERN RUSSIA

A somewhat peculiar type of Russian oligarch had set up a ZOOLOGICAL GARDEN OF WORLD INTELLIGENCE in a remote corner of the Russian Far East with 17 gardeners, 6 organizers, 4 designers and 10 helpers. The wealthy man had originally bought the land suspecting that a new spaceport would be built there to replace the Baikonur spaceport in Kazakhstan. But, as it turned out, it ended up being just a little too far away. And so the oligarch decided to change focus. He was also moved by the proximity to the stars which, despite a certain distance, still symbolized the new space centre to the neighbourhood.

And that is how the INTELLIGENCE PARK came into being. There, among plants, paths, sheds and excavated, already concreted cellars for future buildings, there were images to see. Each of the pictures, set up on poles, designating an example of human intelligence. Moreover, there were collective posters which gave overviews of all the different species of intelligence: 12,000 types of intelligence were currently exercised on earth. In addition to 18,000 historical, archaic examples. Eight hoped-for and planned new types.

No one came. The journey from Moscow or St Petersburg took too long. Even the founder never showed his face in the province. He had, however, sent scouts off into the world to track down ever-new descriptions of special forms of intelligence that had been previously unknown to him and not yet been represented in his garden. Boxes of material lay on site, waiting to be processed. The distance from this 'paradise of intelligence' to the Pacific Ocean and Vladivostok was the same. You could catch a glimpse of the launch pads of the new spaceport, gradually rising into the air, through the bushes and trees.

Wortfeld
„Temperamente der Intelligenz"

rational

schlau

„Voller Witz in den Augen"

kundig

schlau   „Witz im Überlebenskamp"

„Mutterwitz"

Intelligenz im „Rust Belt" an der Ostküste der USA
(einer verwüsteten Industriezone)

Intelligenz der Slums

„Plebejische Intelligenz"

„Voll von Erfahrung"

„Dumm geworden vor Intelligenz"

AKADEMISCHE INTELLIGENZ—unverzichtbar,
nirgends ausreichend ...

Mathematischer Verstand

Orientierung

Überblick

„abstrakte Anschauung"

Tasten

Kontaktintelligenz

FIGURE 119. [Semantic Field 'Temperaments of Intelligence']

Kühles Denken

Unterscheidungs-

Findigkeit

„Erfahrungsgesättigte
Vernunft"

Kristalliner Ver-

„GLÜHENDE MOTIVATION"

WILDE GEDANKEN

ALGORITHMEN /

klug
geistegegenwärtig

GEGENALGORITHMEN

Geistig beweglich

„Sekundenschnell blitzte es in ihren Augen"

„Melanchthons und Reuchlins versöhnende
Intelligenz"

Intelligenz der Fußsohle

Intelligenz der Haut

INTELLIGENZ DER GEFÜHLE

„Außerirdische Intelligenz"

„Fremde, die uns längst besuchten /
Nur dass wir einander nicht erkannten"

„Man kann nicht lernen, nicht zu lernen"

„Unabweisbarkeit der Intelligenz"

„Eigensinn der Intelligenz"

FIGURE 120

'DRINKING SONG
OF THE LIGHTHEARTED LANDSCAPES'

The best successor to Mozart's MAGIC FLUTE, the poet and composer of DAS MÄDCHEN AUS DER FEENWELT ODER DER
BAUER ALS MILIONÄR, Ferdinand Raimund, composed the following song: 'Knowledge, you glowing star, / I see you neither near
nor far / But how I wish that you were mine . . .' In order to find
intelligence, Raimund says, I must get rid of all of my assumptions.
Only then would I know what it was, of what it was made and what
it might bring to pass.

Assuming that intelligence is based on discrimination and that
it is not rooted in any one of our senses, but in the vast spaces between
them—then it would be a rhizome, a root-work: 'intelligence of
feelings'. That would certainly be a light, fleeting, even aeronautical
being.

Rage, courage, the sense of identity, genealogy, prejudice,
hunger, allegiance, ambition, self-realization, desire, powerful
memory—what massive forces these are compared to the attributes
of intelligence, which have a lot of nerve but not all that much mus-
cle! What's more, we humans have been living in a SECOND
NATURE since the Anthropocene, but even more accelerated in the
last 100 years or so. All our individual forces have been dug into
social senses and forces, into abstract systems of control. Embedded
in the commodity fetish: that GREAT ECONOMY which separates
us from the soul's arable soil in which we once grew. We are cloud
animals. The achievements of intelligence lag far behind in the wake.

TIME'S SPHERICAL SHAPE /
THE EVOLUTIONARY
ARCHITECTURE OF BIOMASS AND SOUL

MONDAY, 28 APRIL 2021. DIARY

Richard Langston's in his office at the University of North Carolina, Chapel Hill. Six time zones away from me. The Atlantic between us. Skype bridges the gap. Today we're talking about the difficulty of coming up with a semantic field for 'Differences of Time'.[3]

Is time a solid, liquid, gas or plasma? Can it assume one of these aggregate states or all of them? All this spoken in analogy and metaphorically. If time forms a plasma: does time in this aggregate state then decompose into its elements? What are these elements? And could these fragments then condense in such a way that time has uniformity and radiance? Can time radiate energy like a sun?

Langston points out that translating these kinds of questions into English isn't that easy, nor would it be that easy to find people interested in answering them in a club in suburban Chicago. What kind of club? One that makes vinyl records. Various groups in the area (coming from the Chicago techno tradition) deliver the music, which then spreads to Amsterdam, Moscow and Shanghai. What we do, they say, is called rhythm. 'We're chasing frequencies through our equipment, breaking up wave motion, then reassembling it. That's music.' I don't really think, Langston says, this group is interested in semantic fields. 'But they are practically dealing with different kinds of time,' I reply.

---

3 Richard Langston is the author of *Dark Matter* (New York, 2020) and the translator of the English edition of Negt / Kluge, *History & Obstinancy*. There one can find 'an atlas of concepts' for which he is responsible. We are trying to come up with a similar atlas for *The Book of Commentary*. Hence our Skype conversations, which, during the completion of this book, we have every Monday at 3 p.m. CET.

Let's assume, I say, that we are swimmers. Water creatures. And that we swim in TIME. In the Harz mountains, there are waters that are calm and smooth on the surface. They flow slowly. A few metres deeper, such a watercourse has a *rapid* current. You can feel it with your feet. If, while diving in the water, you get caught in a vortex of this current, and if this happens in a narrow passage, of which the rock bed of the river has several, you can be swept away and drown. This river is called the Kalte Bode (the 'cold' Bode). In some places, it forms pools. You can stand there with your feet on the bottom. Mud. Fish swimming around your legs. Underwater plants. The river of time, I conclude the thought, shows more differences (between the mud and rushing tide) than the water I've described.

The sun that's bathing Langston's study in light (I can see it from my place in Munich, where it's overcast) on the other side of the Atlantic plays a role in our conversation. There's a six-hour difference in its position in the sky between he and I, yet we speak and see each other at the same time. We are simultaneously describing how strange the PRESENCE OF ALL TIMES between aeon and second is for us at every moment. We live in a time wave of 200,000 years, and at the same time in one of about 60 years, as well as in the present day and in the concrete hour and minute. Time, Langston points to a corresponding diary entry by Sergei Eisenstein, has a SPHERICAL SHAPE. This contradicts the idea of the 'arrow of time moving forward'. Time's a fraud, Langston says, when it claims that it's always rushing forward, that it's only working towards progress.

In the attempt to create semantic fields, it seems to us both that *one* word can rarely describe a quality of time streams, time mountains, time grains. We're still wavering on whether it is better to describe time as 'fluid' or 'granular'. Are there such things as sandstorms of time? Tsunamis in which time condenses?

FIGURE 121. A piece of one of Langston's notes,
where he records the results of our conversations.

THE ZONE OF MYSELF

A self in its housing of chitin. So it can fly to all horizons. But
it cannot grow to any size. Nor can it become as 'agile as a gazelle'.
It cannot extend its neck to the highest branches of the trees (like
a giraffe). For that, the ego would have to be constructed as a skeleton. Human imagination is also unable to exist in a solid shell. It
needs to be suspended in a skeletal structure.

THE ARCHITECTONIC EVOLUTION OF PROTEIN MASSES (OF 'LIVING THINGS', OF THE 'SPIRIT')

When the spine and head emerged, evolution split into two lines. In
the group from which we originate, the backboned (the dorsal), the
axis between the skull and the anus ran across the back. A second
form of the axis between 'front' and 'back', the brain and the end of
the body, developed separately. These became the BELLY-BONED
(the ventral), the insects.

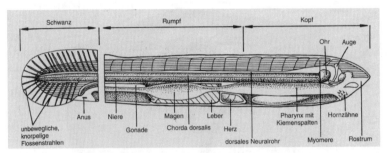

FIGURE 122. The body plan of a so-called craniate (that is, with a skull of hard bone or cartilage). The transition to the vertebrates. From here, the split between us and insects.

AN EVENING CONVERSATION ON THE BEACH

One evening on a beach in Denmark, Bert Brecht and Walter Benjamin debated this 'difference in evolutionary architecture'. In the case of the belly-boned, Brecht said, the biomass was enclosed in a kind of barrel or container. One could certainly hang more protein on a skeleton, a 'bony clothesline', and swing, twist and screw the whole thing in a bolder way than if you were to enclose the biomass as in the body of a ship. Insects lack differentiation. Does, Brecht continued, 'aggressivity out of the spirit of hunger', out of the 'materialism' of socialist revolution, prevent gut feeling, the generous unfolding of all ANIMAL SPIRITS? Would it be easier to organize the forces of human nature in the most diverse directions under socialism in the construction of the 'anti-belly' of ideas and dreams? China is considered to be the 'Middle Kingdom'. Are the Chinese and socialists 'belly-boned'? Are they like ants? What if it had to do with the superior skeletal structure of human beings' elemental power, the antithesis of 'materialism'? Benjamin simply listened, Brecht spoke incessantly, dusk fell, the sea rushed to the shore with great persuasiveness.

COMMENTARY
OF AN EAST PRUSSIAN FORTUNE TELLER

An East Prussian aristocrat, Ulrich von Finckenstein, authorized signatory in a Berlin bank and astrologer. In the 1930s, and even at the beginning of the war, he provided a trusted circle of his peers with predictions about the future. He had a special sense of foreboding. In the 1940s, he predicted that he himself was facing the 'imminent danger of a brutal deprivation of liberty'. He trusted his 'inner oracle'.

These premonitions, on the basis of which he prophesied never consisted of words but, though they did not present any scenes, of signs that he knew how to read. They were always linked to a certain indeterminacy. Finckenstein believed that he was threatened with arrest. So he used his connections within the navy to get himself drafted into a voyage aboard a steamer that—as of 1941—was to land a team of meteorologists in East Greenland. The aim was to establish a secret meteorological station. There, it seemed to the fortune teller, he would be safe from arrest in the German Reich. The steamer, however, was captured by a British destroyer. Finckenstein spent several years in a prison camp (deprived of his freedom, as he had foreseen but imagined differently).

In the days of his freedom, when he was an admired figure in Königsberg, and especially in Berlin society, he was popular with the theologians at Berlin University. Thus, in private, purely on the level of social contacts, he had acquired theological-professional knowledge for the interpretation of religious texts. Now and again, he surprised his mentors, who had academic rank but did not know everything, with certain intellectual about-faces (as he did in horsemanship too).

The tale of Balaam and his donkey (Numbers 22: 21–39), he recited over a few twilight pints in Dahlem, had been misunderstood. This donkey, with Balaam on its back, refused to go on. Nothing could persuade the stubborn animal to alter its obstinacy. The donkey had seen the *angel* blocking the way. Its master Balaam, on the other hand, hadn't seen a thing and continued to strive towards the fateful goal. In Arabic, Finckenstein explained (speaking casually, incidentally, without any lecturing tone, all the listeners were superior to him in scientific rank), the Hebrew word for 'donkey' refers to the pineal gland in the human head. He knew this from his interrogation of an Arab prisoner of war in North Africa. The pineal gland as the 'seat of better knowledge'. Numbers 22 is not really concerned with a stubborn beast of burden, but the lamp of Balaam's soul. Its 'better insight'. In a conversational tone, Finckenstein listed the 'patron saints of 1939':

The 'donkey within me'

'The light in the solar plexus right next to the heart'

The 'farmer within me'

The 'blacksmith within me'

The 'horse breeder within me'

The 'mysterious angel within me' = the adept of secret texts, the 'reader of the starry skies'

With the latter, Finckenstein alluded to his knowledge of astrology, on which he based his predictions.

A GLANCE OUT THE WINDOW OF MY STUDY

In the park, there's a young woman standing in a wall of sun that's surrounding the trees, sniffing her hair. She's holding it in front of her nose like a stalk.

'AREAS FOR FUTURE DEVELOPMENT'

Two women are pushing their carriages through the park, with freshly born children inside them. The babies are outdoors to fill up on oxygen. Up to 90 years of expectation lie ahead of them. An enormous amount of time. You rarely see horses in the city.

THE MURMURING OF
THE PILOT FISH

FIGURE 123 (ABOVE). A pilot fish with its characteristic white stripes.
When excited, the white stripes begin to glow.

FIGURE 124 (BELOW). 'In a convoy'. Pilotfish with shark.

FIGURE 125. The pilot fish's 'nervous' white stripes.

FIGURE 126 (ABOVE). 'Falling Intellectuals and the Mouth of the Large Fish'. From the series: 'James Ensor and the Japanese Ghosts'. Aluminium print, 2020.

FIGURE 127 (BELOW). 'Brothers beneath the Starry Skies'. Aluminium print, 2020.

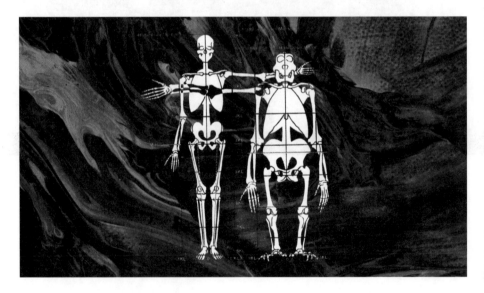

NAUCRATES DICTOR (THE PILOT FISH)

Pilot fish clean the skin of their impressively larger hosts. Which are usually predators. Marine scientists say that pilot fish are excellent navigators. Without them, large predatory fish such as sharks and voracious sea turtles would hardly be able to orient themselves correctly. At night in the tropics, and even in the black of the underwater night, they say, the PILOT FISH INTERNATIONAL correspond with one another. Exchange experiences. A buzz develops. Often over thousands of nautical miles.

Along with ravens, pilot fish belong to the HERALDIC ANIMALS OF INTELLIGENCE. Evolution has proven the value they possess in relation to the giant bodies of predatory fish, what with the latter's tendency to lose their way, and this use protects them.

The quanta of intelligence behave similarly in the human kingdom: unpredictably on the move, hardly muscular, small-scale. Fortune seekers, but navigators too. Tolerated in the maw of real conditions. But one unintentional convulsive swallowing movement of the BIG FISH in whose mouth we live—and intelligence will have disappeared deep inside.

A STORY THAT HAD A GREAT EFFECT ON ME AS A CHILD . . .

My maid Magda often took me to see her father-in-law, a retired civil servant who had once been a sailor, on Richard-Wagner Strasse. He was the father of Magda's bridegroom, Sergeant Major Hans Bügelsack. Though the resident troublemaker at home, there I would fall silent for hours. Listening.

This old sailor was the one who told me the story about how pilot fish live in the mouths of sharks, their hosts. About how the large predators do not swallow them. Indeed, the pilot fish help the big fish navigate, often saving their hosts from the deadly dangers of the seas.

If a pilot fish gets too deep into a shark's mouth or even its oesophagus, the big fish simply burps and sweeps the small fish back towards its teeth with a strong burst of air. The teeth are distributed chaotically in the front of the mouth. Sharks are extremely old animals. A species that has not changed for millions of years. Whatever has been so tried and tested by evolution possesses nobility and knows loyalty. Sharks save pilot fish at any cost. THAT is what the sailor had to report. Just as the pilot fish ensure that their sharks find schools of fish and grind their teeth. Most of the story's details were pure fantasy.

WHY DID THE PILOT FISH *NOT* DISAPPEAR INTO THE BOWELS OF ITS PREDATORS, BUT HUMAN INTELLIGENCE COULD VERY WELL DO SO IN THE ABYSS OF THE MARKETPLACE?

There is a famous biblical story about how an intelligent man named Jonah is swallowed by a big fish but survives in its belly. Then, thanks to his faith in God and a belch, he is spat out on land and lives to a ripe old age as living proof of God.

This incident was vigorously debated in a seminar at Johann Wolfgang Goethe University, Frankfurt am Main, at the time it had been renamed Karl Marx University. Comrades of the Socialist German Students' League (SDS) took the floor. The question was HOW DOES STUDENT PROTEST BEHAVE IN CAPITALISM, HOW DOES INTELLIGENCE DEFEND ITSELF AGAINST BEING DEVOURED? The comrades pointed to the analysis in Marx's work: historically, intelligence is initially subject only to FORMAL SUBSUMPTION UNDER CAPITAL. 'The Archbishop of Salzburg cannot tell Mozart how to compose the Mass that the Church has ordered him to write.' Formal subsumption (subjugation) means indirect rule by capital or the Church. The labour power of industry, on the other hand, the proletariat, is subject to 'REAL

SUBSUMPTION'. Were this to happen in the modern age or to intelligence in the future: what then?

The event was chaired by Hans-Jürgen Krahl. He spoke about the barracking of intelligence, the factory-like recruitment of intelligence's resources under late capitalism. The taking away of the authentic expression of intelligence. That was REAL SUBSUMPTION: the taking away of the means of production, the seizure of the rebellious power of intelligence in the system: that alone was the event horizon. Krahl followed this up with his thesis that it was precisely this, the devouring of intelligence, that would turn its REBELLIOUS POTENTIAL INTO A NEW REALITY. The 'life form of intelligence' introduced into the stomach of capital bursts the 'body' of capital. It forces the 'system' to explode.

One of the comrades wanted to extend this idea into praxis. The expression 'explosion of the body of capital' didn't do anything for her, because capital, she said with a raised voice, had no 'body'. Therefore, she assumed that the rebelliousness of 'intelligence displaced into nothingness' would have to express itself differently. She returned to the pilot fish in the mouth of the predator. How does the pilot fish 'change' and how does it in turn change the predator fish? Did the predator fish end up becoming an intelligent being just because it ate the pilot fish (or a large amount of it)?

The comrades who took part in the debate complained that there was no known example of a historical event on such a scale. In any case, they knew nothing about it. One group agreed that there must always be a way out, a way 'out of coercion and into freedom' (in line with Kant's concept of freedom). And so they proposed—it was a group of Germanists—to speak about it in the grammatical form of the future perfect tense: What will have become of the rebellious student intelligentsia in 50 years' time if it does or does not do something this week? This clarified Krahl's question into a question of political actuality.

REMEMBERING HANS-JÜRGEN KRAHL

Back in those days of the student protest movement in which Hans-Jürgen Krahl was working on his manuscript *Konstituion und Klassenkampf. Zur historichen Dialektik von bürgerlicher Emanzipation und proletarischer Revolution* (Constitution and Class Struggle. On the Historical Dialectic of Bourgeois Emancipation and Proletarian Revolution), I would meet him at his local by Bockenheimer Warte. The manuscript is about the relationship between the INTELLEC-TUAL CLASS and the WORKING CLASS. Krahl was also familiar with the metaphor of the 'pilot fish in the mouth of the shark'. Like me, this image seemed to him to be a good comparison for the 'role of intelligence in the environment of power'.

His manuscript had to do with the observation that, in the history of socialism, the 'proletarian masses' were almost always 'led' by members of the intelligentsia. What qualifies the intelligentsia—which initially had long periods of control over its own means of production (it only had to deliver the results to capital)—to 'lead' the rebellion of the masses? The Marxist theorist Alfred Sohn-Rethel was a research associate at Mitteleuropäischen Wirtschaftstag, a lobbying group for the leading German industrial enterprises, banks and business associations. He had made a significant contribution to a key concept of socialism, a combination of the commodity fetish with the concept of logic. According to Krahl, an intellectual in the centre of power acts as an 'explosive body' for the destruction of that power! Such observations always brought the 'chance of the pilot fish' into the debate's field of vision.

At the Bockenheimer Warte pub, Krahl was protected by comrade Riechmann's giant body. Student comrades and young workers were sitting around the table. Krahl began with a 'training session'. Being shot dead by assassins, something that had already happened to so many other comrades of the workers' movement, was never supposed to happen to this 'revolutionary' spirit, comrade Krahl. Riechmann would have recognized such a person the second they stepped inside. He would have pinned the perpetrator with his shoulders and strong arms. Removed the gun or the knife. That, or his big body would have stood in front of Krahl and taken the bullet, the knife, the deadly weapon.

IN THE JARGON OF THE 1968 PROTEST MOVEMENT

A night-time discussion with Krahl. Not the party, a FUNCTION-ALIST ORGANIZATION, but THE OPEN AND DECENTRALLY SELF-ORGANIZING INTELLIGENCE comes into consideration as the 'head of the proletariat'. 'Head', Krahl added, is a metaphor here and, as an expression, precarious. Because intelligence is not to be found in the head alone. Nor in an academy. The self-organizing and rebellious power of intelligence is located between all heads, in the eyes, it has its seat in the hand, on the skin. Our conversation deepened.

–Intellectual power, just like labour power, is in every proletarian's head. As a substance. Unprofessional.
–Indeed, we're against professionalism.
– . . . but 'power' organizes itself cooperatively, and that looks as if it's been 'trained'.
–Trained or rebellious?
–Rebelliously trained.
–And furthermore, captured in a collectively legible 'script'.
–Namely, in the commodity fetish. The soul's lamp in commodities, the cipher of life. The life script of the producers of these commodities . . .
–And thirdly in happiness. You can gather that up. That's what the poets do.

Krahl didn't want to go that far. I continue to debate with him at night today.

'INTELLIGENCE OF THE SKIN'

In his letter of reply to Albert Einstein, 'Why War?', Sigmund Freud states that it is unlikely that the moral forces in people prevent war or even slow it down. In case of doubt, he writes, the instances of morality prolong the course of war and increase its energy. In contrast, the skin is a 'natural counter-agent'. In the misery of the trenches of Flanders, and under the moon-like conditions of war in the Alps, removed as they were from the human form of existence, unwashed, irritated by fear, this skin responds in the form of allergies. Freud writes that he has seen ghastly markings of such protest on people's naked skin. Similarly, in cases of stress and extreme danger, the outer skin of the pilot fish changes colour. And this is why natives of the Pacific Islands consider the pilot fish 'inedible'. Intelligence of the skin.

A MARCO POLO TYPE'S VISIT TO SILICON VALLEY

I deal in vaccines. In a market regulated by the authorities, you could call me a black marketeer. I buy my black-market goods ex-factory. The pallets of vaccine for Tel Aviv, for example, and for addresses in the Gulf states. This is the foundation of my 'kingdom'. It consists of a few warehouses and hiding places. These depots are always located near transport routes. They are global locations close to 'cash-rich communities'. In the case of West Coast of the US—as wealthy as the southern coast of the Persian Gulf, as Israel, as Hong Kong (still)—'close proximity' is defined as 6,900 miles. Given the trafficability of small aircraft (loading time, flight time, delivery) on earth, that is still a 'short distance in time'. My life-saving vaccines reach the addressees 'promptly'.

At the moment, I'm on the road to Silicon Valley, with shaking bones. This VALLEY: what kind of 'valley' is it anyway? It looks like a plain to me, flat land. Nothing here seems 'rural'. But I wouldn't call any of it 'urban' either.

When I imagine all this land awaiting the construction of an imagined 'spaceport of humanity', a site preparing for radical development, that's what I would say Silicon Valley reminds me of. A collection of individual buildings, warehouses, a plain of sand crumbs ('silicon') and cement ('silicon' as well). Something that, in the future, will cover both land and city. Individual APARTMENT-BLOCK TOWERS IN A NON-LANDSCAPE. This is the seat of the highest possible power of disposition in the world today.

I am a philologist by profession, a linguist. I am also a 'European'. In my two original professions and in my origin from the 'province of Europe', I am 'unrecognizable' here, appearing in one of the meeting rooms. They think that I'm an oddity, a 'native of somewhere'. They are polite. Sitting across me is a mixed population. A pair of Chinese eyes, a pale and freckled Irish face, several Indian countenances and thinking foreheads: where a gifted mathematician comes from, an algorithmicist, is not predetermined. Like a magnet—or a gravitationally highly effective celestial body—the Silicon Valley algorithm centre attracts talent from 'all corners of the world'.

As a 'real human being', however, I still have not arrived. Up to San Francisco International Airport, the journey went smoothly enough, then the change from bus, taxi, fast train, taxi again. My quarters, among the last ones available, are 70 kilometres away from all my meeting points with the decision-makers.

I'd have been happy to present my concept of the ANTI-ALGORITHM here. That would be the sum of all the texts and experiences of the 9,000 years that preceded digitality. From Uruk to the abolition of the gold standard at Bretton Woods.

As I said, it's not my competence but the virus' power of attack that has surprised the congregation sitting before me at plastic tables. Though masters of the digital world, they are not masters of aerosols. And therefore I, double inoculated though I may be (the 'proprietor' of seven 'pharmacies', i.e. secret depots with sufficiently deep-frozen pallets of the vaccine, 'master of the situation'), must wear my mask, just like they do.

FIGURE 128. Conference room. All of us with muzzles over our mouths.

A HORNET'S NEST OF ELEGANT ALGORITHMS

I am visiting this imperium, this HORNET'S NEST OF ELEGANT ALGORITHMS, for the twelfth time. Nothing reminds you of the splendour of ancient palaces where rulers designed their own likeness. 'Being more than appearing'. No, it's the 'nonchalance of exercising power'. The trainers, the sports shirts though no one's playing any sports, the Babylonian variety of expressions: all speech a draft . . . They consider us Europeans to be a grotesque apparition just by the way we sit, by how, dishevelled and shattered, almost 'with the loss of all spirit', we step out of the hotel room we just managed to get and show up at the meeting. They refer to me as 'a Marco Polo who got his directions all wrong'.

What I'm saying about the need to populate the vast empty spaces between algorithmic assumptions with 'oases' is the concept of the ANTI-ALGORITHM. Heraclitus can't be reproduced by a Wikipedia article. This kind of 'spiritual-gravitational heavyweight' belongs *between* the simplifications (= giving simplified commands to a machine called 'algorithm').

A Göttingen School algorithm is a set of instructions, a set of rules, for conceptual processes, for the 'gradual extension of mathematics to the limits of what's provable'. This is the 'via moderna', 'mathematical experience', a scouting on the horizons of the imagination. I am a 'Göttingen School' enthusiast. At lunchtime, after eating a terrible package of soggy white bread with lettuce leaves and rotten ham, each of us recognizing our mutual non-appetite, it becomes apparent that we are becoming more familiar with one another.

This morning I, the philologist, European and advocate of the world spirit, see a completely different problem. I recognize the need for cartography in holographic extension. In other words, the very thing that my counterparts are technically able to envisage to some extent, the 3D industry, instructs us to build bridges between the artefact of the 'informational concentrate' (the size of a fingernail, the reproducible image of the flowering of the classical industry of 1939: the 'best years of our lives') and the real conditions in which we live: our bodies, cells, fears and our courage—by no means compromises, always beings. Before I became a philologist, and long before I became a vaccine dealer, I studied law. I am an advocate for the world that wants to be born again. It would be a pity if my weakness today caused us to miss the NEW BEGINNING. I'm still a bit wobbly from the journey, somewhat paralysed by the slowness of those across from me, who cannot seem to break free that quickly from the routine of their PROGRESS. I notice that they aren't listening to me. At times, it takes from 7 to 12 minutes to decide whether a *development* is working out. I'd like to be understood. At the moment, no one in this room understands me, but they all expect me to deliver the coveted vaccine. Hope—it's as potent as any drug.

NOTES and SOURCES

References to stories, texts and films in Alexander Kluge's *oeuvre* that can be used as supplements to the stations in this book.

[The titles translated into English appear in parentheses. All page numbers refer to the German editions.—Trans.]

→HOW DOES ONE TELL A STORY FROM FAR AWAY?

Telling a story about something the author themselves cannot 'touch' excites me. The unknown itches to be told. The poet Arno Schmidt called this the 'Karl May effect'. Something like this applies, for example, to the stars and to the cosmos.

- The six-year-old within me and the starry sky above me. *In Tür an Tür mit einem anderen Leben*, p. 606.
- Solar camera Jupiter. *Geschichten vom Kino (Cinema Stories)*, p. 15.
- The cosmos as cinema. *Geschichten vom Kino*, p. 44.
- *The Sound of the Planet Uranus & the Song of the Gorillas*. Film, 2021.
- A humming of lamps of the soul. Jacobins flying to the moon in a balloon. *Das Bohren harter Bretter (Drilling through Hard Boards)*, p. 89.
- Metempsychosis according to Fourier. Prolegomena of any rational astrology. *Die Lücke, die der Teufel lässt*, p. 886.
- Stores space / Primary unease / Fly where? *Die Lücke*, pp. 319–88.
- Loss of the planet. *Chronik der Gefühle*, VOL. 2, Chapter 11: Lernprozesse mit tödlichen Ausgang, pp. 827–920.

The Sound of the Planet Uranus & the Song of the Gorillas.
9 min 10 sec

**'THE UNIVERSE SLEEPS
ON ITS GIGANTIC EAR, ITS
PAWS STUDDED WITH STARS . . .'**

→HOW DOES ONE TELL A STORY FROM UP CLOSE?

Stories that deal with the subjective side of human life are called BASIC STORIES. The lion's share of personal experience is made by people in the world of work and in the intimate spheres. Basic stories have to do with the latter, with closeness and separation, with happiness and the search for happiness.

- Foreign languages in love. *Die Lücke, die der Teufel lässt*, p. 213.
- The dear mouth which also kisses dogs. *Die Lücke*, p. 684.
- Secret love. *Tür an Tür mit einem anderen Leben*, p. 117.
- Love lasts the blink of an eye, art is forever. *Geschichten vom Kino* (*Cinema Stories*), p. 67.
- Mass death in Venice. *Chronik der Gefühle*, VOL. 2, p. 461.
- With skin and hair: Basic stories. *Die Lücke*, pp. 437–506.
- Between being alive and being dead / What does being alive mean? *Die Lücke*, pp. 9–104.
- Siamese hands / Between love and barbarism: Basic stories. *Tür an Tür*, pp. 485–533.
- Islands of life and death. *Tür an Tür*, pp. 535–607.
- To what degree is love a republican virtue? *Tür an Tür*, p. 500.
- Is the labyrinth an appropriate metaphor for love? *Das Labyrinth der zärtlichen Kraft* (*The Labyrinth of Tender Force*), pp. 93–113.
- Derivates of the tender force. *Das Labyrinth* pp. 205–33.
- Love makes one clairvoyant. *Chronik der Gefühle*, VOL. 2, p. 371.
- The princess of Clèves. Love politics. The obstinacy of intimacy. *Das Labyrinth*, pp. 441–568.
- Love as a heavy labourer. *Kongs grosse Stunde* (*Kong's Finest Hour*), p. 339.
- The empire of freedom and the empire of necessity in love. *Kongs grosse Stunde*, p. 486.
- Equalization of love and procreation in the world that follows Silicon Valley. *Kongs grosse Stunde*, p. 486.
- The sharp breath of freedom / 'Carmen as the Other'. *News & Stories* from 21 October 1991.

- Cinderella wins the king and is strangled / A famous Chinese epic. *News & Stories* from 22 November 1993.
- 'Your tears provoke my longing' / Tosca and the police chief. *News & Stories* from 27 April 1998.

FIGURE 129. 'On the way to the workshop'.

→COMMENTARIES ON THE ANTAGONISTIC CONCEPT OF REALISM

In the life of the person who examines the facts, there is an emotionally intense COUNTER-REACTION towards realities which grossly disturb the emotions, intense desires, interests, needs and, in general, obstinacy. This resistance to the real from within activates not only in the case of existential threats (I don't want to die!), but already begins in the everyday (I don't want to finish my food!) and possesses political potential: 'If acts of executive power or environmental changes result in gross violations of vital interests, an intensity of defence arises that turns an everyday relationship into a political one.'

If this defence mechanism cannot be materialized and expressed publicly, the political becomes apolitical. Turns into repression and abstraction. The 'anti' is therefore always directed concretely against reality, which does not have my best interests in mind, and fights it either directly (politically) or indirectly (fantastically). The basal phenomenon is just as real as so-called reality. People act internally and externally according to the rules of the ANTI-REALISM OF FEELING, or they are not realists. The poles in anti-realism *both* have the character of reality.

- The sharpest ideology: that reality invokes its realistic character. *Gelegenheitsarbeit einer Sklavin. Zur realitischen Methode*, p. 214.
- The role of fantasy. *Gelegenheitsarbeit einer Sklavin*, p. 241.
- The five senses—sensuality of context. *Gelegenheitsarbeit einer Sklavin*, p. 211.
- The realistic method and the so-called 'filmic'. *Gelegenheitsarbeit einer Sklavin*, p. 201.
- The indestructability of the political. *Kongs grosse Stunde* (*Kong's Finest Hour*), pp. 249–95.
- Can a community say I? *Die Lücke, die der Teufel lässt*, pp. 105–93.
- What does power mean? / Who can I trust? *Die Lücke, die der Teufel lässt*, pp. 507–627.

- Signs of power's decline. *Chronik der Gefühle*, VOL. 1, pp. 147–305.
- The principles of life on Black Friday. *Chronik der Gefühle*, VOL. 1, pp. 127–41.

PROTEGO

ERGO SUM

'I am able to protect, therefore I am.' According to Thomas Hobbes, this is how the king or sovereign speaks: 'fidelity contract versus social contract'.

→HOW DOES ONE TELL A STORY ABOUT AEON? / LONGUE DURÉE / 'THE FLASH OF A SECOND'

- The chronicle of Pangaea up through today. In *Kongs grosse Stunde* (*Kong's Finest Hour*), pp. 527–654.
- The chronicle of a second. *Kongs grosse Stunde*, p. 630.
- *The Chronicle of a Second*. Film triptych. In exhibition at Foundation Beyeler, Basel: *Hommage an Georg Baselitz.*
- Like lucky children of the first globalization. In *Tür an Tür mit einem anderen Leben*, pp. 9–55.
- The long march of basic trust. In *Chronik der Gefühle*, VOL. 2, pp. 921–1010.

→HOW DOES ONE TELL A STORY
ABOUT CROSSROADS (TURNING POINTS)?

- Is there a dividing line between ages? / Paris, June 1940. In *Die Lücke, die der Teufel lässt*, pp. 195–254.
- '*Spring with White Flags*': *The Surrender of 1945*. Film-length, 61 min. 2021.
- *Lamento on the Flooding of the Kali Mines to the South of the Harz*. Film triptych. 2021.
- *The DDR's Last Autumn*. Film triptych. 2021.
- The crush effect (Stories on 11 September 2001). In *Die Lücke, die der Teufel lässt*, p. 85.

→HOW DOES ONE TELL A STORY
ABOUT HUMAN LABOUR POWER?

- Passages from ideological antiquity: Labour / Obstinacy. In *Das fünfte Buch*, pp. 161–221.
- Oskar Negt / Alexander Kluge, *Geschichte und Eigensinn* (*History and Obstinacy*).

→'SCRAPPING THROUGH WORK'

- 'Scrapping through Work' in *Chronik der Gefühle*, VOL. 2, p. 101.
- The attempt to think simply. *Chronik der Gefühle*, VOL. 2, p. 286.
- A Nazi of Science. *Chronik der Gefühle*, VOL. 2, p. 291.
- Bieske's severely cold radar: 'that evil and violence at one point of our globe are felt at all points of it'—*Chronik der Gefühle*, VOL. 2, p. 304.
- *Storage Fees*. Film. In *Früchte des Vertrauens / Finanzkrise, Adam Smith, Keynes, Marx und wir selbst: Auf was kann man sich verlassen?* DVD I: Die Unruhe des Geldes, Nr 14.
- Industrial landscape with sun and moon simultaneously. *Chronik der Gefühle*, VOL. 2, p. 299.

FIGURE 130

Bohrgerät Glück

Auge Kopf Hand Kraft Atem

"Fingerspitzen-gefühl"

FIGURES 131–33

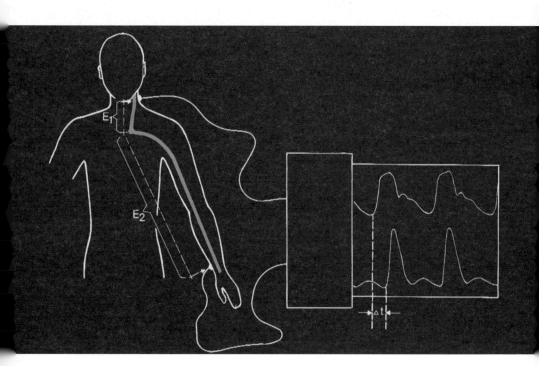

FIGURE 134

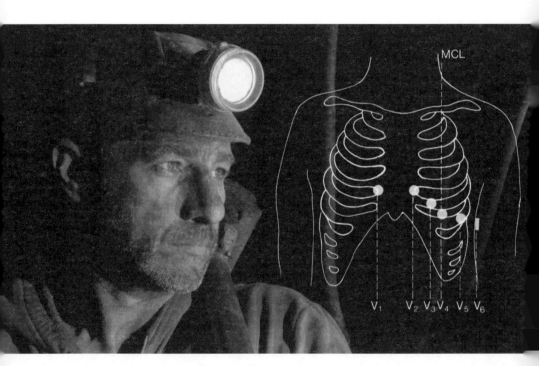

FIGURE 135

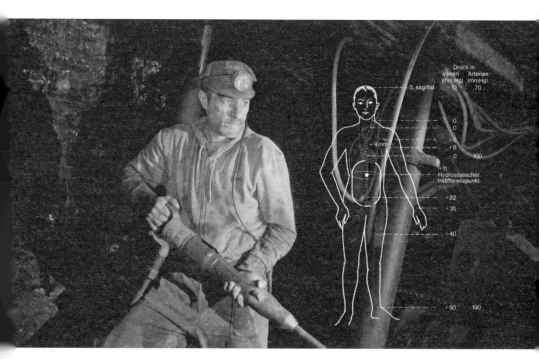

FIGURE 136

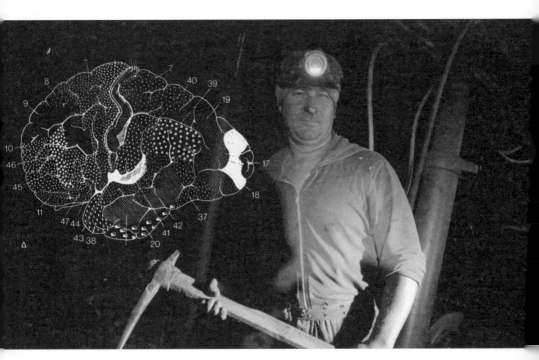

FIGURE 137

FIGURE 138

Tasten, Schrauben, Bohren ...

Schieben, Prüfen,

Atem, Muskeln, Schätzwert

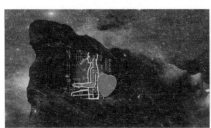

Der Gesamtarbeiter

FIGURE 139

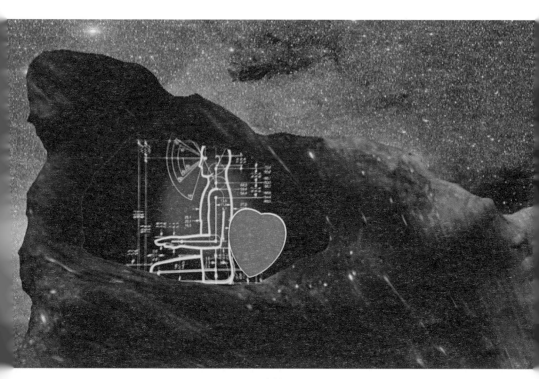

FIGURE 140

FIGURE 141. [The total labourer]

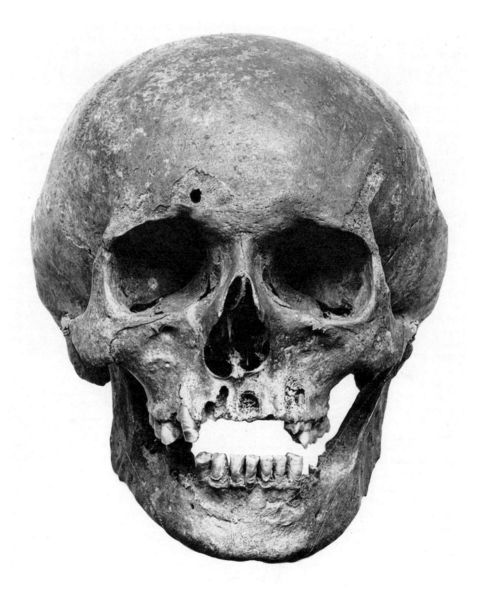

FIGURE 142

RTL 4 DECEMBER 2017, *10 VOR 11*

LEIBNIZ AND THE MATHEMATICS OF SNAKES

Leo van Hemmen:
'Every point on the scale of the senses has its own mind'

Pit vipers are snakes that, in addition to their eyes, have infrared sensors on their heads or 'pits'. In the desert's sea of sand, these snakes' two jaws sway to the rhythm of the waves as their prey approaches. The thermal images through which the data reaches the snake's calculating brain, biophysicist Leo van Hemmen says, are incredibly blurry. Nevertheless, in the end, the maps in the brain created 'with the mathematics of snakes' are so precise that the snake strikes in a flash.

Modern biophysics uses such processes in which several independent senses interact 'multi-modally' to investigate the intrinsic laws of the senses, but the innovative impetus for robots too. The scales on which the elementary processes of perception take place are separated from each other in humans—as they are in snakes. The neurons know nothing about the psychology they are, in fact, building.

Modern biophysics comes to similar conclusions as the great philosopher Leibniz: everything elementary consists of blind monads. And yet these autonomous monads produce a whole that functions as reality. Our human neurons have never seen the starry sky for themselves. And yet we explore the cosmos.

RTL, 15 AUGUST 2004, *PRIMETIME*

LEIBNIZ AND THE DEMONIC

Terrorism, egoism, diversity, harmony

For the philosopher Leibniz, there is no place in the world for true evil. The cosmos and humans' inner world have a 'pre-stabilized harmony'. How does the great thinker fit terrorism and everyday egoism into his world view? Hans Poser, Vice President, Leibniz Society.

FIGURE 143

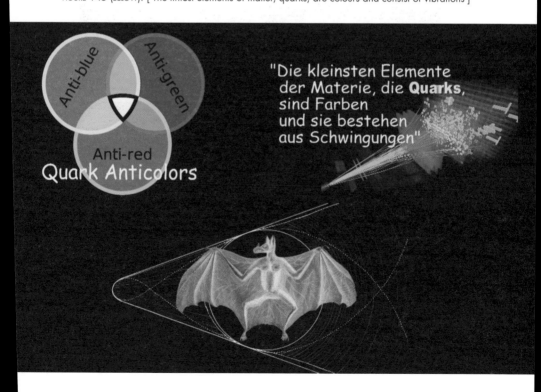

FIGURE 146–48. ['The invention of freedom']

FIGURE 149

FIGURE 150. In my media laboratory on the premises of Arnold & Richter. In three weeks' time, this lab, where I have worked for 30 years, will be vacated. My new work-shop is also located on the ARRI premises.

IMAGE CREDITS

ACKNOWLEDGEMENTS

I would like to thank my long-time editor for his critical, steely-nerved and productive guidance on this book. Ute Fahlenbock did an extraordinary job on the setting of the numerous images. I would also like to thank my trusted colleagues Beata Wiggen, Barbara Barnak and Gülsen Dör.

Alexander Kluge